THE WAX-WORK CADAVER

Johnson and I bent over the prone figure to assess the damage. At first glance it seemed slight. The outstretched pistol arm had broken the force of the fall, and sustained most of the damage. The pistol had flown wide. The index finger was broken clear off, and the rest of the hand was shattered. As Johnson picked up the severed wax finger, my first emotion was one of relief that the damage was no worse.

Then a cold grue of incredulous horror went through me. *Under the cracked wax of the highwayman's shattered fingers were the bones of a human hand!*

IPL Library of Crime Classics®
presents

THE COMPLEAT ADVENTURES OF
DR. SAM: JOHNSON, DETECTOR

DR. SAM: JOHNSON, DETECTOR
THE DETECTIONS OF DR. SAM: JOHNSON*
THE RETURN OF DR. SAM: JOHNSON, DETECTOR*
THE EXPLOITS OF DR. SAM: JOHNSON, DETECTOR*

*forthcoming titles

Dr. Sam: Johnson, Detector

being, a light-hearted Collection
of Recently reveal'd Episodes
in the Career of the GREAT LEXICOGRAPHER
narrated as from the Pen of

JAMES BOSWELL

Including:

the UNMASKING of the *Flying Highwayman;*
the singular Episode of the *Monboddo* APE BOY;
the RECOVERY of Prince *Charlie*'s vanisht Ruby,
the stolen *Christmas* Box, and the pilfer'd
GREAT SEAL of *England;* also,
the DETECTION of the mysterious Visitant
in *Mincing Lane,* and the macabre Affair of
the WAX-WORK CADAVER

by LILLIAN DE LA TORRE

New York: imprinted for INTERNATIONAL
POLYGONICS, LIMITED, Booksellers, at the sign of the
Polygon, and are to be had wherever Books are sold.

1983

DEDICATION  *to* G.S.M., *Esq:*

Sir,

Pray accept my Book; being, tho' not first publish'd, yet my first Fruits; and no less yours, than she by whom 'twas writ.

'Tis fit, that my Tales of Dr. Sam: Johnson *be address'd to him, of whom I first learned to love that great Humanist; by whom, my Invention was corrected and better'd; and in whom, his Virtues live: To enumerate which were tædious; yet cannot I forbear adverting to his Warmth in Friendship, his Courage in Infirmity, his domestick Tenderness; his steady common Sense, his ever refresh'd Curiosity, his catholick Learning; his purging Laughter, and his humane Wisdom.*

All which, redivivus, *you have these fourteen Years past display'd at large to,*

Sir,

Your oblig'd and admiring Servant,

LILLIAN DE LA TORRE

ADVERTISEMENT
to the Reader

THE NINE STORIES of this series take place in England and Scotland between 1763, when young James Boswell met the great Sam: Johnson in Davies's back room in Russell Street, and 1784, when their close friendship was severed by the death of Johnson. They exhibit Dr. Johnson in a new role, a role which, though he assumed it but once, was well within his extraordinary possibilities—the role of *detector* of crime and chicane.

The stories are written as from the pen of James Boswell, who so faithfully recorded Dr. Johnson's sayings and doings in his great biography.

I hope and believe that none of these imaginary exploits of Dr. Sam: Johnson will outrage belief. Each is abundantly possible to the man upon the quickness and accuracy of whose perceptions Boswell commented; who pursued chemical experimentation in Thrale's kitchen garden; who had the address to tackle a man who picked his pocket, and the courage to stand off four foot-pads at once. "He expressed great indignation," says Boswell, "at the imposture of the Cock Lane ghost, and related, with much satisfaction, how he had assisted in detecting the cheat."

James Boswell will be found equally in character, as the amateur of sensation who said of himself, "I have a wonderful superstitious love of *mystery;*" a believer in ghosts and second sight who visited the chapel at Inchkenneth by night only to enjoy (and report) "a pleasing awful confusion;" a lawyer allured by the criminal scene to the extent that he called on Mrs. Rudd the fascinating forger and flirted with her outrageously ("This was experiment," he noted in his account of the interview.), he resorted insatiably to Hackman the lovesick murderer, and upon one occasion at Tyburn, he mounted the condemned man's hearse the better to see him hanged, an act which he immediately wrote up for the papers.

Johnson and Boswell lived out their joint lives in the "full tide of human existence"—eighteenth-century London. The stories in this book are woven about the people who passed that way and the things that might have happened or that did happen in those days. Each story has as its starting-point a mysterious event, or a provocative setting, or a queer personality of the time. I have invented solutions, or personalities, or mysteries, to suit.

In eight of the nine stories, some villain is unmasked. Four of these scoundrels are the fruit of my invention;

but four of them really lived. One of the four was certainly guilty. The other three may be maligned in the positions of turpitude in which not I, but the logic of their stories, has placed them.

The stories are as accurate in language, prose style, historical fact, and background detail as research, albeit light-hearted, can make them. To their making have gone years of closest association with Dr. Sam: Johnson in print.

It does the heart good thus to live with Sam: Johnson. There was something heroic in this ugly, unwieldy creature with his blunted senses, his failing health, his lonely life. Over all he triumphed by sheer greatness. "So much does mind govern and even supply the deficiency of organs that his perceptions were uncommonly quick and accurate," wrote Boswell. His intellect was strong and original; he tried out glazes in Chelsea, verified physiological theories upon himself, and tackled the Greek Testament at sixty-five. Almost as late in life he dared the very real discomforts and dangers of travelling in order to see the Western Islands of Scotland in the company of Boswell. He triumphed over loneliness by the warmth and kindness of his heart, supplying "the vacuity of life" by warm and happy friendships. He roared down sham, and laughed away nonsense.

So deep was his sympathy for the disinherited, the poor who "wanted a dinner," that he had none to waste on the distresses of fashionable sensibility. He gave away all the money he came by, and filled his house with the poor, the old, the friendless, and the quarrelsome—a low surgeon, a black boy, a blind woman, a prostitute. "When asked by one of his most intimate friends," relates Hawkins, "how he could bear to be surrounded by such necessitous and undeserving people as he had about him, his answer was, 'If I did not assist them, no one else would, and they must be lost for want.'"

He would have been astonished by the part he plays in these pages, but I do not think he would have been angry. "Depend upon it," he quoted to Boswell, "no man was ever written *down*, but by himself."

To write about Sam: Johnson, even with unbridled fancy, is to write him *up*. That in these pages, though thrust fictitiously into sensational circumstances, he still comports himself with that common sense, humour, and sense of human dignity which distinguished him in life, is the hope of

THE AUTHOR

TABLE OF CONTENTS

THE WAX-WORK CADAVER, *page 3*

THE SECOND SIGHT OF DR. SAM: JOHNSON, *page 30*

THE FLYING HIGHWAYMAN, *page 55*

THE MONBODDO APE BOY, *page 79*

THE MANIFESTATIONS IN MINCING LANE, *page 108*

PRINCE CHARLIE'S RUBY, *page 138*

THE STOLEN CHRISTMAS BOX, *page 163*

THE CONVEYANCE OF EMELINA GRANGE, *page 192*

THE GREAT SEAL OF ENGLAND, *page 222*

NOTES ON HISTORICAL BACKGROUND, *page 253*

DE LA TORRE'S LIFE OF JOHNSON, *page 258*

ADDENDUM: THE GREAT CHAM, *page 259*

The WAX-WORK *Cadaver*

DR. CLARKE, Successor to Mrs. *Salmon*, and Worker in Wax to Surgeons' Hall, displays Mrs. *Salmon's* famous WAX-WORKS new-furbish'd:

INCLUDING The Royal Off Spring: Or, the Maid's Tragedy Represented in Wax Work, with many Moving Figures and these Histories Following. King *Charles* I upon the Fatal Scaffold, attended by Dr. *Juxon* the Bishop of *London*, and the Lieutenant of the *Tower*, with the Executioner and Guards waiting on our Royal Martyr. The Royal Seraglio, or the Life and Death of *Mahomet* the Third, with the Death of *Ireniae* Princess of *Persia*, and the fair Sultaness *Urania. Margaret* Countess of *Henningburgh*, Lying upon a Bed of State, with her Three hundred and Sixty-Five Children, all born at one Birth, and baptiz'd by the names of *Johns* and *Elizabeths*, occasion'd by the rash Wish of a poor beggar Woman.

Old Mother Shipton that Famous *English* Prophetess, which foretold the Death of the *White* King.

LIKEWISE: Our late most august Sovereign King *George* II. lying in his state Robes, with two Angels supporting the Crown over his Head; also a fine Figure of Peace laying the Olive Branches at his Feet. His Majesty the King of *Prussia;* with our gracious Sovereign's chief General in Germany, Prince *Ferdinand* of *Brunswick.* As also those pernitious Villains and Knights of the Road *Dick Turpin* and *James Maclaine* the *Gentleman Highwayman;* all done to the Life in Wax by the said DR. CLARKE with so much Variety of Invention, that it is wonderfully Diverting to all Lovers of Art and Ingenuity, and may be seen at the Sign of the Salmon near St. *Dunstan*'s Church.

Such is the hand-bill which lies among the *collectanea* for my account of my illustrious friend, Dr. Sam: Johnson, the great lexicographer; where in truth it sorts ill with the stately epistles, pious prayers, and learned dissertations in whose company it lies.

No less ill, to be seen to this day at the Wax-Work, sorts the waxen effigy of my learned friend with its companions; for it is menaced on the one side by the effigy of Maclaine, in the very attitude of "Stand and deliver!"; while it is flanked on the other by the wax-work cadaver of Laurence, Earl Ferrers, who was hanged and laid out in his wedding-suit, and lies thus in the Wax-Work, done in wax for all to see. Between the maccaroni highwayman and the murderous Earl

4

sits my illustrious friend in waxen contemplation. How he came to sit thus forms the substance of my tale.

In the year 1763 I was a young springald of two-and-twenty, new come from my native Edinburgh, and on fire to explore the manifold pleasures of the metropolis. The year was made memorable, and the pleasures of the metropolis were enhanced, by my newly formed acquaintanceship with the *Great Cham* of literature, Dr. Sam: Johnson the lexicographer. Though separated in age by above thirty years, we were mighty cordial together, and made up many a party of pleasure at the Mitre or on the river.

Thus it fell out that on a day in October I burst into my friend's lodging by Inner Temple Gate with Dr. Clarke's broadside of the Wax-Work in my hand, and desired that he would accompany me thither.

"No, sir," replied Johnson, "I saw the Wax-Work in my salad days, and I'll go no more; what have I to do with Dick Turpin and Mother Shipton?"

"Come, sir," I urged, "surely the author of *Irene* will not behold unmoved the waxen history of the Royal Seraglio."

"Sir," said Johnson, "no man stands less in need of instruction concerning the history of the unhappy Irene. But come, Mr. Boswell, if wax-works be your fancy, be guided by me, I'll shew you wax-works that shall astonish and instruct you. Do you but accompany me to Surgeons' Hall, there you shall see every organ of the human frame moulded in wax and coloured to the life. I assure you, 'tis as good as seeing some culprit anatomized."

"I nauseate anatomies," I exclaimed boldly. "Pray, Mr. Johnson, indulge me; for I never saw our late worthy Sovereign in the flesh, and I am ambitious to look upon him portrayed in wax."

"Well, well," said my kind friend indulgently, "I see you must have your way. We'll stay no longer, for 'tis but a step to the sign of the Salmon."

So saying he clapped his plain three-cornered hat over his little rusty wig, and we set out.

We passed through Inner Temple Gate and turned east into Fleet Street. There we stood a moment admiring the bustling activity of the busy thoroughfare. To the west rose the arch of Temple Bar. I saw, and shuddered to see, the shapeless black lumps affixed on poles above it, that had been the heads of the luckless Jacobite rebels.

It was a sunny day, but the wind was high; all up and down the street the wooden street-signs flapped and creaked on their irons over the heads of the passers-by. Past Middle Temple Gate was to be seen the antient sign of the Devil Tavern—a crude St. Dunstan with the tongs ready, and the Devil leering over his shoulder.

"This is an antient work of art, sir," I remarked to my companion, indicating the painting with a smile.

"'Tis an antient house," replied my friend. "This was Ben Jonson's Apollo Tavern, where he lorded it over the wits; and from here by an underground way he made good his escape into the Strand when the watch came to take him for stabbing a fellow-player."

"Pray tell me the tale," I begged.

"Not so, sir," replied Johnson, "for it has been too

The Wax-Work Cadaver

often rehearsed; but I'll tell you another, which not every man knows, that shall serve for your introduction to the Wax-Work."

"Do so, sir," I cried eagerly.

We turned into the wide thoroughfare just as, down the street, the giants of St. Dunstan's Church lifted their heavy clubs and struck the quarter, wagging their heads the while.

"'Twas during the days of the Pretender," began Johnson, "when one night the Duke of Montague makes up a party of pleasure at the Devil Tavern, and Heidegger the Swiss Count made one. No sooner was Heidegger convinced in liquor, so that he lay like one dead, but Montague sends up the street in haste for this very Mrs. Salmon whose wax-works we are to see. She took a cast of his face, he knowing no more than the dead of what she did, and so made a mask in wax and painted it to the life. Montague, sir, turns out a friend in Heidegger's cloathes and the wax-work mask, and carries him the very next night to the masquerade, where Heidegger was employed. Up gets the false Heidegger, and in a voice like the Bull of Bashan cries out for—the Jacobite anthem! The true Heidegger was beside himself."

"Is this the way of it," I enquired curiously, "is a wax-work made thus, from a casting of the features?"

"I cannot say," replied my friend, "but you may soon know, for here we are at the sign of the Salmon."

I looked curiously at the old house, hunched against the old grey stones of St. Dunstan's. The gilded salmon hung on its iron over our heads. A narrow deep-set doorway led to the display. Beside it was affixed a bill; I paused to read it with attention.

My learned friend peered over my shoulder with his near-sighted eyes.

"Here is riches," he murmured. "The Royal Court of England, one hundred fifty figures—the Rites of Moloch—the overthrow of Queen Voaditia—come, Mr. Boswell, let us make haste to view these wonders."

I however, lingered to peruse the bill to its end:

". . . all new-furbish'd and exhibitted by Dr. *Clarke* of *Chancery-lane.*

☞ RUN OFF from his Master, my Apprentice *Jem Blount*, being a tall likely Lad, fresh-colour'd, mark'd with the Small-pox, had on when last seen fustian Breeches, leather Shoes without Buckles, blue Stockings, a red Waist-coat having very particular Copper Buttons like a join'd Serpent, and a dirty Baize Apron. Any Person, who can give any Account where he is, shall have *Ten Shillings Reward*, to be paid by Dr. *Clarke*, Surgeon, of *Chancery-lane*, which will greatly satisfy the said Dr. *Clarke.*

"Come, Mr. Boswell," cried my friend, "you waste time in this reading; for you may depend upon it, *Jemmy Blount* is not a wax-work."

So saying, he propelled me up the narrow stair and into the exhibit of MRS. SALMON'S WAX-WORK.

I own I gazed with awe at the crowded hall. Every appurtenance of majesty adorned the wax-work presentments of the dead Kings and Queens of England. First to strike my eye was the recumbent figure of his late sacred Majesty George II, of blessed memory. Peace, laying the olives at his feet, seemed to quiver with life; the angels, suspended on wires, actually floated in the light air; bent over the bier, as if in reverent grief, a man's figure had life in every limb. I regarded the mourner, a fine figure of a man, tall, broad in the shoulder, soberly cloathed in mulberry broadcloth, with a full light wig hiding his face.

"What artistry!" I cried to my friend. "Does it not seem to you that these angels must stir their wings and fly away, or yonder mourner at King George's bier rise and speak to us?"

The words were hardly out of my mouth when the hair prickled on my scalp and a cry escaped me, for the man at the King's bier rose slowly to his feet and faced us.

"Your servant, sirs," he said easily.

I could only gape.

"Permit me, gentlemen," said the man in mulberry. "It is sixpence to see the wax-works, and I will be your cicerone. Dr. Clarke, gentlemen, at your service."

My companion tendered a shilling before I could recover from my stupor. I stared at the surgeon-turned-wax-worker. I cannot say by what eccentricity or parsimony the man wore a light wig; his long face was the colour of leather, his deep-sunk eyes were dark under heavy tufts of black brow. His half-smile shewed white teeth. His brown hands were the long fine hands of a surgeon.

He took my friend's shilling, finished smoothing into place the robes of the wax-work king on which he had been engaged, and proceeded to display the Wax-Work.

We were like living men in the halls of the dead as we scanned the waxen faces of long-buried Turks and Romans and Englishmen. The silence was oppressive, and our voices when we spoke hardly lifted it. I wished we had visited Surgeons' Hall instead.

My learned companion soon tired of gazing, and began in his penetrating voice a discourse upon the philosophy of wax-works.

"For I hold, sir," said he argumentatively, "that to present to the eyes of the young and the untutored such effigies as these of Queen Elizabeth and the Court of England is at once to instruct and to edify them; but what useful purpose can be served, sir, by perpetuating in wax the ridiculous romantick legend of the too-prolifick Countess or the vulgar prophecies of Mother Shipton? While as to the enshrining of these two ruffians—" he waved a contemptuous hand at Turpin, standing a-straddle in his buckskins, and Maclaine, presenting his pistol, with the crape mask covering his eyes—"what is it but the enshrining crime, and reviving a bad example rightly eclipsed on Tyburn Tree?"

"I am sorry they offend you, sir," said Dr. Clarke candidly, "for it is my intention thus to perpetuate many another object of publick interest, however that interest may have arisen. Maclaine I have only just completed," he eyed the effigy affectionately, "it is the best thing I have ever done; and I have in process no less a malefactor than Earl Ferrers."

"In process?" I cried eagerly. "Pray, sir, will you not gratify us with a sight of it, for I have a great curiosity to see how these things are made?"

The Wax-Work Cadaver

The surgeon hesitated.

"Pray, sir, do," urged my companion, ever eager to be instructed.

"As to how they are made," said the surgeon slowly, "you will learn little in my work-room. These effigies you see, that are the work of my predecessor, are but coarsely cast in wax, and the limbs tied together and so cloathed; and one mould serves for many faces, as you may see if you compare the ladies of the harem with the ladies of the English Court."

"How then is a likeness obtained?" asked Johnson, indicating the well-known piscine face of the late monarch.

"This is my work," replied the surgeon proudly, "for I model direct in the wax and colour it from the life. These faces—" he jerked his head at the Romans and the Turks—"are but masks, they have nothing under them; but *my* faces are built from within. Stay, you shall see. Pray step this way."

He led the way to the door, and stood aside to bow us through. Beside the door, propped on crutches, stood the famous image of Mother Shipton: a gnarled nutcracker countenance, coarse hair crowned with a hat like a steeple, a sombre cloak thrown over the shoulders.

"After you, Mr. Boswell," said my courteous friend with an inclination.

"No, sir, after you."

The contest of courtesy prolonged itself, until, to end it, I bowed and stepped through the door. To my utter amazement, there was a creak and a clatter, and I felt my breech saluted by an unmistakable kick from behind.

I turned dumb-founded, to realize that both the surgeon and my friend had burst into roars of laughter. I stared incredulously.

"Alack, Mr. Boswell, this by itself repays my shilling," declared my friend, wiping his eyes. I could not believe that it was he who had thus assaulted me; but it was surely not the surgeon? My perplexity was resolved when my friend, still laughing, bade me stand back.

"I had taken precedence of you at first," he remarked, "but I have been here before."

So saying, he stepped over the door-sill; when with a creak and a clatter the witch-like figure by the door lifted her jointless leg and delivered a well-placed kick. My cumbersome friend eluded its effect dexterously, and grinned back at me from the threshold.

"How is this managed?" I asked the grinning surgeon.

"'Tis done by clock-work," replied Dr. Clarke. "As you step on this board on the threshold, a trip is actuated that sets the figure in motion; 'tis the very Devil to keep it oiled, but the results repay the exertion."

Speaking thus, he led us down the stair and through a backward passage into his work-room.

It smelled of hot wax, with a musty effluvium. Long windows looked into a yard filled with miscellaneous lumber. In the room was a vat as long as a baker's kneading-trough; a glowing brick oven big enough to roast an ox; and a long table, fit to carve an ox, in the center of the room.

The Wax-Work Cadaver

At the table stood a young man, a tall likely lad, fresh-faced, marked with the small-pox, wearing leather shoes without buckles and a dirty baize apron.

On the table before him was a collection of limbs in wax, which he was colouring with a dilution of cochineal. Johnson bent to examine them more closely; but my eyes were rivetted on the waistcoat of the fresh-faced young man. Above the baize of the apron the buttons shewed, very particular buttons of copper, shaped like a joined serpent.

The young man set down his brush and turned with anxious mien to his master.

"What news of my brother?" he asked in a heavy voice, knitting his brows.

"None, Micah," replied Dr. Clarke. "I went down to Water Lane again this morning, but never a hair of him has your mother seen; the young runagate is off to Sadler's Wells, as like as not."

The tall young man continued to frown; he shook his head slowly.

"Jem never run off, and not told me," he said heavily, "Jem never did a thing without he told me; by cause I'm his elder, d'ye see, and he does as I bid him. Three days he's gone, sir, and never a word of him; 'tis not natural, and that's flat."

"Be easy, Micah," said the surgeon, "he'll return when it suits him, I'll be bound."

Micah Blount said no more. He took up his brush and went back to his cochineal. His broad hands were surprisingly deft.

Dr. Clarke indicated the scattered limbs.

"This is Earl Ferrers," he remarked, shewing his white teeth in a grin.

I regarded the fragments with interest.

"Earl Ferrers was a fine figure of a man," said the surgeon. "I saw him hanged; he died with great decency, with the aid of a trap which was mechanically depressed and so turned him off with the dignity becoming his high station."

He picked up a waxy arm.

"This arm is moulded, not cast," he remarked. "With a tall man, do you see, Mr. Boswell, the limb is longer in every proportion, every little bone of the hand is elongated; we cannot cast such limbs in the same moulds as served for Mother Shipton. They must be modelled as if the bones lay beneath. Look, here is the radius bone, here the wrist bone, you may see how the wax shapes around them. Would not you take this for an arm of flesh indeed?"

"Where is the head?" enquired Johnson.

For answer the surgeon took down a wax head where it hung on the wall.

"Is it modelled also?" asked my friend.

"No, sir, 'tis cast. I was at Surgeons' Hall when Earl Ferrers was anatomized—"

"How, anatomized!" I exclaimed in horror. "An Earl anatomized like an ordinary cadaver!"

"Yes, sir; for if he was an Earl, he was also a murderer, and the blood of his murdered steward cried aloud for justice. I was present at the scene, and made a cast from the face; so the likeness is exact, although a cast is used. Here is the wig; Earl Ferrers died in his own brown hair."

"Will there be a pall?"

"No, sir. The Earl died, and was buried, in his wedding-suit."

The surgeon called up the back stair. An answer came from above, and presently Mrs. Clarke descended, bearing a sumptuous white brocade garment with rich silver embroidery.

"If this is not the very suit he died in," said the surgeon proudly, "'tis its twin, for Mrs. Clarke is a very Arachne with her needle."

The plump little woman beamed and bobbed; her pale eyes went into slits as her fat cheeks lifted in a grin. She hung the garment carefully against the wall.

Johnson was shaking his head over the table full of the *disjecta membra* of the dead Earl. I peered out a doorway into a dark passage, which seemed to lead into the cellars below. It smelled damp and decayed.

"Come, gentlemen," said Dr. Clarke at my elbow, "if you would see how a head is moulded, you must follow me. We shall examine," he went on, mounting the stair, "the head of Maclaine the highwayman, for I have never done a better."

He tossed aside the flapped hat and stripped off the crape mask.

"You may see, gentlemen," he said, "how the face is, as it were, built up from within. Maclaine had a plump cheek, yet you may trace that there is a cheek-bone beneath."

My near-sighted friend peered at the feature indicated. The surgeon was alight with sombre enthusiasm; we had clearly struck on his ruling passion. He tipped the figure toward us.

"Look," he cried, "at the shape of the head. This is no bullet head or ball of wax. The skull is longer than it is wide, and so I have modelled it. The skull, gentlemen—"

There was a clatter on the stair, and the apprentice burst into the hall. His broad face was full of consternation. In his hand he held a blue apron; it was marked with a dreadful splash of red. The surgeon looked at him impassively, still supporting the inclined figure of the highwayman.

"What do you here?" he asked. "Get back to your work."

"The apron," stammered the lad, " 'tis Jem's, I know it well. I found it but now, 'twas stuffed into the shed with the coals."

"Be easy, boy," reiterated the surgeon, "I am perswaded that Jem has run off to Sadler's Wells; and what 'prentice would be such a blockhead, as to run to Sadler's Wells in his 'prentice garb?"

As Micah stood irresolute, my bulky friend was seized with one of those convulsive movements, to which, alas, he was always subject; he lurched heavily against the wax figure, and it fell to the ground with a crash.

The surgeon turned in a fury. His anger fell, not on my friend, but upon the lad who had interrupted us.

"Dolt!" he rated the heavy-witted apprentice. "Blockhead! My masterpiece—a wax-work built upon new principles of natural philosophy—shattered! It was worth twenty Blounts! Be off with you! Back where you belong!"

Johnson and I bent over the prone wax figure to assess the damage. At first glance it seemed slight. The outstretched pistol arm had broken the force of the fall, and sustained most of the damage. The pistol had flown wide. The index finger was broken clear off, and the rest of the hand was shattered. As Johnson picked up the severed wax finger, my first emotion was one of relief that the damage was no worse.

Then a cold grue of incredulous horror went through me. *Under the cracked wax of the highwayman's shattered fingers were the bones of a human hand!*

My memory of the next five minutes is confused. I remember the face of the apprentice as he gave way before the fury of the surgeon, and backed down the stairs, with the red-stained apron still in his hand. I remember we came away quickly, saying nothing, my brain reeling with our hideous discovery.

At Inner Temple Lane I would have stayed with my wise friend, but he sent me abruptly about my business. This piqued me; and although I knew him to be fully capable of bringing the affair to whatever conclusion prudence and right dictated, I resolved to take a hand in the game and see whether I did not hold a trump or two.

The event justified me. It was with triumph that I called in Inner Temple Lane the next evening after supper. Johnson was from home; but I determined to await his return.

The full moon was mounting the sky when he at last appeared, in high good humour.

"Where have you been so long, sir?" I cried peevishly.

"Where every good Christian should go; to church," he replied, "and where you, in these villainous weeds?"

"By Water Lane into *Alsatia*," I replied, naming the lawless district that lay south of Fleet Street.

"In what *bousing-ken*, with what *morts* and *culls?*" my companion questioned me in thieves' cant.

"With none," I replied, "with one Mistress Blount, of whom I have learned much of her missing son; most notably I have learned wherein he differed from Maclaine the highwayman."

"Why, as for that," my companion humoured me, "they were of a size, being tall likely fellows both; and had each a plump pudding face, if Jemmy may be judged by Micah."

"Ay," I replied, "but they were not to be confused, none the less, for Jemmy Blount was *lacking the forefinger of his right hand*; but the gentleman highwayman had his five fingers all complete."

My companion started.

"Did he so!" he cried, "now this is a lesson in *false generalization!*"

He threw on the table before him two finger bones, grey and brittle; to one, fragments of the rosy wax still adhered.

"Deceivers, lie there," he cried; and seized his three-cornered hat.

The Wax-Work Cadaver

"Come, make haste, Mr. Boswell," he cried.

"Whither?"

"To the Wax-Work."

"At midnight?" I cried aghast.

"'Tis not midnight," replied my friend, "the bells of St. Dunstan's have barely gone eleven; but if it were midnight or dawn, there is not a moment to lose."

"What must we do?" I panted, trotting up Fleet Street at my friend's heels.

"Look at the *middle* finger of Maclaine the highwayman," replied my friend; and fairly ran along the footway.

Soon he was thundering on the narrow door. The sound reverberated through the empty street for a long moment. Then the two-pair-of-stairs window was flung open, and a head came out in a night-cap.

"I must see Dr. Clarke," cried Johnson.

"Alack, sir," replied a woman's voice, "he's from home."

"Let me in!" shouted Johnson.

"Yes, sir."

The narrow old house lay still as death. Next door the old grey stones of St. Dunstan's gleamed in the moon and threw a deep shadow on the face of the Wax-Work. The silence bemused my sensibilities. I seemed to hear movement in the old house, a board creaking, a door quietly pulled to. After an eternity of expectation, there came a step on the stair, and a white-faced serving-wench opened the heavy door.

In the shadow a barrow of potatoes was waiting by

the door to trip me; I cursed it, and hastened to follow my friend and the servant wench as they mounted the stair. In the two-pair-of-stairs sitting-room we found the mistress shivering in her bed-gown by a dying fire. She shuddered as she bade the girl cloathe herself and fetch coals to mend the fire. Her fat face was the colour of dough.

"Ma'am," says Johnson civilly, "where's your husband?"

"He's gone," said the little woman, and quivered. "He's left me."

"When?"

"Last night. He only lingered till he'd done the dead Earl wax-work, and then he went. I saw him go. I was abed, and trying to sleep, when I heard the front door slam. I looked out at my window, and there he was below me on the door-step. I saw him very plain by the light of the moon. He'd his mulberry broadcloth on, and a scarf about his throat against the night air. His hat was flapped, and he carried his portmanteau. I called to him, and he made off down Fleet Street as if the Devil was after him. Alack, sir, he's gone for good." The woman began to cry. "I knew it, I knew it'd come to this, when he started in with his nasty bones and anatomies."

My friend looked very grave. He had no consolation to give her.

"Pray, ma'am, admit us to the Wax-Work."

"You have but to go down, Mr. Johnson; the door is not locked."

"You will accompany us, ma'am."

The Wax-Work Cadaver

The woman shrank at this, but Johnson was adamant. She took up the candle and followed us.

By the light of the single candle I liked the wax-works hall as little as she. It smelled to me of death. The highwayman lay where he had fallen. In the alcove beside him was extended the new wax-work, the hanged Earl in his white-and-silver. I admired, albeit with a shudder, the still face and the long aristocratic hands joined palm to palm upon the breast.

Johnson went directly to the prone figure of the highwayman and took up the broken hand. He beckoned imperiously for the candle, and I was left beside the wax-work cadaver in the half-dark. To a man of my sensibility, the experience was harrowing. I am never free, at a wax-works, from the conviction that the figures behind me are stirring with inimical life. I seemed to hear stealthy breathing beyond the periphery of the candle's glow. My spine crawled, and the palms of my hands felt wet.

Suddenly the air was rent with scream upon scream of terror. My companion started to his feet; Mrs. Clarke almost dropped the candle.

"Rouze up the apprentice!" cried Johnson. "Give me the candle! Come, Boswell!"

Mrs. Clarke only lingered to lock the door behind her. My friend lingered not at all, but ran full tilt down the stair and through the lower passage towards the screams, which seemed to emanate from the yard.

It was the wench who was screaming. She stood fully cloathed by the shed and distended her throat with scream after scream. The candle flickered in her hand.

She found words as she pointed blindly towards the shed, where the sliding of the coals had laid bare a motionless, outflung hand.

" 'Tis Jem," she wailed. "Jem said it, the vaults is full of dead men, and we'll all be murdered in our beds."

I was by Johnson's side as we flung the coals aside and uncovered a nude body. It had no head.

"Quiet, girl," said Johnson disgustedly as he laid hold of the still, slippery figure, "have you never seen a wax-work before?"

Another candle came through the work-room, and Mrs. Clarke stood in the door-way regarding the headless figure with horror.

"O lack," she cried, "is it Micah?"

"Micah?"

"Micah's not in his bed," she said from a dry throat, "he's gone. *Where is Micah?*"

My friend looked gravely at the headless figure, the long hands with fingers not spread, the swell of the radius bone and the wrist bone.

"Come," he said, "let us go back to the Wax-Work."

The trembling women brought their candles. Passing through the work-room, Johnson paused. The smell of hot wax was gone, but the place smelled more musty than ever.

The brick furnace was cold. Johnson opened the fire-door, and, taking a candle, held it within. I peered over his shoulder.

"These are strange ashes," said my friend, "they are

the ashes neither of wood nor of coals, but of cloth. Pray, Mr. Boswell, reach me the poker."

He turned over the layers of blackened cloth. There was a tinkle, and he drew out of the mass a blackened thing about the size of a shilling. I held the candle as he wiped off the soot. It was a very particular button, like a joined serpent.

"Jem Blount's!" I cried.

We mounted the dark stair. Mrs. Clarke turned the heavy key in the lock, and again my friend and I entered the Wax-Work. The women hung back; if truth were told, I longed to hang back with them.

My friend led me straight to the recumbent figure of the murderous Earl, lying with closed eyes and joined palms in the candle-light.

I shuddered as he touched the wax of the face, then with a jerk pulled loose the wig of brown hair. I closed my eyes as I held the candle close, then opened them with loathing to behold the skull beneath.

It was not a skull. It was not a battered head. It was a smooth expanse of uncoloured wax. My friend unsheathed his pen-knife; the blade slipped in easily to its full length. The head of the wax-work cadaver contained nothing but wax.

"Tschah," said Johnson disgustedly, "we waste time. This is the Earl's own head, cast from his death-mask. Now the hands—"

He slashed the wax of the near hand. It peeled back in a thin integument; under it was a hand of flesh, stiff and cold.

"So," said my friend, "the head is gone in the doctor's portmanteau."

"We must lay an information," I cried, "and set up the hue and cry."

"Ay," responded Johnson, "if we cannot ourselves lay the murdering villain by the heels. Let us go."

At the word I was through the door in a trice. Beyond the threshold a sense of something missing, something wrong, halted me.

I smiled as it came to me.

"Why sir," I called to my friend as he lingered, surveying the room about by the light of his candle, "now the master is fled, all is at sixes and sevens; even the famous parting salute of old Mother Shipton has ceased to operate."

"What, sir, no kick on the rump?" cried my curious friend. "Come, sir, you have sidled by or leapt through, or the lady had not failed you. You shall see, she will not fail me, for I shall take care to step rightly."

So saying, Johnson set down his candle-stick, and trod firmly towards the door. There was neither a click nor a clatter, but the foot of Mother Shipton lifted in a mighty sweep of skirts behind Johnson's back; when to my utter surprise my sturdy friend wheeled, caught the lifted heel, and brought the cloaked figure to the floor with a bone-shaking crash. The steeple hat rolled aside; the hair went with it. Johnson presented a pistol at the side of the head. I hurried up with my candle.

"You have caught the mad surgeon!" I cried.

"No, sir," replied Johnson, stripping the wax mask

from the face beneath, "but I have caught his murderer."

I advanced the candle, and looked into the sullen face of Micah Blount.

There was no fight in Micah Blount. He marched meekly enough to the watch-house, and there we lodged him for safe-keeping. Early the next morning we had him before the magistrate.

Micah made a full confession:

"I knocked in his head," he mumbled in his heavy voice, "and then I wondered where to hide him, for I had then no conveniency to make off with the body; nor did I dare to burn it, for the mistress would be sure to smell it. Then I thought of the Wax-Work. I cloathed him like Earl Ferrers, and coated the head and hands with wax; but 'twould not do. In the end I took off the head and laid out the body in the Wax-Work with the wax head to it. First I thought to melt down the wax body, but then I thought better of it, for I would need it when I could come by with a barrow and take the body off; so I hid it under the coals in the shed."

"Why did you burn the waistcoat with the copper buttons?"

"Blood," said Micah; his eyes looked inward.

"Yet how came you," I cried, "to be wearing your brother's waistcoat?"

"'Twas mine," said Micah, "there were the two alike. They were my mother's work, and the copper buttons were some my uncle came by in the French wars."

"So then," said Johnson, "you donned the doctor's cloathes, for you two were of a size, and put on his wig, and flapped his hat over your face and took the head away in his portmanteau."

"Ay."

"And when one called to you from the window you ran as if the Devil were at your heels; how could you know that, looking down on you from above in the moonlight, your mistress would see only a tall man wearing her husband's cloathes, and think you the surgeon himself."

Micah said nothing.

"And tonight you returned for the body, for it must be removed before the odour betrayed that it was other than wax. How did you hope to carry it safely off?" enquired Dr. Johnson.

A light dawned on me.

"The barrow!" I cried. "The barrow of potatoes!"

Micah nodded.

"'Twixt midnight and dawn every costermonger is abroad with his barrow," he said. "Under the potatoes I might have wheeled him swiftly and safely down Water Lane till I came to the river, and so flung him off Dung Wharf, as I flung his head the night before."

The bereaved woman wailed loudly.

"How could you," she sobbed, "how could you treat your kind master so?"

Micah ground his teeth.

"He killed my brother," he cried passionately. "He killed Jem and put him in a wax-work."

"Ay did he," struck in the serving-wench, "and for

why, Jem found the vault in the cellars where he hides the bones of all the men he kills. Jem told me so, he was mortal afeared of the doctor after he saw them heaps and heaps of bones lying in the vaults, and the doctor killed him to keep his tongue from wagging."

Micah's eyes were full of tears.

"Poor lad," said Mr. Johnson with regret, "Dr. Clarke never killed anybody."

I stared in amazement.

"What of the blood on the boy's apron?"

"Not blood, Mr. Boswell—cochineal."

"Then how came the highwayman to be built upon bones?" I demanded.

"Ay," struck in the wench, "and whence came them piles of bones in the cellars? The doctor, he kept the passage locked, but Jem got in and saw 'em, piles and piles of bones lying about."

"I carried the highwayman's finger home with me," Johnson related, "and when the wax was peeled from it any eye could see that it was no fresh bone, it was old and brittle. To make sure, I called upon my old friend the sexton of St. Dunstan's, and he admitted me to look upon the bones of the charnel-house, where they have been shovelled out to make room for the newly dead under the church floor. He gave me such another finger bone, of one who had been dead these hundreds of years, before the new church was built and the new churchyard made up the lane."

Johnson sighed.

"'Twas a painful reminder of mortality," he said, "smelling of the grave, with the dust of ages over all.

'Twas with horror I saw that there were footprints in the dust. I followed them, and so found the passage that connects St. Dunstan's with the Wax-Work, for all these old edifices are honeycombed beneath with passages leading from one to another. I knew then where the doctor had found the highwayman's bones, and how his *scientifick* bent had caused him to build his wax-works like one doing an anatomy in reverse, from the inside out."

"Then why did you run so quickly to the Wax-Work when you heard about Jem Blount's finger?" I asked.

"Because the bone I had erected my speculations on," replied my learned friend, "was a *right forefinger*. I had to be sure that the surgeon had not supplied a deficiency with the charnel-house bone; I had to see for myself that the other fingers were not the fingers of Jem Blount. They were not; they were all charnel-house bones."

"How," I enquired curiously, "were you so sure that the surgeon was the cadaver and not the murderer?"

"The face was gone," replied my perspicacious friend, "but the hands were there. They were not the broad hands of Micah, but the surgeon's fingers of the doctor."

"I marvel," I admitted, "how you smoaked Micah in the weeds of the wax-work witch."

"I did not," replied Johnson, "though I thought it possible that he might be lurking about; his secret was not safe while the wedding-suit of Earl Ferrers covered the cadaver of his murdered master. But I did not smoak him until the machinery, which had worked the day before, failed to operate. Even then it was but a surmise. I tempted him with my words. If he had not fallen into my trap, and moved, as a human being must, like a human being, not a clock-work, he might have got clear off; for a clock-work which has failed once may fail twice, and rouze no suspicion."

"What is this," enquired the magistrate, who had heard thus far with keen interest, "of Jem Blount's right forefinger?"

"'Tis missing," replied I.

"Did this boy wear a red waistcoat with very particular copper buttons?"

"Ay."

"Then," said the magistrate, "I can lead you to the boy. He came to me three days gone with a cock-and-bull story of his master having a heap of bones in his cellar; but he was brought to confess that he was a runaway 'prentice, and I could not credit him; and in short, he was committed to gaol for correction, and there he bides."

"Look to the young man!" cried Johnson.

Micah's face was a sickly green. As I watched him, he let go the bar he leaned on and slowly slid down in a heap.

"'Tis a sturdy rogue," said the magistrate, as the unfortunate boy was hauled to his feet. "Pray, Mr. Johnson, how had you the address to take him single-handed?"

"'Twas not done with address," replied Johnson with a smile, "'twas done with an empty pistol, which I made bold to borrow from my wax-work friend, James Maclaine, the gentleman highwayman."

THE SECOND SIGHT OF

Dr.   *Sam: Johnson*

S IR," said the learned Dr. Sam: Johnson to the
Laird of Raasay, "he who meddles with the un-
canny, meddles with danger; but none the less for that,
'tis the duty of the philosopher, diligently to enquire
into the truth of these matters."

All assented to my learned friend's proposition, none
dreaming how soon and how terribly his words were to
be verified, and his intrepidity put to the test.

No premonition of events to come disturbed the
pleasure with which I saw my learned companion thus
complacently domesticated upon the Isle of Raasay. Our
long-cherished scheam of visiting the Western Islands
of Scotland was now a reality; and it was in acknowl-
edgement of the plans of the Laird for exploring the
wonders of the isle that the respectable author of the
Dictionary uttered these words.

As he did so, he gazed with complacency upon his
companions by the Laird's fireside; a group of High-

land gentlemen, shewing in face and bearing that superiority which consciousness of birth and learning most justifiably supplies. Of the family of MacLeod were the Laird himself, a sensible, polite, and most hospitable gentleman, and his brother, Dr. MacLeod, a civil medical man of good skill. These gentlemen shewed a strong family resemblance, being tall and strongly made, with firm ruddy countenances; genteelly apparelled in sad-coloured suits with clean ruffles.

Their companions in the ingle-nook by the glowing peat fire were two brothers, Angus and Colin Mac-Queen, sons of the incumbent rector of the parish of Snizoort on Skye. They resembled one another, being lean, light, and active, with bony dark faces; wearing suits of scholarly black, and their own heavy dark hair cut short.

The elder, Mr. Angus MacQueen, was a learned young man, a close observer of the natural phænomena of the island. He filled the trusted post of tutor to Raasay's heir. The younger son, Colin, new returned from the University, had all his elder brother's wide and curious learning, but displayed withal an ill-regulated instability of mind and a hectick behaviour, poorly held in check by respect for Raasay and my learned companion.

Dr. Samuel Johnson's character—nay, his figure and manner, are, I believe, more generally known than those of almost any man, yet it may not be superfluous here to attempt a sketch of him. His person was large, robust, I may say approaching to the gigantick, and grown unwieldy from corpulency. His countenance was naturally of the cast of an antient statue, but somewhat disfigured by the scars of that evil which it was formerly imagined the royal touch would cure. He was now in his sixty-fourth year, and was become a little dull of hearing. His sight had always been somewhat weak, yet so much does mind govern and even supply the deficiency of organs that his perceptions were uncommonly quick and accurate. His head and sometimes also his body shook with a kind of motion like the effect of a palsy; he appeared to be frequently disturbed by cramps or convulsive contractions, of the nature of that distemper called St. Vitus's dance. He wore a full suit of plain brown cloathes with twisted-hair buttons of the same colour, a large bushy greyish wig, a plain shirt, black worsted stockings, and silver buckles. He had a loud voice and a slow deliberate utterance, which no doubt gave some additional weight to the sterling metal of his conversation. He had a constitutional melancholy the clouds of which darkened the brightness of his fancy and gave a gloomy cast to his whole course of thinking; yet, though grave and awful in his deportment when he thought it necessary or proper, he frequently indulged himself in pleasantry and sportive sallies. He was prone to superstition but not to credulity. Though his imagination might incline him to a belief of the marvellous, his vigorous reason examined the evidence with jealousy.

Such was my learned friend during our visit to the Western Islands; and thus it was that on this first evening of our sojourn on Raasay our talk turned on the topography, the antiquities, and especially the superstitions of the Isle of Raasay.

Dr. Johnson had professed himself eager to enquire into our Highland phænomenon of second sight.

"Sir," said Angus MacQueen, "I am *resolved* not to believe it, because it is founded on no principle."

"Then," said Dr. Johnson, "there are many verified facts that you will not believe. What principle is there why the lodestone attracts iron? Why an egg produces a chicken by heat? Why a tree grows upward, when the natural tendency of all things is downward? Sir, it depends on the degree of evidence you have."

Young Angus MacQueen made no reply. Colin MacQueen rolled his wild dark eyes on the awe-inspiring figure of my friend as he asked:

"What evidence would satisfy you?"

"Whist, then, Colin," interposed his brother, "let past things be."

"I knew a MacKenzie," Dr. MacLeod said cheerfully, "who would faint away, and when he revived again he had visions to tell of. He told me upon one occasion, I should meet a funeral just at the fork of the road, and the bearers people I knew, and he named them, too. Well, sir, three weeks after, I did meet a funeral on that very road, and the very bearers he named. Was not that second sight?"

"Sir," said my friend, "what if this man lay a-dying, and your MacKenzie and the whole town knew who his friends would be to carry him to the grave? —Ay, and by the one nearest way to the graveyard?"

"What do you say then to the women of Skye," said

the honest Laird, "who stopped me on the road to say that they had heard two *taisks*, and one an English one—"

"What is a *taisk*?" I ventured to enquire. It is the part of a chronicler to omit no opportunity to clarify his record.

"A *taisk*, Mr. Boswell, is the voice of one about to die. Many of us in the Highlands hear *taisks* though we have not the second sight."

"Sir," said Dr. Johnson, "it is easy enough for the women of Skye to say what they heard. Did *you* hear it?"

"I have not the gift," said the Laird of Raasay, "but returning the same road, I met two funerals, and one was of an Englishwoman."

"Is there none in the Isle of Raasay with the second sight?" enquired my learned friend.

"There is indeed," replied Colin MacQueen in a low voice. "There is an old wife on the other side the island with the second sight. She foresaw my brother's murder."

"How, sir!" exclaimed Dr. Johnson. "Murder! I had no intent to distress you."

"I will tell you the story." Young MacQueen's eyes glittered in the fire-light. "Rory was younger than I, and meddled with the lasses where he had no concern. Old Kirstie comes one night to Angus and me, and falls to weeping, crying out that she has heard Rory's *taisk*, and seen him lying dead with his head broke. Wasn't it so, Angus?"

"It was so," said the young tutor sombrely.

The Second Sight of Dr. Sam: Johnson

"And did it fall out so?" I enquired.

"So it fell out, for Angus was there and saw it," replied young Colin, "and if 'twas a grief to us, it broke old Kirstie's heart; for it was her own son killed him. A strapping surly ghillie he was, Black Fergus they called him, and he broke Rory's head for him over the bouman's lass."

"Did the villain suffer for his crime?" enquired Dr. Johnson, profoundly struck by this tale of moral obliquity.

"He did, sir, though we have neither court nor judge upon Raasay since the troubled days of the '45; but rather than be took he flung himself into the sea; and his mother saw him in a dream rising up out of the sea dripping wet, with his face rotted away."

" 'Twould interest me much," said Dr. Johnson, "if I might meet with this aged Sybil."

"Nothing is easier," replied Dr. MacLeod, "for to-morrow I propose to shew you the strange caves of our eastern coast, and the old woman lives hard by. You shall interrogate her to your heart's content."

"Sir," said Dr. Johnson, "I am obliged to you. What is the nature of the caves you mention?"

"They are sea caves," replied Dr. MacLeod, "of great age and extent. No one has ever explored all their ramifications."

"My young friend MacQueen," added the Laird, bowing to Angus, "who is botanist, lapidarian, and antiquary of our island, knows them better than any man; but even he has never penetrated to their depths."

"He fears the Kelpie," said young Colin recklessly.

"The Kelpie?" I echoed.

"A water-demon," said Colin. "He lives in the Kelpie Pool under the Kelpie's Window, and he eats men."

"Such is the belief of the islanders," assented Angus MacQueen. "In their superstition they connect this supernatural being with a certain natural orifice in the cave wall, giving upon a deep pool of the sea."

"The pool is bottomless," struck in Colin, "and under it sits the Kelpie and hates mankind."

"It is impossible," pronounced Dr. Johnson, "by its very nature, that any depression which contains water should lack a bottom."

"This one does," muttered Colin.

" 'Tis perfectly true," said Raasay, "that the Kelpie Pool has never been sounded."

"Thus do we see the credulity of ill-instructed men," cried Dr. Johnson, with a glance of fire at young Colin, "who because a thing *has never been done,* conclude illogically that it *cannot be done.*"

"Tomorrow you shall see the Kelpie Pool," said the learned young tutor, "and judge for yourself. I can promise you also some interesting petrifications; and you shall see there a device which I have constructed to measure the rise and fall of the tides."

"I shall be happy to be instructed," replied Dr. Johnson civilly.

"Pray tell me," I enquired, "is the Isle of Raasay rich in fauna?"

"We have blackcock, moor-fowl, plovers, and wild pigeons in abundance," replied Dr. MacLeod.

JOHNSON: "And of the four-footed kind?"

36

The Second Sight of Dr. Sam: Johnson

MacQueen: "We have neither rabbits nor hares, nor was there ever any fox upon the island until recently; but now our birds are hunted, and one sees often the melancholy sight of a little heap of discarded feathers where the brute has supped."

Boswell: "How came a fox to Raasay? By swimming the channel from the mainland?"

MacLeod: "We cannot believe so, for a fox is a bad swimmer. We can only suppose that some person brought it over out of pure malice."

Johnson: "You must set a trap for him."

MacQueen: "I think to do so, for the remains of his hunting betray where he runs."

Boswell: "Now had you but horses on the island, we should give Reynard a run."

This said, by mutual consent we all arose. Dr. Johnson and the Laird strolled off with Mr. Angus MacQueen to behold the stars of these northern latitudes. Dr. MacLeod, yawning, sought his bed; young Colin disappeared from my side like a phantom into the night; and I was left alone to the pleasing task of arranging my notes of the evening's discourse.

The morrow dawned wet and stormy, being one of those Hebridean days of which Dr. Johnson complained that they presented all the inconveniencies of tempest without its sublimities. Our enforced confinement was made pleasant by the learned discourse of the Reverend Donald MacQueen and his no less learned son; till, the storm abating, the younger man left us near sundown, to inspect his sea-gage at the edge of the island. He parted from Dr. Johnson on terms of mutual respect, and promised to bring him some specimens of petrifactions.

The night came on with many brilliant stars; and we congratulated ourselves on the prospect of a fair dawn for the promised ramble about the island.

Colin was at my bedside next morning between five and six. I sprung up, and rouzed my venerable companion. Dr. Johnson quickly equipped himself for the expedition, and seized his formidable walking-stick, without which he never stirred while in Scotland. This was a mighty oaken cudgel, knotted and gnarled; equipped with which the doughty philosopher felt himself the equal of any man.

We took a dram and a bit of bread directly. A boy of the name of Stewart was sent with us as our carrier of provisions. We were five in all: Colin MacQueen, Dr. MacLeod, the lad Stewart, Dr. Johnson, and myself.

"Pray, sir, where is Mr. Angus MacQueen?" enquired Dr. Johnson.

"Still on the prowl," said his brother carelessly.

"Observing the stars, no doubt," said Dr. MacLeod. "No matter, we shall surely encounter him in our peregrinations."

We walked briskly along; but the country was very stony at first, and a great many risings and fallings lay in our way. We had a shot at a flock of plovers sitting. But mine was harmless. We came first to a pretty large lake, sunk down comparatively with the land about it. Then to another; and then we mounted up to the top of Duncaan, where we sat down, ate cold mutton and bread and cheese and drank brandy and punch. Then we had a Highland song from Colin, which Dr. Johnson set about learning, *Hatyin foam foam eri*. We then walked over a much better country, very good pasture; saw many moorfowl, but could never get near them; descended a hill on the east side of the island; and so came to a hut by the sea. It was somewhat circular in shape, the door unfastened.

We called a blessing on the house and entered. At the far end an old woman was huddled over a peat fire. As we entered, she dropped the steaming breeks she had been drying before the glowing peat, and redded up for company by shuffling them hastily under the bedstead.

"Well, Kirstie," Colin MacQueen greeted her, "here's Dr. Johnson come all the way from London to ask you about your gift of the second sight."

To our utter astonishment the wizened old creature dropped to her knees and began to keen in a dreadful voice, rocking herself to and fro and wringing her hands.

"Come, come, my good creature," said the humane Doctor, "there's no occasion for such a display, I'm sure," and he benevolently insinuated half-a-crown into her clenched claw-like hand.

The aged Sybil peeped at it briefly, and stowed it away about her person; but she continued to keen softly, and presently her words became audible:

"Alas, 'tis no gift, but a curse, to have seen what I have seen, poor Rory gone, and my own son drowned, and now this very day—" The keening rose to a wail.

39

"We are causing too much distress by our enquiries," muttered my friend.

But the aged crone caught him by the wrist.

"It is laid on me to tell no less than to see."

"What have you seen today, then?" enquired Dr. MacLeod soothingly.

"Come," said Colin roughly, "there is nothing to be gained by lingering."

"Angus! Angus! Angus!"

"What of Angus?" asked Dr. Johnson with apprehension.

"I have heard his *taisk!* I have seen him lying broken and dead! He's gone, like Rory, like my own son that's drowned. Ai! Ai!"

"Come away," cried Colin, and flung out at the door. My friends complied, and I followed them, but not before I had bestowed some small charity upon the pathetic aged creature.

Colin led the way, walking heedlessly and fast. My friend and I perforce dropped behind.

"This is most remarkable," said Dr. Johnson. "If we should indeed find that the young man has met with a misfortune—which Heaven forfend—"

"We may speak as eye-witnesses of this often-doubted phænomenon," said I, concluding his statement.

"Nevertheless, sir," pronounced the learned philosopher, "man's intellect has been given him to *guard against credulity*. Let us take care not to fall into an attitude of superstitious belief in the old dame's powers. As yet her allegation is unsupported."

By this time we were come to the cave. It lies in a

section of the coast where the cliffs mount up to a threatening height, with a deep sound under, for a reef of jagged rocks some way out takes the pounding of the sea.

Dr. Johnson shewed especial curiosity about the minerals of the island. Ever solicitous for the improvement of human comfort, he enquired whether any coal were known on the island, "for," said he, "coal is commonly to be found in mountainous country, such as we see upon Raasay."

"See," he continued, "this vein of black sand, where otherwise the sand is white."

He gathered a handful; it stained his hand, and he cast it away.

"It is surely powdered coal," concluded my learned friend, punching at the deposit with his sturdy stick.

"Sir," I ventured, "it more nearly resembles charcoal."

"Coal or charcoal, 'tis all one," returned my friend. "Did I live upon Raasay, I should try whether I could find the vein, for there's no fire like a coal fire."

"Come, let us enter the cave," cried Colin MacQueen impatiently.

To my surprise the ghillie who carried our provisions unconditionally refused to enter the cave, alleging it to be haunted; a circumstance which was confirmed to his untutored mind by a strange echo from within, as of footsteps walking, that seemed to sound over the breakers.

"I'll not go in," said the lad stubbornly, " 'tis full of wild-fire these days, and something walks there."

" 'Tis your fox that walks there," observed Dr. Johnson, poking at a pile of feathers hard by the entrance.

"Well, my lad, if you won't come you may e'en stay here," said Colin MacQueen impatiently. "I fear neither fox nor fox-fire, and I'm for the cave. Come, gentlemen."

He led the way up a sloping incline and through a low entrance-way. Dr. Johnson had to stoop his great frame as he crowded through. Within, our footsteps rattled on the pebbly path. Colin carried a torch, which gleamed upon the rising roof and upon the petrifications that hung from it, formed by drops that perpetually distil therefrom. They are like little trees. I broke off some of them.

The cave widened and grew lofty as we progressed. Dr. Johnson was much struck by the absolute silence, broken only by the noise of our advance, which re-echoed ahead of us.

I drew Colin's attention to certain places on the floor, where partitions of stone appeared to be human work, shewing indeed the remains of desiccated foliage with which they had once been filled.

"In the days of the pirates," he explained, "this cave was a place of refuge. These are what is left of the beds. Here," he continued, "the cave divides. The left-hand arm slopes down to the sea, where a wide opening provided shelter for boats and a hiding-place for oars. Half-way down, there is a fresh spring. We take the right-hand turning, gentlemen."

"In times past," contributed Dr. MacLeod as we ascended the right-hand slope, "the cave sometimes served as a refuge for malefactors; but it invariably proved a trap."

"How so, sir?" I asked, "with a fresh spring, escape by sea or land, and the unexplored fastnesses of the cave to lurk in?"

There was a puff of air, and the torch with which Colin was leading the way was suddenly extinguished. At first the blackness was pitchy.

"You may proceed without fear," spoke Colin out of the darkness, "provided you always keep the wall of the cave at your left hand. I will endeavour to restore the light."

"Colin knows this cave as he knows his own house," Dr. MacLeod assured us.

We groped our way forward.

"Thus it was, in darkness on this ascent, that men waited to take or destroy the outlaw," Dr. MacLeod took up his narrative. "Just around this bend we come into light."

He spoke truly, for already a faint ray was diluting the darkness. As we rounded the bend we saw, ahead and close at hand, an irregular opening through which we could glimpse the sky.

"Whoever takes shelter in the innermost recesses of this cave," said Dr. MacLeod, "must pass by that opening whenever thirst drives him down to the spring below. A marksman stationed at the bend can pick him off as he passes against the light."

"That's the Kelpie's Window," said Colin at my

elbow. I started, and then in the uncertain light perceived him where he leaned in a little recess striking a light with flint and steel.

"Press on," said Colin, "I'll come behind with the torch."

I own it oppressed me with gloomy thoughts to climb in the darkness this path where savage and lawless men of the past had died. My venerable companion is of more intrepid mould; he and Dr. MacLeod pressed forward undismayed.

"I was on this path not three months since," pursued the physician, "when Black Fergus the murderer took shelter in these caves."

"Did you take him?" enquired Dr. Johnson with interest.

"We did not," said Dr. MacLeod. "We waited here in the dark, off and on by relays, for three days and three nights."

"Did not he come down?"

"When he came, he came running; and before we could take aim, he had flung himself into the sea."

I was powerfully struck by this narration. I seemed to see the hunted figure, driven by thirst to a watery grave.

We attained the top of this sinister incline, and stood in the Kelpie's Window, a sheer 100 feet above the black waters of the Kelpie Pool. Height makes me flinch; I retreated behind a rock which jutted out beside the opening.

Dr. Johnson stood firm and viewed the craggy descent with curiosity. The cliff fell away almost perpendicular, but much gashed and broken with spires and chimneys of rock.

"From this point Black Fergus flung himself into the sea," mused Dr. Johnson. "'Tis a fearful drop. His body must have been much battered by those jagged rocks below."

"We never recovered his body," replied Dr. Mac-Leod. "He had sunk before we reached the window, and he rose no more."

Colin came behind us with the torch alight.

"He must rise to the surface in the evolution of time," said Dr. Johnson. "—What is that at the edge of the Kelpie Pool?"

The physician stared fixedly below.

"It is certainly a body," he pronounced.

"'Tis Black Fergus," cried I, peeping in my turn.

Colin leaned boldly out to see.

"That is never Black Fergus," he said. "—Good God! 'Tis my brother!"

He turned and plunged down the dusky slope, carrying the torch with him.

"Wait, sir!" cried Dr. Johnson.

"I fear he is right," said Dr. MacLeod quietly, "that broad sun-hat is certainly Angus's. I must go to him."

He in his turn ran down the slope, following the diminishing gleam of Colin's torch.

It was indeed the unfortunate young tutor. His grief-stricken brother drew the body gently to land, and we made shift among us to bear it to the mouth of the cave. The terrified ghillie wrung his hands and babbled about the Kelpie; but Dr. MacLeod bade him hold his tongue and run to the big house for bearers.

"Poor lad," said Dr. MacLeod, "those petrifications have been the death of him. He must have over-balanced and fallen from the Kelpie's Window."

"I don't understand it," cried poor Colin. "Angus had no fear of height; he could climb like a cat."

"Nevertheless, he fell from the Kelpie's Window and drowned in the Kelpie Pool," I said with a shudder.

"Not drowned," said the physician, "he was dead when he hit the water. He must have struck his head as he fell; his skull is shattered."

The bearers arriving, we carried the unfortunate young man to his patron's house and laid him down.

This sad occurrence, as may be imagined, cast a pall over Raasay; all retired early, with solemn thoughts of the mutability of human affairs.

The night was advanced when I awoke with a start and was astounded to behold my venerable companion risen from bed and accoutered for walking in his wide brown cloth greatcoat with its bulging pockets, his Hebridean boots, and his cocked hat firmly secured by a scarf. I watched while he stole forth from the chamber, then rose in my turn and made haste to follow.

Lighted by a fine moon, the sturdy philosopher crossed the island at a brisk pace. I caught him up as we neared the opposite coast. As I came up with him he whirled suddenly and threw himself in an attitude of defence, menacing me truculently with his heavy staff.

"Sir, sir!" I expostulated.

The Second Sight of Dr. Sam: Johnson

"Is it you, you rogue!" exclaimed he, relaxing his pugnacity.

"What means this nocturnal expedition, sir?" I ventured to enquire.

"Only that I have a fancy to interrogate old Kirstie farther about the second sight," responded he.

"You do well," I approved, "for we have had a convincing if tragic exhibition of her powers."

"Have not I warned you against an attitude of credulity?" said the learned Doctor severely. "I must understand more of her powers before I may say I have seen a demonstration of the second sight."

"What more can you ask?" I replied.

By now we were within sight of old Kirstie's hut. Without replying, Dr. Johnson astounded me by striking up an Erse song in a tuneless bellow.

"Sir, sir, this is most unseemly!" I expostulated.

"*Hatyin foam foam eri,*" chanted Dr. Johnson lustily, striding along vigorously.

A boat was drawn up in a cove; Dr. Johnson rapped it smartly with his stick as we passed it. Then with a final triumphant "*Tullishole!*" he thundered resoundingly on the door of the hut.

The little old crone opened for us without any delay, and dropped us a trepidatious curtsey. The close apartment reeked of the remains of the cocky-leeky standing at the hearth. We had interrupted breakfast, for a half-consumed bowl of the stewed leeks and joints of fowl stood on the rude table.

"So, ma'am," said Dr. Johnson bluntly, "Angus MacQueen is dead like his brother."

The old beldame began to wail, but Dr. Johnson most unfeelingly cut her short.

"We found him dead in the Kelpie Pool with his head broke."

"He should never have gone in the cave!" whispered the aged Sybil. "He had my warning!"

"There's Something lives in that cave," said Dr. Johnson solemnly.

"Ay! Ay!"

"There's Something wicked lives in that cave, that comes forth to kill the blackcock by night, and hides in the upper reaches by day."

"Ay!"

"Have you seen it in your visions?"

"Ay, a mortal great ghostie that eats the bones of men . . . Alas! Alas!" the keening broke forth afresh.

"Then, ma'am," said the intrepid philosopher, "I have a mind to see this ghostie."

Hefting his heavy stick, Dr. Johnson left the hut. The woman burst forth into a clamour of warning, admonition, and entreaty, to which my friend paid little heed. Having bestowed a small gratuity, which served to intermit the old dame's ululations, I hurried after the venerable Doctor.

I caught him up at the cove. The declining moon was bright and clear.

"That is MacQueen's boat," I recognized it. "Who has brought it here?"

My only answer was a touch on the arm.

"Be quiet," said my friend in my ear. "Take this—"

he pressed a pistol in my hand, "and when we come to the cave—"

"You will never go into the cave at this hour!" I gasped.

"You need only go as far as the fork. Watch what I do, but take care not to reveal your presence. I have a mind to conjure up the Kelpie."

There was no gainsaying my learned friend. So it was done. I own it was rather a relief than otherwise, after the pitchy blackness of the first ascent, to come in sight of the moonlight streaming through the Kelpie's Window. I shrank gratefully into the shelter of the shoulder of rock where Colin had stood that morning. I thought no shame to breathe a prayer for the intercession of St. Andrew, patron of Scotland.

My lion-hearted friend mounted steadily, till at last I saw him stand in bold relief against the moonlit sky in the ill-omened Kelpie's Window. He stood foursquare without shrinking, his cocked hat tied firmly to his head, his heavy stick lost in the voluminous skirts of his greatcoat. What incantation he recited I know not.

Whatever incantation the intrepid initiate recited, it served to raise the Kelpie. There was a slip and slither of stealthy footsteps in the cave above; and then he came down with a rush and a rattle of pebbles. I saw his bulk dimly in the half light, with the great club raised; then my friend wheeled nimbly into the shelter of the rock that had served me that morning. At the same time he struck down strongly with his heavy stick,

49

and with a horrible cry the threatening figure overbalanced and tumbled headlong.

I hastened up the slope. At the top, my friend stood motionless and grave. At the foot of the cliff the fallen figure lay horribly still at the pool's edge.

"If he appear to his mother this time," muttered Dr. Johnson, "I'll know that she has the second sight."

"It mazes me," I remarked when once more we sat together at the Laird's fireside, "how in a record of second sight thrice confirmed, you, sir, managed to read the unsupernatural truth."

"Man's power of ratiocination," returned Dr. Johnson, "is his truest second sight."

"Doubtless," remarked Colin MacQueen, "old Kirstie, poor thing, was just as amazed at the learned Doctor's perceptions as we were at hers."

"Pray explain, then, how ratiocination led you to the truth."

"Sir, 'tis my earnest endeavour to instruct myself in your Highland phænomenon of second sight, of whose existence I have heard so much. I repeat, I am willing to be convinced; but of each demonstration I remain a skeptick. I ask: Is second sight possible? and I reply in the affirmative. Of each separate occurrence I then ask: Is *this* second sight? Could not it be something else? I have yet to hear of the case that would not admit of some other explanation. Such was my frame of mind when first I heard of old Kirstie and her feats of second sight."

"She prophesied Rory's death," said Colin.

The Second Sight of Dr. Sam: Johnson

JOHNSON: "Nay, sir, she *warned* you of his danger. Her reputation for second sight enabled her to do so without betraying her son. She foresaw what happened, not by second sight, but by her knowledge of her son's murderous frame of mind."

BOSWELL: "Then her story of her son rising out of the sea before her in the night was a pure invention."

JOHNSON: "Nay, sir, 'twas pure truth, save for the one detail that he was alive."

MACQUEEN: "How knew you that?"

JOHNSON: "Sir, I had concluded before I heard of this second apparition that the first one was a lie. If the second was a lie, it had one of two motives: if her son was dead, to add to her reputation for second sight; if alive, to contribute to his safety by confirming his supposed death. Thus far had ratiocination carried me when we visited her hut and heard her third prophecy. I had no faith in this third apparition, which I took, wrongly, to be a second warning."

BOSWELL: "Why a warning?"

JOHNSON: "Because, sir, I saw in the hut that which convinced me that Black Fergus was alive and on the island."

BOSWELL: "What?"

JOHNSON: "Why, sir, the great pair of breeks which we caught her drying at the fire, that she quickly hid under the bedstead. Think you that that poor wizened body had been wearing them, even were the women of Raasay given to masculine attire?"

"But with my own eyes I saw him leap into the sea and rise no more," objected Dr. MacLeod.

"You saw him leap," returned Dr. Johnson. "I saw when I stood in the Kelpie's Window how a strong and intrepid swimmer could leap outward and take no harm, for the Kelpie Pool is deep and calm, and for his life a man can swim a long stretch under water. Had you looked along the cliffs instead of down into the pool, Dr. MacLeod, you might have seen his head breaking water, like a seal's, to breathe. So it was that he came dripping to his mother out of the sea by night, and she comforted him, and hid him in the cave, and they plotted how he should reappear disguised when the nine-days' wonder had died down."

"Did ratiocinating on a single pair of sodden breeches tell you all this?" I rallied my learned friend.

"Not so," replied Dr. Johnson. "I concluded only to keep a sharp eye for signs of where she had hidden him. By the cave I saw the remains of his hunting—we have scotched your fox, Dr. MacLeod—and the charcoal of his fire ground into the sand; and in the cave we saw the fern he had couched on. From Dr. MacLeod I learned of the fresh spring and the chambers above; and I saw the Kelpie's Window and the pool below. Then we found the unfortunate young Angus, and the thing was certain. I knew at once how he had met his death."

"Why? Why did Black Fergus wish to harm him?" burst forth Colin MacQueen bitterly.

"Your brother ventured into the cave, torch in hand, to fetch those specimens of petrifications he promised me. There he came face to face with his brother's murderer, and knew him. So much is certain. I think he fled, and was struck down from behind."

"How came he in the Kelpie Pool, then?"

"Ratiocination tells me," replied Dr. Johnson, smiling slightly, "that guilt and terror obscured the man's reason. Instead of hiding the body where it might never have been found, he endeavoured to simulate an accident, by flinging the body from the Kelpie's Window. He then swam or waded by night to his mother's hut and implored her to facilitate his flight. There he lay hid while the old beldame dried his garments."

"Was he, then, in the very house when the old woman 'prophesied' Angus's death?"

"Was he elsewhere, without his breeches?" countered Dr. Johnson. "When I saw Angus lying murdered, I knew who had done it, I knew what he must do next. I resolved to stop his flight."

"Why you? Why single-handed?"

"Since the '45, there is no law on Raasay, save what is brought from the mainland. I, an Englishman, a stranger, might most safely take justice upon myself. By night, I returned to the hut."

"How dared you seek him out on his own ground?"

"I preferred to face him on ground I had chosen. By the ostentatiousness of my arrival I gave such warning as drove him from the hut to his hiding-place in the cave. Mr. Boswell will confess that though I am scarce fit for Italian opera, my rendition of an Erse song has a peculiar carrying power. For the same purpose I thundered, sir,—" turning to Colin, "upon your boat, which the murderer had stolen and beached, ready for his flight. Having thus assured the murderer's presence in the cave, I entered in search of him."

"Good heavens, sir!" cried Colin impetuously, "to venture thus into the lair of a wild beast, and hope to surprize him ere he can surprize you!"

"I had no such hope," replied my intrepid friend. "He was sure to perceive me and attack me first. I permitted him to do so, only choosing my ground with some care."

"The Kelpie's Window hardly seems like favourable ground."

"On the contrary," replied Dr. Johnson. "If I was to bait my own trap, I had to have visibility, a quality provided in the whole cave only by the Kelpie's Window. There also shelter is provided, as Mr. Boswell found."

"Do you mean to say, sir," cried Dr. MacLeod, "that you stood in that orifice, contemplating such a declivity, and permitted a desperate murderer to creep up on you in the dark?"

"I expected him; I detected his approach; I was able to evade him at the crucial moment. That he fell from the Kelpie's Window was no part of my plan, for I had counted on taking him with my pistol."

"Sir, sir," I cried, "you took a grave risk thus staking your life on your hearing."

"Nor did I so," replied Dr. Johnson, half smiling. "You forget that Black Fergus had been supping on *cocky-leeky*. It takes neither ratiocination nor second sight, sir, to detect the proximity of your pervasive Scottish leek!"

THE

Flying Highwayman

S IR," remarked my illustrious friend Mr. Sam:
Johnson, "I am sorry to hear of the insolent behaviour of your landlord; but you need not take the
law of him in order to be quit of your bargain. For consider: if he determines to hold you, and the lodgings
must be yours for a year, you may certainly use them as
you think fit. So, sir, you may quarter two lifeguardsmen
upon him; or you may send the greatest scoundrel you
can find into your apartments; or you may say that you
want to make some experiments in natural philosophy,
and may burn a large quantity of assafœtida in his
house."

I was torn between laughter and admiration at the
wonderful fertility of Johnson's mind; but betwixt the
two I was still determined to carry the matter before the
magistrate, if only to acquaint myself at first hand with

the police of the great metropolis. I had not resided in London many months, and being a raw Scotch lad of twenty-three, I still looked with eagerness upon the crowded scene and desired to be a part of it.

Yielding to my whim, Dr. Johnson carried me with him to the publick office in Bow Street, and thus I came to have a part in the strange affair of the Flying Highwayman.

"You will find here," he instructed me as we turned out of Drury Lane, "the most famous magistrate in the kingdom. Henry Fielding the novelist sat here till his death, and now his brother John sits in his room. Stay, this is the house."

I looked with interest upon the tall, narrow structure, and hastened to mount the exiguous stair and come into the presence of the magistrate.

We found Sir John Fielding in the publick room. 'Twas a long, empty chamber. At one end and along the sides extended benches, now deserted, for 'twas past dinner-time. One or two nondescript men stood about; but 'twas upon Sir John Fielding, seated in his great chair, that my eyes became rivetted.

I saw a burly man in middle life, with a strong, handsome face. He was decently attired in brown stuff with horn buttons, and wore his own hair, prematurely white, combed in loose curls. In his hand he held a light wand, and about his head over his eyes he wore a narrow band of black silk. He turned towards us as we entered—not his eyes, for they were tight shut; but he turned his whole frame and inclined towards us with parted lips.

The Flying Highwayman

I saw with a shock that the famous Westminster magistrate was blind.

Sir John greeted Sam: Johnson as an old friend, and me as a new one; and of my vexatious affair it need only be said, that by Sir John's instructions all went off to a wish, and my impertinent landlord plagued me no more.

"Pray, Sir John," said I then, "will not you acquaint me with the police of this metropolis?"

"I will do better than that," replied the blind magistrate with a smile. "You shall see it at first hand. I am now to visit the watch at Stamford Hill turnpike, and I shall be honoured if you and Dr. Johnson will accept of a place in my carriage."

We consented eagerly, and soon we were bowling briskly along on the Hertford Road, leading north out of London. As we rode, Sir John explained our errand.

"You must know, Mr. Boswell, that the metropolis is plagued by miscreants of every description, by Abram coves, by sky-farmers, by the running-smobble; most of all by the gentlemen of the high toby."

"Highwaymen," glossed my learned friend.

"To remedy which evil," pursued the blind magistrate, "there has recently been established the horse patrole, thief-takers in my employ, well mounted, who patrole the turnpikes and raise the hue and cry so soon as they hear of any robbery upon the highway; for now every idle 'prentice who can come by a horse takes to the high toby, and that with too little fear of capture. One such, whom we have striven in vain to capture, is he whom we know only as the Flying Highwayman. He haunts this very road, out Enfield way. The horse patrole watches for him at Stamford Hill turnpike to the south of Enfield, and mans a barrier by Turner's Hill to the north; but barrier nor pike stays him no more than a bird; he comes and goes at will like a ghost. I am resolved he shall be taken, and I make this visit to the turnpike and the barrier to hearten up my brave lads of the patrole."

Chatting thus, we came to the turnpike. 'Twas but a long pole across the road, fitted to swing upon a stock or stump at one side. Barriers on either side prevented the wayfarer from going around and so cheating the turnpike man of his toll. The house of the turnpike man was close by. A man on horseback was at the alert by the side of the road. Our chaise drew up at the pike, and the man came to the chaise-side and saluted Sir John.

"Ah, Barrock," said Sir John at the sound of his voice, "and where is Watchett? Sure you have not permitted him to leave his post?"

"He's rid on patrole, if you please, sir," replied the fellow hoarsely. He was a stumpy, powerful fellow in middle life, with a broad blank face.

"Being," he added, "but a young 'un, d'ye see, and new to the patrole, and having scant patience for waiting here at the barrier."

"Very good, Barrock, so he's not doing his patrole at the Rose and Crown with the serving-wench on his knee. Is all quiet here?"

"Dead quiet, sir. Never a rider has passed over the barrier since dinner-time."

The Flying Highwayman

'Twas as the man spoke that Sir John lifted his head and listened.

"Here's a rider coming now," said he.

I listened, and heard nothing. 'Twas a full minute before my less sharp ears caught the beat of horse's hoofs, and longer before the animal appeared, coming towards us from the Enfield side of the turnpike. For a moment I thought we might be face to face with the Flying Highwayman. The rider was young and strong-built, with heavy dark brows and a resolute jutting chin. He wore a long sand-coloured horseman's greatcoat; on his shoulders the dust of the road lay thick, though by its dun colour scarce visible. As he drew near the pole I saw the wicked long horse-pistols riding loose in his saddle-holsters. He put his grey to the barrier, cleared it at a bound, and came to us in the chaise.

"All's clear, sir," he reported to Sir John in a piping boyish voice, " 'twixt here and the barrier; and no rider has come over the barrier this two hours past."

'Twas Watchett, the restless lad of the horse patrole.

Instead of answering, Sir John once more raised his head to listen.

"Here's a wayfarer coming," said he, "and this time on foot."

Dr. Johnson peered near-sightedly into the gathering gloom; from which gradually emerged a strange and bedraggled figure.

'Twas a woebegone young man of fashion that stumbled towards us. His attire was rich, but marred with dust and disarray, and indecorously scanty. He wore once-snowy buckskins, and boots of Russia leather, and a shirt of finest linen, richly embroidered and beruffled with lace—and nothing else. As to his person, he was of middle size, and well-made. He had a noble profile and a handsome head, but made strange and bare by the fact that he had no wig, only his own fair hair in short curls. He smelled of otto.

'Twixt chattering teeth he cursed the Flying Highwayman. Watchett and Barrock exchanged glances of dismay as the newcomer approached the chaise-side. When he saw my venerable companions, he gave over his profane swearing and altered his tone.

"Your pardon, gentlemen," he said suavely, "for appearing before you in this disarray; for which you must not blame me, but the Flying Highwayman, whom I have but now to my disadvantage encountered upon the road. The scoundrel has had, not only my purse, but my phaeton and pair, and my very garments as well. Pray, can you not help me to some rag to cover me?"

Almost before he spoke I had doffed my greatcoat and thrown it around him, a courtesy which he acknowledged with a graceful salute.

"Sir," replied Sir John, "you have fortuned to come upon the right man, for I can help you to what you stand most in need of, namely, justice, and your goods again. Sir John Fielding, at your service, sir."

The modish young fellow bowed low.

"William Page, of Waltham Cross; yours to command."

"Say then, Mr. Page, where you had the misfortune to encounter this pernitious miscreant."

The Flying Highwayman

"Not a quarter-mile below the Rose and Crown."

Without more ado Sir John despatched the men of the horse patrole to ride thither in pursuit. Then we repaired to the house of the turnpike man to hear the story at large.

The turnpike keeper was a little weasel of a man with quick beady eyes. He set before us gin and small beer, a meagre entertainment which appealed to none of us save the shivering victim. Of the gin he downed a full four fingers, not without a grimace of distaste, before he told his tale.

"You must know, Sir John, my elder brother is Lord Mountcairn. My father being lately dead, Mountcairn takes the estate, d'ye see, and I'm left with my choice of the horses or the women. I take the horses, they're the less kittle cattle. I've as pretty a pair of matched blacks to my phaeton as you'll see in Middlesex, and I drive them myself, and now this confounded knight of the pad has got 'em, curse him!

"Well, sir, I left my house at Waltham Cross to drive to London, and coming over the barrier I most particularly enquired if the road were clear, for this Flying Highwayman is the scourge of that stretch of road. 'O yes sir,' says they, 'for here's Watchett has ridden off but now, and he says all's quiet as the grave. You may drive to London in peace.' Peace! Ha! I had scarce passed the Rose and Crown, when out of a copse steps this black-avised scoundrel. He'd a dun greatcoat about him, and a half-mask over his eyes, and dark hair tied behind, and a chest like a barrel. He rode a grey horse, and presented two deuced long horse-pistols, and 'Stand!' says he, 'Stand and deliver.' A brace of horse-pistols is a great perswader, Sir John and gentlemen. I stood, and I delivered. I delivered my purse, and my phaeton and pair, and the cloathes off my back, and the very wig off my head, and trudged off down the London road with the great black-browed scoundrel laughing behind me."

"Sure, sir," said Dr. Johnson thoughtfully, "this is something new in highwaymen. I muse what he wants with your cloathes and your wig."

"Sir," replied Sir John, "the whims of these gentry are past finding out. I have known in my time one knight of the high toby, that absolutely required two ladies, whom he robbed, to walk a minuet before him; and another who at pistol's point forced a clergyman, his victim, to preach him a sermon upon the text, *Thou shalt not steal.*"

" 'Tis well, at that rate," remarked Mr. Page, "that the Flying Highwayman proved a fancier, neither of religion nor of dancing, but only of horse-flesh and haberdashery; I had scarce satisfied him else."

Suddenly Sir John turned his closed eyes towards the door. It opened, and Barrock entered.

"Your phaeton, sir," he cried to Mr. Page, "I've brought it back safe and sound; as likewise, sir," turning to Sir John, "we've taken him that had it."

With that through the open door stepped Watchett, urging by the collar a bow-legged youth in the striped vest of an hostler. He bent his black brows in a dark scowl upon his captive, and shook him a little as if to shake speech out of him.

The Flying Highwayman

"Which I am hostler at the Rose and Crown," the bandy-legged fellow whined, "and I'm innocent, me Lord."

"Innocent!" cried Watchett, "when I caught him in the inn yard, red-handed with the phaeton! One of the horses was gone, and he was just upon loosing the other from the traces when I rode in and caught him at it."

"One of the horses was gone!" cried young Page in agony. "The finest matched pair in the county, and one gone! Where is my horse, villain?"

"I don't know, indeed, your Honour," cried the miserable boy. "I found the phaeton in a copse, indeed, indeed I did, with one horse gone and the other standing in the traces, and so led him gently to the inn, where indeed, me Lord, I meant only to refresh the beast before informing the horse patrole."

"Pray, Watchett, did you search the stables?"

"I did, sir, but never a black horse did I find."

" 'Cause why?" retorted the young hostler stubbornly, " 'cause never a black horse was there, bar him was still in the traces."

Sir John probed the youth with rigour, but no better answer could he get, and at last we all trooped out to inspect the recovered phaeton.

'Twas a luxurious vehicle, fit for a lord, and the single black in the traces was a glossy, handsome animal. I noted the empty pistol-holders by the side of the vehicle. The seat was richly upholstered, and on it, neatly folded, reposed Mr. Page's missing cloathes. All was there—the brocaded coat, the laced waistcoat, the fine cocked hat, even the handsome powdered wig. Only the purse full of guineas was still missing. Sir John, though he could not see the equipage, inspected all with nose and fingers, even going so far as to inhale the otto given off by the powdered wig.

"Past question," he remarked, "Mr. Page, this gear is yours."

The young fellow laughed as he donned his coat once more.

"And happy am I to have it," he replied. "Depend upon it, from this day I'll take good care to carry pistols in yonder empty holsters. I'll not rest, till this miscreant of the pad be laid by the heels."

"I muse," replied Sir John, "how it is to be done; for the man wears a cloak of invisibility."

"He must be decoyed into the open," declared Dr. Johnson.

"How, decoyed?"

"We must provide him a traveller to rob, who shall take care to be well armed in secret. Once he has come forth, he may be taken, be he never so invisible at the turnpikes and barriers."

"How shall I find such a traveller? My men are known."

"I will gladly make one in the scheam," cried young Page eagerly.

"No, sir," replied Dr. Johnson, "for having once been robbed, you also are known. But come, Mr. Boswell, let us take this adventure upon ourselves; 'twill be something to tell in Edinburgh."

"With all my heart, sir," I cried.

"You must take care to have gold about you," suggested Watchett, "and shew it at the inns and turnpikes; for I am perswaded, that the scoundrel hath friends at both, who keep him advised, and it may be turn the other way as he goes past the barriers."

Ay, thought I, picturing the weasel-face turnpike man —and not a thousand miles from here.

"Gold!" exclaimed Dr. Johnson. "Nay, sir, if I must find gold, the adventure is ended before it begins."

"It is for the magistrate to find the gold," replied Sir John, "for Watchett is in the right, you will scarce flush the Flying Highwayman from his covert without it. The men of the horse patrole shall be close at hand to take the scoundrel."

"No, sir," replied Dr. Johnson, "for the same spies who report the gold, are sure to report also that Sir John Fielding's people are on the roads, and so our scheam will fail. No, sir, we shall be very well. Mr. Boswell, in the character of a postilion, will be armed with a pair of horse-pistols, and between us we shall take him."

"You must have help, sir," cried Sir John.

"If we are to have help, it must be of a private person," replied Johnson firmly.

"You are right," cried Page, "and in this I may be of use to the scheam; for if the Flying Highwayman will scarce assail me a second time, he can be under no apprehension if I am seen on the road; for on that road, and at the inns and turnpikes, I am as well known as the Hertford coach, passing nigh as often between my house in the country and my house in town."

We accepted of this offer. Sir John promising us a purse of twenty guineas, we parted to prepare against the adventure of the morrow, Dr. Johnson and I to Fleet Street, Mr. Page to Waltham Cross. We agreed to rendezvous betimes the next evening at the Rose and Crown.

The next day's sun was setting as we paid our toll at the Stamford Hill turnpike. The lad Watchett of the horse patrole sat on the stile eating an apple; his horse cropped grass. The boy ignored us ostentatiously. I did not see Barrock. With one of his frequent convulsive starts, Dr. Johnson contrived to spill the purse of guineas, at which the turnpike man stared. Then he turned the long pike, and we rolled into the stretch of road haunted by the Flying Highwayman.

'Twas a new experience for me, riding postilion on the lead horse in my buckskins and tight cap. I touched the horse-pistols in their holsters, and was reassured. I longed to be riding in the chaise with my illustrious friend, who never discoursed better than when elevated and inspired by the pleasures of rapid motion to which he was so addicted; but it was not to be, and I kept the horses at a lively trot, wondering every minute whether we should ever reach our rendezvous at the Rose and Crown.

I wondered the more as twilight fell, for slowly the conviction was growing upon me that we were being followed. I seemed to hear our horses' hoof-beats re-echoed from a distance; yet when I turned, the road was bare and empty. I fear I turned often to stare along the dusty road, with its dark copses on either side, its squalid little hedge-ale-houses sheltering who knows what? It was with relief that I saw ahead the lights of the Rose and Crown.

I left the chaise standing in the yard, and together we entered the common room of the inn and called for refreshment. A buxom, masterful woman presided at the tap—Hester Palmer, hereditary mistress of the old house. The pot-boy took the filled tankards from her brawny hand, and slapped them down on the bare oaken table before us. Dr. Johnson regarded the man with interest. He was no boy, being on in years, lame in one leg, and but sparsely provided with teeth. But for us the room was empty. The antient drawer leaned against the table, ready for a bit of talk.

"Ye'll be London gentlemen?"

"Ay," said Dr. Johnson, according to plan, "we're for London tonight, and sorry I am to be benighted, for we carry a purse of gold, and here's an ill strip of the road by reputation."

" 'Tis so, sir," assented the pot-boy eagerly. " 'Tis the worst stretch of road north of London, I'll be bound, and has been since the great days of Dick Turpin. Ah, Turpin! There was the greatest of all the lads on the scamp. I mind him many a time, striding into this very inn with his pockets full of gold."

"This very house!" I exclaimed.

"And why not?" croaked the antient pot-boy, "for he married the landlord's daughter, and more by token there she stands at the bar, Mrs. Richard Turpin as ever was, though the name's forgotten these many years."

The door creaked open. On the threshold stood a sturdy young man muffled to his lips in a long sand-coloured horseman's greatcoat. He wore a flapped hat pulled down about his brows, presenting to our gaze no more than a bold nose and a bit of tanned cheek. He was swarthy as a gypsy.

He stood motionless in the doorway and swung his eyes slowly about the room. He raked with his glance the virago at the bar, the empty tables, and ourselves in our corner. Satisfied, he strode in and took a place in a sheltered settle well back from the fire. Mistress Palmer brought him a pot, and for a while their heads were together in close converse.

"Ah, Turpin!" the antient was rambling on, "no thief-taker ever took Turpin. He lay snug in his cave, him and Tom King, just over the river," he pointed in the general direction of east—"and Mistress Hester victualled them from the inn. I was the hostler's boy then, and many's the time I've carried the hamper, ay and eat with Turpin and King too, and drunk at the mouth of the cave."

"Where is this cave?" enquired Johnson.

" 'Tis but a trot, sir, for a man on a horse, but for all that 'tis not so easy found, I'll warrant you, without you was shewed the way."

"Yet if no thief-taker ever took Turpin," I struck in, "how came he to be hanged at last?"

"Alack, sir, 'twas all along of his high spirits. He went down into Yorkshire, d'ye see, for the better pre-sarving of his health; swinging in a rope, said he, he had a mortial aversion to, for his prophetical great-grandmother had formerly told him, it was a plaguy dry sort of death. Well, sir, here he was, living quietly at York, when he takes a notion to a bit of sport, and discharges his piece at his landlord's cock. 'You do me wrong, sir, to shoot my fowl,' cries the landlord. 'O ho,' says bold Turpin, 'is it you? Do but stay till I have charged my piece again, I'll shoot you too.' Sir, the curmudgeonly old hunks swore the peace against him; and when they had him, by ill luck they learned who he was. Oh, sir, he swung with spirit! 'Don't hurry,' says he to the crowds hastening gallows-wards, 'there'll be no fun till I come!' On the scaffold he kicked off his boots among the crowd, to make a liar of his old mother, who often said, he was a bad lad, and would die in his boots."

To all of this discourse Dr. Johnson listened with rapt attention, as the fowler learns the habits of the birds, or the courser notes the ways of the hare. Now, however, the discourse was cut short by the arrival of William Page.

He came in with a rush. Under the brooding eye of the brown young man, Dr. Johnson tried to frown him off, but to no avail. He rushed up to us.

He was splendidly attired in a raspberry-coloured coat with gold upon it, a laced waistcoat, a great cocked hat, and a pea-green greatcoat reversed with fawn. His newly powdered wig, clubbed behind, set off his handsome, fresh-coloured face.

"All is well," he cried, "I came over the Turner's Hill barrier but now, all is in order, and no such horseman as we seek has passed the barrier. Neither did I pass anyone on the road, save an old clergyman ambling along on his pad. Depend upon it, our man, if he but comes, will come from another direction."

"Ay," cried I, "from Turpin's cave, may be."

"There's no great mystery in this," mused Dr. Johnson. "In my early days in London, just such a Flying Highwayman exercised the wits of the town. 'Twas simple in the end—the daring miscreant would put his horse to the turnpikes, and so clear them while the turnpike man was still withinside. The great thing is, not to worry our wits in surmise, but to lay the fellow by the heels and so resolve all at once. Come, let us go."

He paid the scot accordingly, with a great display of guineas, and we descended to the inn yard. There we found our chaise, Mr. Page's phaeton, and the stranger's grey, all under the care of our acquaintance of Stamford Hill, the bandy-legged hostler who had been found in possession of the phaeton.

Mr. Page scowled upon him. I felt for the sporting gentleman, for in the traces of his phaeton, instead of his darling matched blacks, stood an ill-assorted pair—the remaining black, incongruously yoked to a nondescript bay. He was a man of action, however; instead of mourning over his severed pair, he strode to the phaeton-side and without a word corrected the priming of his pistols.

"Allow me, Mr. Boswell."

He did the same for mine. Somehow the action pierced me with a new realization of the danger involved in our nocturnal adventure.

"Let us go," said Johnson resolutely. "Do you, sir, follow us. 'Tis a matter for nicety, to keep so far behind, that the Flying Highwayman will not take alarm at our confederacy, yet so close that one may come to the assistance of the other. Pray look to it, gentlemen."

"Trust me, sir."

With these words I leaped to horse and in my character as postilion guided our chaise out of the inn yard. Mr. Page mounted his phaeton and followed. The bandy-legged hostler watched us go.

We turned into the road and proceeded at a good pace towards Stamford Hill. No sound was to be heard save the jingle of our harness. On either side we passed darkened cottages, or quiet fields and copses. I loosened my pistols in the saddle-holsters.

We had passed Houndsfield, and were proceeding through dark coverts, when behind us I heard the hoofbeats of a horse ridden hard. Another moment, and the beast had drawn up level with the lead horse.

"Stand!" cried the rider, and caught my bridle. "Stand and deliver!"

My reply was resolute. I snatched the loosened pistols and fired point-blank at the menacing figure. I heard the highwayman laugh as my pistols flashed in the pan. He dragged our team to a stop, and pranced his horse to the chaise-side.

"Pray, sir," says he to Dr. Johnson in a soft, light, caressing voice, shewing pistols in his turn, "pray oblige me with your purse, for you see there's no help for it."

My usually intrepid friend shewed no fight. He regarded the pistols the highwayman presented, and handed out his purse without a word. I stared at the highwayman as he weighed it.

He sat like a centaur upon William Page's black. He was well-set and elegant, modishly attired in a long dun horseman's greatcoat reversed with some dark material. Lace ruffles fell to his knuckles. He wore dark hair, unpowdered and clubbed behind, and his laced hat was flapped. His shoulders were dusted with white, and he smelled of otto. His face was entirely covered by a black lace mask. Behind the cobwebby thing his eyes gleamed.

"What's this, Dr. Johnson," says he softly, "cockleshells? Curling-paper money?"

"As to that," says my friend, "I am but a poor man—"

"You are richer than this," cut in the highwayman, "by Sir John's twenty guineas; so out with them, for I'll not be trifled with."

"Sir," said Johnson heavily, "I'm loath to have it known that I delivered Sir John's guineas without striking a blow for them. Pray, give me such a Gadshill scar as I may shew—oblige me by putting a ball through the crown of my hat."

The highwayman gave a chime of laughter.

" 'Tis a shrewd old fogram. Well, sir, so be it."

The blast of the horse-pistol was deafening. It tore a gaping hole through Dr. Johnson's respectable old cocked hat.

"Here's your battle-scarred bonnet," said the highwayman contemptuously, "so you may deliver with a clear conscience. Over with it."

"Sir, my friend Boswell has also a character to lose. Come, Bozzy, reach him your coat that he may put a ball through the tail."

At this outrageous proposition I stiffened.

The Flying Highwayman

" 'Pon honour, sir," I began haughtily.

"No words, sir," thundered Dr. Johnson, "do as you are bid."

"Ay," seconded the highwayman with a sneer, "do as your governor bids you, for by God if you don't reach it me, I'll as lief put the hole into you as into your coat."

Sullenly I obeyed, and a second blast shook the copses as the highwayman emptied his second pistol into my coat.

Here was an ignominious ending to our adventure! I strained my ears to hear if our ally in his phaeton were not at hand; and sure enough I heard far off the beat of horse's hoofs.

"Now, sir," says the Flying Highwayman in his affected, girlish voice, "I've obliged you by marring your apparel, do you oblige me with Sir John's guineas."

"Pray, satisfy my curiosity in one thing," replied Dr. Johnson. "Say, how you contrive to come over the turn-pikes?"

"I jump them," replied the knight of the road shortly, "and so no more words, but out with your gold, for I'm not such a fool as to stand here prating while your ally approaches."

"If I must," said Dr. Johnson, and slowly drew Sir John's purse from his breast. The highwayman leaned forward impatiently to snatch it. The hoof-beats were nearing now at a gallop.

As the highwayman stretched forth his hand, suddenly my burly friend caught his wrist in a grip of iron. With an oath the highwayman set spurs to his horse, an ill-considered act which merely served to seal his doom; for as the startled creature shied, my muscular friend, so far from relaxing his grip, with one powerful impulse fairly pulled the marauder from his horse.

"Yield!" cried Dr. Johnson triumphantly. "Yield, for you've shot your bolt!"

The breath was out of him. In a trice I had leaped to earth and secured him, just as still another rider gallopped up and reined in beside us.

"You have taken him!" he cried.

'Twas Barrock, the thick pursuer of the horse patrole. I looked at him astonished. He wore a venerable full-bottomed wig and clergyman's bands.

"Disguise," said he with a grin. "Sir John set us to watch over you, but in our own persons 'twould not do."

I thought privately that no clergyman's blacks could make the man look other than a thief-taker. He looked precious odd as he competently took up the sullen highwayman, masked as he had fallen, and bound him securely into his saddle, and thus we drove him before us towards Stamford Hill. I momentarily expected the phaeton to catch us up, but it never appeared; though as we neared the turnpike I again had the disagreeable sensation of a horseman at our backs.

At Stamford Hill Sir John Fielding awaited us, taking his ease in the keeper's house. He turned his closed eyes towards us as we entered.

"Well, Mr. Page," he said, "have you had good sport, and did you take your quarry?"

"Mr. Page is not with us, sir," I explained regretfully, "here are only Dr. Johnson and myself, and honest Barrock, and," I added with pride, "the Flying Highwayman, whom we have taken."

"Mr. Boswell is mistaken," said Dr. Johnson instantly. "Mr. Page *is* of our number, as I have known from the first."

I stared. My companion turned to the pinioned malefactor and stripped the lace mask from the face, the wig from the head. I looked into the pink-and-white countenance of William Page Esq:, the sporting gentleman. His spirit was unbroken; he laughed in my thunderstruck face.

Before a word was spoken, there was a diversion. Into the room strode the gypsy-face young man of the inn. He plucked off his hat to Sir John, and I saw his face. 'Twas Watchett—stained, and by the light of the candles hastily and inexpertly stained, with some dark dye—but indisputably Watchett.

"Here's a coil, sir," he cried. "Here's your phaeton left in a copse, Mr. Page, sir, and your other black gone from the traces; for though I followed you I did not follow close enough, and when I came up with the phaeton the mischief was done."

"The mischief was done indeed," said Dr. Johnson grimly.

"So," said Sir John to our captive, "this was your scheam, eh, for coming over the barriers?"

"By jumping?" I puzzled.

"No, sir," replied Dr. Johnson. "I fed him that explanation, and then gave him cause to feed it back again in his guise as the Flying Highwayman. No, sir, he passed the barrier driving his phaeton, in his character as sporting younger son. Once past, he had only to conceal the phaeton in some copse, turn his coat, change his wig, and ride off on one of his blacks. The robbery done, back to the phaeton, and whisk! the Flying Highwayman had once more flown away."

"Yet, pray, sir," demanded the magistrate sternly, "how were you so foolhardy as to complain to me, that you had yourself been robbed by the Flying Highwayman? Do you hold so low an opinion of Sir John Fielding, as to court his investigation?"

Dr. Johnson forestalled the highwayman's answer.

"He could do no other. Yonder hostler lad found his phaeton and his discarded cloathes hid in the copse, and made off with them. How else account for them, if the truth were not to be suspected, than to complain that they had been stolen? Nor did he single you out for his dupe, but rather complained to all he might meet."

BOSWELL: "Yet how could you smoak Mr. Page in this disguise?"

JOHNSON: "Sir, I was on the look-out for a vehicle or cart which might pass the barriers unsuspected. Now in this whole affair we had no other vehicle than the phaeton. My attention was thus drawn to the victim of the robbery himself. To what end would his cloathes and phaeton be first taken, at risk to the thief, and then abandoned? But suppose they had been, not taken, but *left*. Then all becomes clear. I watched Mr. Page carefully. I could not prevent him drawing the charge from Mr. Boswell's pistols; but I could, and did, devise a scheam for the harmless discharge of *his* pistols; which you, Mr. Boswell, thought very ill of me for carrying out."

BOSWELL: "How came it, that at the turnpike Mr. Page—" at the respectful appellation the detected highwayman bowed ironically—"the masquerading highwayman," I amended, "when he described the Flying Highwayman, described Watchett to the life?"

JOHNSON: "Why not, when Watchett in the flesh had been by so recently? I'll ask you suddenly to describe a non-existent person, what can you do better than to limn the last stranger you have seen?"

BOSWELL: "Yet what thought you, sir, when you beheld our highwayman to be a girlish youth with dark hair?"

JOHNSON: "A girlish voice may be assumed; and as to dark hair, he who doffs a powdered wig may don a black one; yet cannot pass safe from detection, if he turns his greatcoat before he changes wigs, and sprinkles his shoulders with powder."

BOSWELL: "Dust, surely?"

JOHNSON: "No, sir. The greatcoat was dust-coloured; 'twas the white powder of a wig that marked it so plainly. Yet the fellow wore a black wig."

"Yet Sir John Fielding," I marvelled, "though he could mark none of these things, knew the man at once."

The great Middlesex magistrate smiled.

"I know three thousand malefactors by ear—"

"Yet Mr. Page did not speak."

"—and many more by *nose*. The man reeks of otto. Take him away."

In fine, all was as Dr. Johnson said. The pseudo-gentleman's first missing black was found straying under saddle by the river-side, and his highwayman's disguise and his pistols finally came to light in the haystack where he had hidden them. Sir John was prodigiously gratified, and in deference to the request of Dr. Johnson, the Flying Highwayman was spared hanging, that plaguy dry sort of death, in favour of transportation to his Majesty's plantations in America; where I hear he hath turned honest, and raises a numerous progeny.

THE
Monboddo Ape Boy

SIR," said Dr. Johnson, "he who affects singularity, must not complain if he becomes the object of publick curiosity."

I laughed, but made no comment.

"If Lord Monboddo," continued my learned friend severely, "avers that the ourang-outang is the cousin-german of man, he must expect the mob to believe that he peoples his estate with apes. If he speculates upon chymistry, he must put up with a rumour that he has found the philosopher's stone and changes base metal to gold."

My illustrious friend's strictures upon this original Scottish philosopher boded ill for the events of the next

79

twenty-four hours, for as he spoke every revolution of our chaise wheels was carrying us nearer to Monboddo. Journeying northward from Edinburgh in late August of the year 1773, bound for the Highlands of Scotland, I was unwilling that Dr. Johnson should pass by Monboddo when by a short drive we might see the estate and its ingenious owner, James Burnet, a Lord of Session under the title of Lord Monboddo. It was so concerted between us, for although Dr. Johnson deprecated the infidelity of Monboddo's speculations on the nature of man, there were several points of similarity between them: learning, clearness of head, precision of speech, and a love of research on many subjects which people in general do not investigate.

Our road led through rolling moors devoid of any tree. The ragged grey clouds hung low. Nevertheless we drove along at a good pace, preceded by our out-rider and only attendant, my servant Joseph Ritter, a Bohemian, a fine stately fellow above six feet high, mounted on a sturdy grey; whom we presently despatched before to apprise Lord Monboddo of our coming.

Though the day was lowering and the landscape barren, the rapid motion of the chaise imparted to Dr. Johnson that peculiar pleasure which he took in the mere state of rapid motion; and he answered with indulgence and good humour when I ventured to dispute his proposition.

"Nay, sir," said I, "how can the foolish inventions of rumour discommode so learned a philosopher as Monboddo?"

"You are wrong," returned my learned friend, "to

think that the ill-conceived opinions of men may do no harm to him upon whom they are laid. You see here these two men who carry a bucking-basket between them—"

I observed the pair with interest as the chaise came up to them. They were an ill-assorted pair, plodding along ahead of us supporting between them by means of poles a very Falstaff of a pannier. The man behind was a red-faced, pig-eyed, burly clod dressed like a countryman in dirty leather breeches and a short-skirted frieze coat. The man in the lead was a very different sort. His light eyes were half-closed in a pasty, bony, coffin-shaped face, set off by a large cocked hat and a dirty trickle of torn lace at throat and wrist. They never raised their heads as the chaise passed them in a rolling cloud of white dust.

"I see them," I replied, still staring over my shoulder. "What then?"

"Why, sir," said Dr. Johnson, "let us say that I conceive the unfounded notion that these ruffians have abducted the heiress of Lothian, and are bearing her bound hand and foot in yonder pannier to Aberdeen, where in a mock marriage the thick lout will wed her to the thin one."

"Then," cried I, laughing heartily, "I should much commend your invention, and set you on to commence playwright; but the honest lads would plod on with their burden no whit discommoded by our fantastick notions."

"This is true," replied Dr. Johnson, "only so long as I hold my tongue. But when once I set the story going, 'twill not be long before your honest lads are laid by the heels and brought before the Aberdeen magistrate to answer the question, 'Where is the heiress of Lothian?' —which being unable to answer, they'll be much discommoded before word can be brought that the lady is living peacefully at home."

"And when their pannier is turned out," I added, still laughing, " 'tis ten to one 'twill be found to contain Lord Elibank's plate that they've stolen from Edinburgh, for if ever I saw a hanging countenance 'tis yon white face with the dirt-coloured ruffles. So I conceive that by your foolish tale they might be discommoded by the hangman in the end."

"*Quod erat demonstrandum,*" said my learned friend in high good humour.

"Why, that yonder pair of gallows-birds won't bear investigation is clear," I protested in serious vein, "but sure one of the Lords of Session stands too high to be harmed by the fantastick gabble of the vulgar. No sensible man believes that Lord Monboddo has in train to wed his daughter to the Lithuanian Wild Boy."

"Nor," added Dr. Johnson, "that he sits at Monboddo making gold as a cook makes pyes, and piling the ingots in the cow-shed. But that it is so believed in the streets of Edinburgh is a sharp-edged fact upon which Lord Monboddo may one day cut himself."

"Surely," said I, "Lord Monboddo is not to be blamed for what the unlettered may believe."

"Not so," returned Dr. Johnson, "for he makes people stare when the Court of Session rises and he walks home in the rain, followed by his wig riding in state in a sedan-chair; and the truth of this eccentrick behaviour lends colour to every fantastick tale about him. He who eats and drinks and bathes with singularity, may be believed to be singular in the chymistry and natural philosophy of his life as well."

Chatting thus, we reached the gates of our philosophical friend's domain in good time. It had begun to rain, and the treeless moorland looked dreary. We were met by a spry little man in a rustick suit and a round hat. This was our host himself, who with old-fashioned courtesy had come down to his gate to greet us.

We saw a thin man of low stature, with a sharp nutcracker face of sardonick cast. The lift of his short upper lip gave him a countenance forever upon the verge of risibility; but his sharp lower jaw, with strongly hooked nose bent down to meet it, and his sharp little eyes under grizzled tufts of brow, depicted the shrewd observer upon the multifarious activities of mankind. He was then in his fifty-ninth year, in full vigour of mind and body.

I could not forbear contrasting the little philosopher with my companion, the learned lexicographer, as they greeted one another complaisantly. Dr. Johnson was the Scotchman's elder by some five years; in figure he towered over him, being tall and strongly made. His thick figure was attired in a decent brown stuff suit of urban cut, with black worsted stockings and buckled shoes; on his bushy grizzled wig he had firmly planted a plain cocked hat. His heavy face was marred by the scars of scrofula; but there was benevolence in his glance, and an expression of philosophical common sense about his broad firm chin. He spoke in a loud voice with slow deliberate utterance.

"Sir," said he courteously to Monboddo, "you are most obliging. Pray, sir, will you not step into the chaise and ride with us to your door? You must be wetted to the marrow."

"No sir," replied Lord Monboddo uncompromisingly, "I will not step into your chaise. I do not ride in chaises. I hold that man was born to ride on a horse's back, not to be dragged at his tail in a box."

I looked for a stern rebuke at this new instance of our host's affectation of singularity, but Dr. Johnson was complaisant.

"Then, sir," he replied instantly, "we will descend and walk with you."

Lord Monboddo was delighted.

" 'Tis but a step," he said eagerly, "and on the way I will shew you my new plantations of turnips, which I have but newly introduced into Scotland."

The turnip plantings were devoid of interest, being bare and streaming with rain; but it was indeed not far from the gate to the house. Monboddo is a wretched place, wild and naked, with a poor old house; though there are two turrets which mark an old baron's residence. Lord Monboddo pointed to the Douglas arms upon his house, saying that his great-grandmother was of that family.

"In such houses," said he in his reedy tenor, "our ancestors lived, who were better men than we."

This was too much for Dr. Johnson.

The Monboddo Ape Boy

"No, no, my lord," he cried loudly, "we are as strong as they, and a great deal wiser."

We passed through the low doorway into a lofty, draughty old hall; but Lord Monboddo led us directly to the great kitchen, where a deep fire burned on the open hearth. There we dried our steaming cloathes, and debate on the primitive state of mankind was deferred.

That done, Lord Monboddo set us down to a rustick feast of mutton and boiled turnips, quoting from Horace:

> "Lucullus, whom frugality could charm,
> Ate roasted turnips at the Sabine farm."

In true Attick style the table was strewn with late roses, and roses garlanded the flagons filled with *mulsum*, a kind of sweetened wine. Assisting us to more turnips, the ingenious philosopher set forth his theory of alimentation.

"I hold," he declared, "that man is benefitted by a nice balance of animal and vegetable nourishment. Another turnip, Mr. Boswell? We are told, that man in a state of nature subsists upon vegetable substances such as roots and berries; and 'tis very clear that man in a state of nature is man at his happiest. Another turnip, Dr. Johnson?"

"No, sir," replied Dr. Johnson, "I will *not* have another turnip. I will have another cut off the joint. Man in a state of nature is not so happy nor so wise as I am; and to my happy and wise state I hold roast meat to be a great contributor."

"Why, sir," protested Monboddo, " 'tis allowed, that

Peter the Wild Boy was never so happy and healthy as when subsisting on the fruits of the earth, gathered by his own uninstructed endeavours, in the forests of Hannover. So also said Memmie Le Blanc, the Wild Girl, whom I saw in Paris through the good offices of M. Condamine, 'tis now eight years gone."

"Then," replied Dr. Johnson, "the girl Le Blanc perceived what you would be at, and framed her answers accordingly. I'll offer the girl Le Blanc a good cut off the joint, and you'll offer her a turnip or a dish of berries, and we shall soon see which she will take."

"Would it were possible," said Monboddo wistfully. "I offered what I could to bring Memmie Le Blanc into England, but 'twould not do. I would have brought her up at Monboddo, and taught her to speak."

"Had she a tail?" I enquired, knowing Monboddo's weakness.

"I will not say," replied Monboddo, "that she had not the vestige of a bump upon her rump; but indeed, though primitive man had a tail, we have lost it by the attrition of long sitting on it."

Dr. Johnson jerked his head restlessly, and swallowed a mouthful of mutton. I was glad when the entrance of a serving-man created a diversion.

"'Tis a pair of bumpkins, my Lord," said he, "has brought a specimen to shew your Lordship."

"Admit them," said Monboddo instantly. The servant stood aside, and into the room stepped the lout in the leather breeches and his companion in the cocked hat, which he did not remove. They set their pannier down in front of the little philosopher.

The Monboddo Ape Boy

"What have you brought me?" demanded Monboddo eagerly.

" 'Tis an ape, like," mumbled he of the leather breeches.

"My man," said Dr. Johnson, "the ape is not indigenous to Scotland."

" 'Tis not exactly an ape neither," said the bumpkin, "though we caught it in a tree. You may say 'tis an ape boy."

"An ape boy!" cried Monboddo. "Let me see it at once!"

The lout made as if to unfasten the pannier, but the white-faced man laid a finger on his arm.

"Now, sir," said the bumpkin hastily, " 'twas mortal hard to catch, and we ha' carried it for miles. Sure you'll not be stingy with us. What's a guinea to you, my Lord? Ay, or five, or ten?"

"So," said the Lord of Session. "Well, I'll buy it of you, my lads, if a guinea apiece will do it."

The weatherbeaten face fell.

"Make it two apiece, my Lord," he whined.

"I'll not buy an ape boy in a poke," said Monboddo sharply. "Turn it out; if 'tis to my liking, I'll bargain with you."

The ruddy man shook his head, muttering, "Two guineas apiece;" but again the coffin-faced man laid a finger on his arm. He overset the basket and unfastened the catch. Out crawled on hands and feet, dirty and touselled and emaciated, naked as the day he was born, an undeniable wild boy.

Lord Monboddo was delighted. Without ceremony

he laid hands upon the frightened creature, and proceeded to investigate his small posterior for a tail. There was none.

"Sure, sir," remarked Dr. Johnson, "you are a logician indeed, for I see you reason by the method."

"How so?" I enquired.

"The learned advocate," replied Johnson, "is seen to reason *a posteriori.*"

The bony-faced man greeted this sally with a suppressed snort, but his weatherbeaten companion ignored all save the matter in hand.

"Will he do, my Lord?" he enquired impatiently.

"You must say how you came by him," replied the little philosopher.

The wild boy squatted on his hams and watched with bright eyes from beneath his tangled mat of hair. He was small and wiry, perhaps as much as ten years old. There were fresh scratches on his skinny arms, and a bruise on his dark cheek. He watched Lord Monboddo without blinking.

"Caught him in a tree," replied the man, adding as an afterthought, "eating nuts."

"Where?"

"This side of Montrose."

"Can he speak?" enquired Dr. Johnson.

"Never a word. He's a real wild ape boy, my Lord, and they said at Lawrencekirk you'd pay us well for him."

"A guinea apiece," said Monboddo firmly.

The lout began to whine, but he took the guinea the Scotchman handed him and backed off. The whey-faced man pocketed a guinea in his turn, and between them they manœuvred the pannier out at the door and were gone.

"What a fortunate thing!" exclaimed Lord Monboddo. "I will communicate with M. Condamine at once. I will write a report for the Select Club. A real wild boy!—Here, sir, what are you about?"

With his own hands my revered friend was shovelling turnips onto a plate.

"Why, my Lord," replied Dr. Johnson coolly, dexterously slicing a large cut off the joint and laying it on a second plate, "why, my Lord, 'tis not every night a man has it in his power to test Lord Monboddo's theories by actual experimentation. Here, boy."

He laid both plates on the floor where the wild boy still squatted warily. Unhesitatingly the scrawny half-starved creature chose the mutton. He did not grovel into it with his snout like a pig, but took it up in both hands like a squirrel with a nut, tearing at it ravenously. When it was gone, he curled himself up into a ball under the table, and instantly fell into slumber; nor could Lord Monboddo's impatience awaken him again.

"Let the lad sleep," said Dr. Johnson. "We shall get nothing further from him till he is rested. Pray, my Lord, will you not let us enjoy the sight of your chymical experimentations?"

"Gladly," replied Lord Monboddo. "Pray step this way."

He led the way down a passage towards one of the ancient turrets, and unlocked a massive door with a large brass key which he took from his pocket. We entered a lofty vaulted room furnished with every device for chymical experimentation. A kiln stood on one side, supported by a very St. Dunstan's battery of pokers, tongs, shovels, and besoms. Vessels of clay in tortured shapes were crowded on the walls. Over a brick oven a closed copper bubbled monotonously through a long spiral of glass.

Lord Monboddo took from his pocket a second brass key, and unlocked the heavy chest which stood by the door.

"I hold, sir," said he, "that every metal is composed of infinitesimal particles, smaller than any yet rendered out; I do not despair of so reducing them; and when I have done so, what shall hinder me to build these atomies again into new combinations? I may thus produce one metal from another; or I may produce by reduction and combination metals wholly new, stronger and more useful than any yet known."

"Why, sir," said I, "then you may turn lead into gold if you will."

"You will have the philosopher's stone," concurred Dr. Johnson.

" 'Tis my view," said the eccentrick Lord of Session, "that only that has value which is useful. I would rather turn gold into iron. I have gold."

He laid in my hand a yellow ingot of about the bigness of my little finger.

"This is gold," said he. "I will reduce it, and turn it to iron or tin, if I can."

The Monboddo Ape Boy

I surveyed the rows of ingots in the brass-bound chest.

"Is it all gold?" I gasped.

"Not so," replied Lord Monboddo, "for I will as gladly turn iron into tin, or tin into iron, if it may be so. This is tin."

He handed me a duller, lighter finger of metal.

"This is lead—this is iron—this is silver—"

My learned friend and I observed the metals with interest.

"How will you go about to reduce—I should say to transmute—these metals?" enquired Dr. Johnson.

"Sir," replied Monboddo, "liquefaction has failed. I design to use pressure, when once I can devise some means of producing a pressure sufficiently great."

"Well, sir," said Dr. Johnson, "lock up your treasure chest, for all men are not such philosophers as we, to despise a bar of gold if it may be easily come by."

Lord Monboddo wielded the ponderous brass key and pocketed it. He then walked to the narrow windows and dropped the bars of the heavy shutters.

"You do well," approved Dr. Johnson, "to make this room impregnable, for gold is a strong temptation."

"Nay, Dr. Johnson," replied Lord Monboddo, "I trust my people. I lock and bar behind me, only because the slightest meddling, though well-intentioned, might bring to naught a chymical investigation on which I had spent weeks of labour."

He locked the oaken door behind us as we left, and the second key joined the first. The wild boy, awakened from his cat-nap, was frisking in the corridor. As we stood by the door in a contest of courtesy as to who should be first down the passage, he loped swiftly towards us, and before we could move he had scaled Monboddo like a tree.

"God bless my soul!" cried the wiry little Scotchman.

For a moment the wild boy clung about our astonished friend's neck, mopping and mowing; then with a leap he ascended into the ornamental cornice over the door and squatted there on hands and haunches.

"Come down!" cried Monboddo in alarm. "Alas, he'll do himself a mischief."

"He who can climb up," said Dr. Johnson calmly, "can climb down. Let us leave him here. He is like a puppy; you shall see, he will follow fast enough."

We walked away slowly. I watched out of the tail of my eye. The bright eyes of the wild boy followed us to the turn of the passage. Then with a leap he was down and running after us as fast as his hands and feet would carry him.

"He is indeed like a puppy," mused Monboddo as he sat by the kitchen fire. The wild boy, squatting at his feet, nuzzled the Scotchman's thin hand, and was rewarded by a pat on the head.

"I'll teach him to speak," says Monboddo in a happy waking dream, "I'll teach him to wear cloathes and write."

"And to subsist on a vegetable diet?" enquired Dr. Johnson slyly.

"Yes, sir," replied Monboddo innocently. " 'Twill be a great vindication of my theories. He shall be tended and instructed; I'll make him a lawyer. He shall learn

The Monboddo Ape Boy

to be grateful for the day when I bought him from yonder rough lout."

The wild boy chewed softly on his finger.

"See," says Monboddo happily, "he caresses me. This is a great argument that gratitude is innate in the human species."

"If that be indeed gratitude," responded Dr. Johnson, " 'tis a great argument that knowledge of the English language is innate in the human species. How otherwise could he apprehend the benefits you intend him?"

"By instinct," said Monboddo, "the wild thing knows by instinct who is his friend." He softly scratched the wild boy's touselled head.

"It may be," said Dr. Johnson. "None the less, I advise you against putting your finger in his mouth."

"Gentlemen," said I, creating a diversion, "the hour grows late. Let us retire. Pray, Lord Monboddo, what is to be your ape boy's place of rest? Must we put him in a tree?"

"He shall have a pile of clouts by the fire," responded the benevolent little philosopher. "He shall have better when I have taught him cleanly habits."

The ape boy took kindly to the warm nest by the fire. We left him burrowed into it, and took leave till morning.

Dr. Johnson and I lay in one commodious chamber together. Retiring first, I jotted down, as is my custom, the interesting events of the day, and the wise comments made thereon by my philosophical friend. When I had finished, and still Dr. Johnson lingered, I ventured to take the candle and sally forth in search of him.

I found him, to my unutterable amazement, painfully clambering down from the cornice above the chymistry room door; I gaped at him.

"What do you here, Bozzy?" demanded he in a subdued voice bursting with annoyance.

"Nay, sir, what do *you?*" I demanded in my turn, suiting my tone to his.

He dusted off his decent brown small-cloathes, and suddenly he grinned at me.

"I had a fancy to see if the wild boy had left any nuts in this tree."

"And had he?" I asked stupidly.

"Yes, sir," said Dr. Johnson. "Two. Write it in your note-book, Bozzy: where the wild boy can climb, there can climb the old scribbler from London."

"With the aid of a stool," I remarked, indicating the bench my friend had used to make the ascent.

"Take up the stool, then," said Dr. Johnson. "It belongs at the bend of the passage."

We were awakened betimes by blood-curdling screams from without, which continued as we hastened below.

"In Heaven's name," cried Dr. Johnson to a passing domestick, "what is the meaning of this horrible outcry?"

The man laughed.

" 'Tis only the wild boy," said he. "You must know, Lord Monboddo thinks to do himself good by going nude in the morning air in his chamber, and mighty pleased he is that his wild boy exposes himself from morning till night without any respect for Christians.

The Monboddo Ape Boy

Well, sir, when my lord has aired himself thoroughly, he goes next, for his health's sake, to bathe in a stream of living water which he has led through a commodious little bathing-house hard by. Now, sir, as the wild boy is well aired too, Lord Monboddo must needs carry him along to bathe for *his* health's sake; but the little animal, I take it, will have none of it, for he's screaming bloody murder down there. Look, here he comes."

The wild boy came streaking across the door-yard and clambered breathlessly up to the roof of the lean-to, where he clung wild-eyed and panting. He was as dirty and black as ever; clearly Lord Monboddo's bathing regimen was less than attractive to his primitive mind.

"This is cruelty," cried Dr. Johnson, who never loved cold water. "Come, come down, boy."

The wild boy eyed him with dumb distrust. Dr. Johnson signalled him with his great hand. The wild boy shook his head stubbornly.

"Here, Bozzy, fetch the joint. He'll understand that."

He understood it indeed. He came down at once. It was a sight to see the learned philosopher standing in the misty morning feeding gobbets of mutton to a dirty, hairy, naked wild boy.

His *al fresco* breakfast over, the little animal ran in and quickly fell asleep by the fire, just as Lord Monboddo came trotting back from his bath, looking chopped and red and feeling self-righteous.

Dr. Johnson cut short his disquisition.

"I've lived sixty years without cold water, and I'll not take to it now. Let us hear no more of this."

It came on to rain, and Dr. Johnson declined as firmly to join our host in a circumambulation of his borders. Lord Monboddo made us free of his library, and with profuse apologies left us to inspect the progress of some sort of rain-trenching in his turnip fields.

I settled down by the fire with Dodd's sermons, and I may have nodded a little. As I jerked up my head I saw out of the tail of my eye the bare-footed ape boy flitting like a shadow out at the door. I followed softly. A chronicler must neglect no means of observation that may enrich his record.

The bare feet pattered lightly down the long passage to the chymical room. The door was ajar. He slipped inside, and so did I after him.

Behind me the door swung to with a click, and the key grated in the lock.

"Mr. Boswell," said Dr. Johnson quietly. "This is a lucky chance. I have a mind to try a little transmutation of my own, and you shall be my assistant."

"I know nothing of chymistry," I replied doubtfully, though willing to be of help. I recalled the Doctor's chymical experimentations at Streatham, mostly explosive in nature, and shuddered slightly.

" 'Tis not a chymical transmutation," replied my friend, "but a human one. I have a mind to teach Monboddo's wild boy how to speak."

"This is the task of years," I protested, "and Lord Monboddo will scarce thank you if you begin at the wrong end, and set his theories at naught."

"Lord Monboddo will thank me indeed," said Dr.

The Monboddo Ape Boy

Johnson gently, "if he comes home and finds that I have taught his wild boy to speak between breakfast and dinner."

"How is this to be accomplished?" I enquired.

"Very simply, sir," replied my learned friend, "as you would teach a jack-daw to speak. We'll take out the fold of his tongue as a huntsman worms a whelp, and then we'll split the tongue to the root, but carefully, for I would not slit his throat; and you shall see, he will speak to us like any Christian."

I regarded my old friend with horror. He proposed this hideous surgery upon his friend's wild boy in easy and gentle tones, a slight smile of benevolence playing about his lips.

"Come, Bozzy," said he, "don't be squeamish. Our proceedings will be of inestimable benefit to knowledge. 'Twill pain the subject, I grant; but his screams will go unheard behind these thick walls, and Monboddo will thank us in the end."

I found no words to reply.

"You may take the tongs," pursued Dr. Johnson. "I fancy the carving-knife will serve my turn. But first we must secure our subject. Do not move, Bozzy, he must not be alarmed. I'll just approach him gently—"

As he spoke these words in an even, gentle tone, Dr. Johnson was already moving towards the unsuspecting wild boy. But as he came within arm's reach, his victim suddenly gave an uncontrollable scream of terror, and bolted towards the locked door. He seemed to understand that it was locked, for he wasted no time wrenching at the handle, but scaled the door-frame in an ecstasy of fear, and clung trembling above the lintel. Dr. Johnson smiled grimly.

"Come down," he said, "come down. What's your name, eh? Dick? Tom? Come down, I'll not hurt you."

Still the wild boy clung to the cornice.

"I know you understand me," said Dr. Johnson sternly. "Speak but two words, and I promise I will protect you."

The wild boy gazed down with stiffened lips.

"Come, sirrah," said Dr. Johnson, "what is to be the word? There is a word?"

"Witcher and ridge," whispered the trembling boy.

"And the time?"

"Midnight."

"Tonight?"

The wild boy nodded.

"Come down, then, boy," said Dr. Johnson. "I will be your friend."

The skinny frame slid lightly to the floor. The bright eyes searched my friend's face, and then the child burst into a passion of weeping.

"Here, boy, don't do that," said my benevolent friend anxiously. "Come, I'll get you something to eat." He took the grimy hand in his. "But remember, don't ever eat turnips."

But though this strange exchange cemented a stranger friendship between my friend and the dirty, naked child, so that they spent the rainy day in one another's company; and though the wild boy had indeed spoken two words; nothing of this was said to Lord Monboddo when he came home in the gloaming. The wild boy again sat under the table and ate generously off the joint, without turnips, eating eagerly from his thin fingers. Again we sat by the kitchen fire, and the wild boy sat against Monboddo's knee. Again we retired betimes to our commodious chamber, and the wild boy lay among his clouts by the fire.

'Twas hard on midnight when Dr. Johnson rose and huddled himself into his greatcoat. He slipped a pistol into my hand.

"Come," he said, "but lightly, for Monboddo is a poor sleeper."

We passed quietly, without a light, to the door of the chymistry room, which Johnson opened with the key. A shadow came down the passage towards us.

" 'Tis Ritter," Johnson breathed in my ear.

My man-servant took his stand beside me. He was armed with a cudgel. With infinite quiet Dr. Johnson set the door close.

We stood so for interminable minutes, hearing the old house creak and whisper around us, and the fire in the brick oven sigh and crack. Then I heard the click of a drawn bolt, and in a moment I was aware of movement in the passage, guarded and almost soundless. Another second, and the door swung silently inward.

"Stand," cried Dr. Johnson, thrusting his pistol against a dark shape. I found the second man's ribs with the muzzle of mine.

"Bing avast!" cried a thick voice. "The young Abram cove has betwattled us!"

"Stubble your whids," drawled a second voice. "We yield, sir."

"Secure the child," cried Dr. Johnson. "Ritter, strike a light."

It was not clear to me how Ritter was to hold the slippery child and strike a light at the same time; but he contrived it, for when the candle's rays strengthened and revealed the strange scene, they fell first on the terrified face of Monboddo's wild boy, held fast by the tangled hair.

They fell, too, on the pale coffin-shaped physiognomy of the man of the pannier, and on his burly companion.

"Ruffin cly thee, Jem," muttered the latter between his teeth, "hast whiddled the whole scrap, eh?"

"Shut your bone-box," said the pale-faced man. "I'll take care of Jem." He smiled dangerously. He spoke negligently well, like a Mohock. The skinny boy shrank back against his captor.

"Make them secure," said Dr. Johnson to Ritter. My servant produced a quantity of rope. He bound the false wild boy with a prodigious number of loops, and laid him on the bench.

The heavy-set man shewed fight when his turn came, but Ritter tapped him under the ear, and he gave no more trouble. He too was bound and stowed away. The second man cursed us with quiet dignity. He too was made secure.

"What's to be done with these gentry?" I enquired.

"We'll carry them to Aberdeen in the morning," replied Dr. Johnson.

The Monboddo Ape Boy

"And ask them for the heiress of Lothian?" I suggested.

"Why, you read them aright after all," acknowledged Dr. Johnson. "But we cannot leave them here. I'll carry the fine gentleman with the foul tongue to the lean-to, and do you and Ritter transport his accomplice to the bathing-shed. 'Tis damp, but sturdy, and will keep him close till time to depart."

So it was done. I returned to our chamber bursting with curiosity to question my astute friend about the events of the night. What was my disappointment, then, to find him already asleep in his bed, and beside him, shorn and washed, albeit somewhat sketchily, and attired in a ruffled shirt much too large for him, Monboddo's erstwhile wild boy. I was forced to blow out my candle and retire unsatisfied.

When I awoke the morning sun was streaming through the casement. I looked across at the bed opposite. It was empty. Dr. Johnson had arisen, and to my surprise very betimes, for the sun was only just above the horizon; and he had taken the now civilized wild boy with him.

I made haste to rise in my turn, and followed him down. As I entered the kitchen, what a sight met my eyes! There sat the wild boy at the breakfast table on a sturdy chair, supported for the increase of altitude by a heavy copy of Foxe's *Martyrs*. He was still swathed in the amplitude of my learned friend's ruffled shirt. A session at the pump had left him glistening with cleanliness and washed away the dark stain which his accomplices had applied. His dark hair had been unskilfully shortened, and stood up in wet spikes all over his small head. A plate before him was piled with viands, and he was plying knife and fork, though not elegantly, yet with assurance.

My learned friend sat beside him, eating oat cakes, and drinking tea. Opposite him the little Scotch philosopher was neglecting his chocolate to watch fascinated his small guest's gastronomick feats. Somewhere Dr. Johnson had found the remains of last night's mutton; he was plying his small friend with collops as fast as he could eat them. The *radicivorous* Lord of Session was mute with disapproval.

I took my place and opened my mouth to give expression to the questions which were thronging there; but Dr. Johnson imperiously signed for silence, and bestowed another gobbet on the now civilized wild boy.

At last the boy heaved a sigh of pure repletion, and pushed back Foxe's *Martyrs*. Dr. Johnson set down his fifth cup of tea (for it is slander to allege, as did Mrs. Blacklock in Edinburgh, that the great man was accustomed to consume *twenty-two* cups to his breakfast).

"Now, my dear sir," cried Lord Monboddo, "pray lay aside this air of mystery and reveal to me how you have achieved the civilization of this young savage in the space of twenty-four hours. This is certainly a notable achievement, and one which I am eager to communicate to my friend M. Condamine."

"Sir," replied Dr. Johnson gravely, "you owe it to the address of this young savage, as you call him, that the danger is passed that your hoard of gold may be rifled—"

"Pshaw, a trifle," ejaculated Monboddo.

"And your chymical researches brought to naught."

"How!" cried Monboddo. "Who are these miscreants? They shall be punished!"

"They shall indeed," promised Dr. Johnson. "With the help of Mr. Boswell and the man Ritter we have laid them by the heels, and I propose to transport them to Aberdeen with the luggage in our chaise; for they are clearly London cullies, and none of your home-grown product."

"Sir," cried the little philosopher, "I am indebted to you. Pray disclose how you came to uncover the plot against me."

"My Lord," replied my friend, "'twas this worthy boy who disclosed the plot to me; he has served you well, and I recommend him to your protection."

"He shall be protected," promised Lord Monboddo. "I'll educate him myself; I'll make him a lawyer."

The wild boy slipped down from Foxe's *Martyrs*, and leaned shyly against Monboddo's chair. The benevolent little Scotchman patted the thin shoulder.

"There's a good boy," he said. "Pray, Dr. Johnson, does he understand me?"

"Perfectly, my Lord; if you do not address him in too philosophical a strain."

"I marvel how you attained such a result, sir."

"You must understand, my Lord, that your wild boy is a creature uniquely wild, not at all to be compared to Peter or to Memmie Le Blanc, being wilder than either and yet sharper. By little and little as he gains confidence he will speak to you; but you are by no means to question him about whence he came, but rather erase it from his memory. I adjure you to feed him well, and not confine his diet to the vegetable kind, for you have seen that out of instinct he chose the joint."

"He shall be carnivorous, Dr. Johnson."

"Then, sir," said Dr. Johnson, "as I perceive our chaise is at the door with the brave Ritter in attendance, we will take our leave."

"Sir," replied Lord Monboddo, "I'm like the Romans, 'happy to come, happy to depart'."

We parted with great kindness. Stowed out of sight, the pale-faced man could be heard cursing steadily in his well-modulated, cultivated voice; but his words were muffled. As we sat in the chaise ready to depart, the former wild boy leaped from Monboddo's side, swarmed up the side of the chaise, and clung about Dr. Johnson's neck, whispering farewells in his ear.

"Have no fear," said Dr. Johnson to him kindly, "obey good Lord Monboddo in all things, and all will be well."

The boy nodded his touselled head, and ran back to cling to the skirts of the little Scotchman's coat, as the chaise rolled out of the door-yard.

As we rolled swiftly along on the highway to Aberdeen, the cursing of the white-faced man died away to sulky silence; which Dr. Johnson suddenly broke with a great shout of laughter, giving himself up to it, rolling his great frame from side to side as he bellowed out his mirth.

The Monboddo Ape Boy

"Ho, ho, Bozzy," cried he, "did you mark the face on the little philosopher when his wild boy chose the good roast mutton? I'll warrant you that will stop his cant about alimentary *balance*. Ho, ho, the brave wild boy!"

"Sir," said I severely, "in my judgement Lord Monboddo has been abused. Trust me, you knew when you tried him with the mutton and turnips that the boy was no wild boy."

Dr. Johnson stopped laughing and looked at me.

"That is so," he said, "but how did you know?"

" 'Tis clear," I replied, "that you proposed a Torquemada's trick on the wild boy only to learn from his behaviour whether he understood what you said or no. He betrayed himself, and subsequently you were able to force from him a confession of his part in the plot."

"Bravo, Bozzy," cried Dr. Johnson. "But, indeed, the lad had no stomach for the scheam, and played his part only out of fear. I had only to promise him protection, and he was quite ready to admit the robbers into the trap in which we took them."

BOSWELL: "How could he admit them into a house so closely locked and barred?"

JOHNSON: "With the keys."

BOSWELL: "Surely he could not hope that Lord Monboddo would let him come at the keys."

JOHNSON: "He had not been an hour in the house when he adroitly slipped them from our friend's pocket before our eyes."

BOSWELL: "Yet though he came by them, how could he keep them? He could hardly conceal them about him."

"Why," said my learned friend, laughing, "you saw him conceal them."

"*I* did?"

"And you saw me recover them; though your haste to think me gone quite mad prevented you from asking what I meant by the nuts in this tree."

"Over the door!" I cried in a burst of enlightenment.

"Just so," replied Dr. Johnson, nodding vigorously. "I recovered them, and frustrated any attempt that night. When the next day I found the lad ready to fall in with my scheam to entrap the miscreants, I restored the front door key long enough for him to use it."

"What foreign tongue," I enquired curiously, "does the boy speak?"

"That is no foreign tongue," replied my widely-learned friend, "but thieves' cant, very common in London and the country over. Nor does the boy speak any more than he has picked up from his criminal companions in this adventure."

"I marvel where they found a boy so agile and apt for the part," said I.

"Nothing is easier," replied Dr. Johnson. "I will go into Edinburgh and buy you twenty such."

"Twenty wild boys?" I demanded incredulously.

"Twenty *chimney-sweeps*," replied Dr. Johnson.

"What will Monboddo do with a chimney-sweep?" mused I.

"Educate him," replied Dr. Johnson. " 'Tis a sharp lad, and will do well at the law. I would have sent him back to Edinburgh, but the lad had taken a prodigious fancy to Monboddo. 'Twill amuse the little philosopher; and sure an Edinburgh street urchin is wild enough boy for anybody, and will vastly interest **M. Condamine**."

"I cannot think," I confessed, "how you smoaked the imposture in the first place."

"Why, sir," replied Dr. Johnson, "yonder lout who did the talking had no sooner opened his mouth than he was out with a whooping great lie. We caught him, says he, in a tree eating nuts—nuts in August! And as to catching him in a tree, pray whoever heard tell of a tree in Scotland?"

THE MANIFESTATIONS
IN *Mincing*
Lane

"Sir," said Dr. Johnson, "the manifestations of the Cock Lane Ghost were a nine-days' wonder; and so may this be."

He gave me the letter that he had been reading. The boy who had brought it waited stolidly by the door.

Writ in a sprawling hand on a yellowing scrap of old laid paper, I read:

SIR,

One who was an admiring Spectator, when Dr. Johnson interviewed the Cock Lane Ghost, makes bold, to recommend to his Consideration the Plight of Mr. Gudgeon, the worthy Sexton of All Hallows Staining. Mr. Gudgeon's Daughter, an estimable and pious young Lady, has suffered considerable Distress of Mind, in Consequence of the Activities of such a rapping Spirit as infested Cock Lane. Mr. Gudgeon would take it very kindly if Dr. Johnson would look into the Matter; as would also,

Sir,
Your obliged humble Servant,
illegible scrawl

The Manifestations in Mincing Lane

I looked up from the paper.

"Is this a jest?" I enquired.

"Not so," replied Dr. Johnson. "My illegible friend is the Rector of All Hallows Staining, a most respectable man. If he says Scratching Fanny is walking again, 'tis so."

We were sitting together, as we so often did, over our wonted table at the Mitre Tavern. The business of dining was happily over, and we were taking our ease in the smoky wainscotted room. 'Twas in the autumn of 1769. My distinguished friend was then in the full plenitude of his powers, and I longed to see his giant intellect grapple with those problems of the other world which held so powerful a fascination for his philosophical spirit of enquiry, as for my more volatile curiosity.

I glanced at the sleepy-looking boy, waiting for his answer, and read off the reverend Rector's postscriptum.

"P. S. Mr. Gudgeon resides in Mincing Lane by Clothworkers' Hall."

"Come, then," I cried eagerly, "let us call on the good sexton in Mincing Lane."

"I am very well where I am," returned my learned friend lazily.

"Parson bade me say," said the stolid boy, "Miss did see a napparition last night a-floating in the air. So Gudgeon says, he bade me say."

"An apparition!" cried my curious friend, rising. "Floating in the air! Why, this is an improvement over Cock Lane!"

I seized the moment.

"Run, boy," I said, "and say that we will come down to Mincing Lane directly."

My learned friend surveyed the house in Mincing Lane, a beetling dark half-timbered old place, perhaps a couple of centuries old.

"This is a most proper site," said he, "for a haunting. I'll lay a little the old place has a history."

"It may be," said I; "but do you then credit the reverend gentleman's story?"

"Sir," replied Dr. Johnson, "I credit that the young woman believes in her apparitions; and I hold that in just such a house an hysterical miss may most likely give way to her fancies."

He rapped smartly on the nearest door. The door was opened a crack, and a lowering, bottle-nosed, pockscarred visage peered at us through the aperture.

"Mr. Gudgeon?" enquired Dr. Johnson affably.

A red-rimmed eye blinked suspiciously. The bald red head jerked.

"Next door," said the surly creature, to my surprize in accents of breeding.

"Pray excuse a stranger," began Dr. Johnson courteously, but his polite inclination was met by the slamming of the door.

We then perceived that the broad dark front of the old dwelling presented to the street two similar doors, side by side, and we hastened to announce our arrival by a sounding summons at the second door. This time the door was set wide'for us, and we were greeted by a broad motherly woman in a brown stuff gown. About

The Manifestations in Mincing Lane

her feet clung a pair of babies in leading strings, a sulky little boy and a most exquisite Fragonard of a little girl. In the sunlight their hair gleamed like spun raw silk, the woman's like tow. The woman identified herself as Mrs. Gudgeon. She was contemptuous when we disclosed our errand.

"Mally? The silly chit has a touch of the mother, naught else, believe me. I'd take the besom to her, were she mine. Lying in her bed the live-long day, and the best bed in the house she must have, too, and never lifting a finger to the housework, because, forsooth, she sees things! Sulky and pouty as she's been these three weeks past, since we sent off young George Tucker the carpenter's boy—mark me, 'tis all one of her tricks. Sir, if you're a clergyman or one of them learned doctors you'll be doing your Christian duty if you bring down the hussy's pride a little and make her see reason. Spectres indeed! I'm fair disgusted with her fits and her folly. Ah, well, thank God she's none of mine! The first Mrs. Gudgeon was a fool, and Gudgeon's no better. This way, sir."

Sweeping the two babes before her, the muttering woman led us up a narrow pair of stairs and past a closed door to where another heavy dark doorway led into the back room of the old house. Without knocking, the woman burst through the door and abruptly addressed a figure half hidden in the curtains of a massive bed.

"Come, then, Mally, leave off your snivelling and attend, for here's Dr. Johnson come to show you your duty and do you good. —No, precious, wait for Mother in the passage, your sister Mally's a bad girl and not fitten to be spoke to. — Mally! Did you hear me?"

The girl on the bed lifted her long dark lashes from her white cheeks for a flash of time, then veiled her eyes again. She was no more than fifteen, slim and undeveloped, with a round pale childish face and a small colourless mouth. She lay on the pillow in a cloud of soft dark hair.

As we gazed at the expressionless face, a long lank figure unfolded itself from a low chair on the other side of the bed. This was Gudgeon, the sexton of the old church of All Hallows Staining. The man was all run to bone. His dangling hands were enormous. His stooped and cadaverous figure towered above the sturdy height of my learned friend. His long bony countenance surmounted a great knob of an Adam's apple, and was crowned with lanky unkempt locks of long dusty black hair.

"Let the lass be," he said in a rumbling bass.

"Let her give over her sojering, then," said his wife pettishly, and flounced out of the room.

I looked about the gloomy chamber. It was panelled in walnut, and had been fine in its day. The little thick leaded panes of the window gave upon a wide court and thence on the churchyard of All Hallows Staining; but only a trickle of dusty light came through. The room was sparsely furnished with a flimsy chest and a chair or two, and dominated by the great brass-bound bedstead sailing like a barge on the worn bare floor, canopied meanly in scanty homespun curtains.

"Your servant, Dr. Johnson," said Gudgeon. "I'm

grateful to you, sir, for coming, for I'm concerned for my girl." His bony hand smoothed the coverlet gently.

"Why, sir," returned Dr. Johnson kindly, "if Mally's a good girl and says her prayers with attention, I'm sure she has naught to fear, she'll have no more dreams."

"Yes, sir," said the girl Mally meekly. "Please, sir, they wasn't dreams."

"Of course they were, my child," Dr. Johnson assured her. "You are to tell me, my dear, what have you been dreaming?"

The child's lip quivered. Gudgeon began the story for her.

" 'Tis now two nights gone," he said, "that my girl woke us all with screaming and crying, and when we came to her she swore that she'd heard the spirits rapping at her bed head and moaning and mumbling and trying to tell her something. She was fair beside herself, screaming and crying that she'd lie in that room no more."

"Now I find," said Dr. Johnson, "that the child has sense. Let her lie elsewhere and she'll lie in peace."

" 'Tis not so easy done, sir," rejoined Gudgeon. "Our gear is but scant, and there's no bed for Mally but this one."

"Let it be moved, then."

" 'Tis fixed where it is, and so we found it when we moved here last year. The little tykes lie with us in front, and my sister on a pallet by the kitchen fire. No, sir, Mally must still lie here and conquer her dreams."

"Well, sir, and so Mally lay in this chamber again last night."

"Ay, and 'twas worse than before. Last night she saw It."

"What did you see, my dear?"

The child's eyelids flickered up.

"It was in the air," she said. "The wall melted, and It was in the air."

"What was in the air?"

"It held a corpse-candle before It," whispered Mally. "It was in Its shroud, and I could see Its face all white, all but the finger-marks. There was a screech, and I opened my eyes, and there It was in the air."

"Then what did It do?" asked Dr. Johnson gently.

"Then It came down and walked on the floor, and It bent over me." The small voice died dry in the child's throat. The frightened eyes closed.

"Then she cried out," Gudgeon finished the tale, "and I bundled on my night-gown and came to her, and stayed by her the same as the night before."

"Did you hear anything?"

"Naught at all. Come morning I told Rector, and he said 'twas the same like Cock Lane, and so he was so good as to send to you, sir, and I beg you'll study this out."

"Sir, I'll do so." Dr. Johnson prowled about the room, knocking and tapping on the wainscot.

"Hark," he said, "hear how hollow the panelling sounds over against the other room, and how thick where the house wall gives on the garden." He sounded the side walls. Behind the bed the wall was thick; but opposite, the panelling resounded hollowly.

The Manifestations in Mincing Lane

"This is no house wall," said he, looking questioningly at Gudgeon.

"That is so, sir," replied Gudgeon, " 'tis but a partition, for we dwell in but half a house, and Mr. Harkebus the surgeon has the other half. But come, sir, let us leave the lass to rest."

He led us to a lower room, where his buxom wife sat plying her needle. Beside the fire sat a gaunt woman, so bony and long that I knew her at once for Gudgeon's sister. Her skinny fingers impelled her knitting needles in jerks. She bobbed her head at us, but said nothing.

"Well, sir," said the wife crisply, "I hope you have spoke seriously to Mally and made her see her duty."

"She'll never sleep again," said the thin woman abruptly. Her voice was deep and hollow, like a tired man's. "She'll never sleep again till the ghost is laid that haunts this house."

Dr. Johnson looked at the craggy features attentively.

"What ghost, ma'am?"

"There's more than one ghost could haunt this house," muttered she.

"The house has a history, then?"

The woman made no reply. Gudgeon answered for her.

" 'Twas from this house that the Master of the Clothworkers' Company was led, and with him the priest he was harbouring, in the troubled times of Elizabeth. He was hanged, drawn, and quartered for treason."

The gaunt woman gave a snort.

" 'Tis never him," she asserted, "for the spectre Mall saw was all in one piece." Dr. Johnson looked surprized at this specimen of close metaphysical reasoning.

"The Clothworkers sold the house," continued Gudgeon, "though their hall is so close at hand; but he who bought it fared no better. 'Twas gutted in the great fire; he refurbished the shell, and built the second door and turned it into two houses, as part of his daughter's portion; but in the end they say the same daughter's husband was the death of him, and the house got a bad name. In my memory, in the years I've lived hereabouts as sexton of All Hallows Staining, it has been let to a parcel of riff-raff."

"Riff-raff indeed," snorted the buxom wife, "and in my opinion that Harkebus is the worst with his winebibber's nose and his anatomies. Depend upon it, if the house is haunted indeed, you may thank Mr. Harkebus and his body-snatchers."

"There was another," said the thin sister in her hollow voice, "brought up from the river in the same basket, not above two days since. Drowned he was, and now Harkebus has got him."

"You see!" said Mrs. Gudgeon, and bit off an end of thread.

" 'Tis never him," said the gaunt woman, "though I grant them that's drowned do walk. But this is never him—'cause why? 'Cause this one is dry and in his shroud, 'stead of coming a-dripping and all over seaweed. The drowned anatomy will haunt Mr. Harkebus, as like as not. He'll haunt him in the garret where he cuts them up, he will, dripping river-water and river-weed."

"Hold your tongue, Pall," said Gudgeon sharply.

"I hope," said Dr. Johnson seriously, "that Miss Gudgeon does not talk in this strain to Miss Mally."

"Oh, don't she, though," exclaimed Mrs. Gudgeon, adding not quite under her breath, "Old crow!"

"*I* know," exclaimed Miss Gudgeon, her voice rising to a rusty screech, "*I* know who lived in this house in his prosperity, ay and Mally's sleeping in his very bed. *I* know who lived in this house till they hanged him."

"This sort of thing," frowned Dr. Johnson, "must be powerfully unsettling for the child."

"Who, Miss Gudgeon?" I asked eagerly, unable to restrain my curiosity. "Who lived here till they hanged him?"

"Ah!" said Miss Gudgeon. She beckoned me mysteriously to a tall press that stood in the corner. Scrabbling in rags, she drew forth an untidy, much-thumbed pile of broadsheets. Lugging them to the fire-light, she squatted awkwardly down beside them and began to turn them over. Dr. Johnson peered over her shoulder, and chuckled.

"Why," said he, "my friend Thomas Percy should see these broadsheets. He'd call them treasure trove, and make them into a fourth volume of reliques of ancient poetry. The Diceys, eh? Why, these are great specimens of their art. What's this? A ballad! *A True and Perfect Relation from the Faulcon at the Bankeside: of the strange and wonderful aperition of one Mr. Powel a Baker lately deceased, and of his appearing in several shapes, both at Noon-day and at night, with the several speeches which past between the spirit of Mr Powel and his maid Jone and divers Learned men who went to alay him and the manner of his appearing to them in the Garden upon their making a circle, and burning of wax Candels and Jenniper wood, lastly how it vanished.* Small wonder Mally sees things in shrouds! What would you have us do, Miss Gudgeon? Make a circle and burn jenniper wood?"

Miss Gudgeon tossed her head, and went on turning over the coarse grey paper of the broadsheets. I picked up one at random: *A Terrible and True Relation of one Melcher a Cut-purse who being taken at his Trade, for the which he was hanged at Tyburn, was expeditiously cut down and conveyed thence by his Friends; and being by GOD's Mercy restor'd, doth to this day ply the trade of a WATERMAN, a very notable example of GOD's just Judgements. 1661. God save the King.*

"God save Melcher!" I added, laughing heartily.

Dr. Johnson scanned the crude rhymes of Melcher's recrudescence, as Miss Gudgeon with a triumphant nod and a cadaverous smile handed me still another ballad. I read out the title:

"*An Account of the notorious High-way-man, Viz. WHITE WILL by Name; with his Compact with the Devil, in token whereof he was mark'd with the Divil's Fingers, as many can attest; his Robberies on the Great North Road; his Scheam to commence Gentleman beyond the seas; with the manner of his taking, and how he was turned off at Tyburn, and his last dying Words of Repentance. 1768.*"

The Manifestations in Mincing Lane

"Last dying words of repentance!" said Gudgeon contemptuously. "I saw him turned off. He never said a word. Jack Ketch was in a hurry, and turned him off and bundled him away to the indignation of the holiday-makers."

"Ah," said Miss Gudgeon. "White Will! 'Twas here in this very house he set up for a gentleman before they took him; and many's the time I've seen him at All Hallows Staining, wearing his Mechlin lace and a ring on his thumb."

"Indeed, ma'am," says Dr. Johnson, wearying of the subject. "Well, Mr. Gudgeon, as to the strange manifestations in the back room—"

"The house is haunted," cried Miss Gudgeon, breaking in, "and 'tis White Will that haunts it. My niece has seen him plainly." She held a bony finger on the margin of the ballad and nodded triumphantly. I read out the stanza she indicated:

> "He was prenticed to the Devil
> Which same doth appear,
> The Devil's claws upon his cheek
> In scarlet doth appear
> The which with daubs of white clay
> He made to disapear."

"A fustian verse," cried the learned critick in disgust.

"Nevertheless it was so," insisted Miss Gudgeon, "and my niece saw him walking in his shroud, with his face all white, *except for the marks of fingers.*"

"Why, so she did," said Gudgeon slowly.

Even Dr. Johnson looked impressed.

"Well, well, Miss Gudgeon," he said thoughtfully, "if you dwelt upon this knight of the road and his fate in your niece's presence, perhaps all is explained. Nevertheless, I would ask the privilege of watching tonight in Miss Mally's room, with my astute friend Mr. Boswell, to ascertain whether White Will will submit himself to philosophick scrutiny or no."

"I'll watch with you," cried Miss Gudgeon.

"And I," said Mrs. Gudgeon; "you will have need of a person of sense about you."

"Why, 'tis better so," assented Dr. Johnson, much to my surprize. "Do you join our wake too, Mr. Gudgeon; and pray, could not you perswade your neighbour the surgeon to make one? Say to him that we desire the presence of a medical man."

"I will try," replied Gudgeon, "but indeed his temper is uncertain, and I cannot vouch for him."

Nevertheless, Mr. Harkebus readily consented to make one; we found him drinking hot tea by the fire when we returned to Mincing Lane after supper. Miss Gudgeon was embroidering her theory of the apparition's identity into his inattentive ear.

"Yes, yes, you may be right, ma'am," said Mr. Harkebus absently, eating bread-and-butter. His hot red eye was sardonick. Portly Mrs. Gudgeon regarded him with aversion.

"Pray, ladies," said Dr. Johnson, "do you be so kind as to repair to the child's chamber and see that all is ready for the night. Be particular to search the child and the bedstead and make sure that she has no way of producing these noises by mechanical means."

"You may count upon me," replied Mrs. Gudgeon grimly. "The chit shan't diddle me, you may be sure."

Dr. Johnson shook his head as the two women mounted the stair with determined tread.

"I hope for the child's sake," he observed to me in a low tone, "that these manifestations are indeed of supernatural origin, and not a wilful freak of her own. 'Twill go hard with her if she is caught out by her step-mother."

"Think you the child is mad?" I murmured in reply.

"Perhaps rather the bony spinster. The events of the night will show," replied my philosophical friend. "If 'tis the step-mother, there's method in it."

Upon summons from above, we men mounted the creaking stair and solemnly took our places in a circle of chairs about the bed. The white-faced child lay wide-eyed in the middle of the great bed. It was the watchers who drowsed as the silent minutes passed. The dark-panelled walls seemed to advance and recede into darkness as somnolence overtook me in that silent circle; when suddenly the silence was broken by a sharp triple knock, thrice repeated. The child moaned; someone in the circle drew in a sibilant breath. Sitting beside the bed, Dr. Johnson reached for Mally's hand.

"Bozzy," he said to me in a low voice across the bed, "take the child's hand in yours; and let every one of us stretch out his hands to his neighbours."

I took Mally's small cold hand in mine, and accepted

in the other palm the bony fingers of Miss Gudgeon. The darkness was intense. Dr. Johnson called our names around the circle. Unless two sitting together lied in concert, we now knew that Dr. Johnson, Mr. Harkebus, Mrs. Gudgeon, Gudgeon, his sister, and I sat finger to finger in the darkened room, with the moaning girl in the bed closing the circle. The triple raps came again, more insistent.

"This is no trickery," muttered Mr. Harkebus hoarsely.

" 'Tis an unquiet spirit," said the hollow voice of Miss Gudgeon. "We must alay it."

"We must speak to it," said Mr. Harkebus, "and 'twill answer by rapping. 'Twas so in Cock Lane."

"Why, then, I will speak to it," said Dr. Johnson sturdily, "and let it make answer, rapping once for *yes* and twice for *no*."

"Once for *yes* and twice for *no*," repeated the surgeon in as firm a voice. "So be it. You shall speak first, Dr. Johnson."

"Then say," cried Dr. Johnson in an awful voice, "whether you be a human thing?"

In the tense silence a single rap sounded. Miss Gudgeon's bony fingers tensed in mine. Her words came in a rush.

"Whether you be—" her voice stuck in her throat— "*White Will?*" My scalp prickled at the awful import of her question, and the chill ran down my spine in flakes as the single sharp rap answered *Yes*.

I wet my lips with my tongue. No power in earth or heaven could have kept me from asking the question I had so often posed in vain. I gasped it out as if I had been running:

"Whether you seek our prayers?"

The two raps came immediately, quick and negligent. I felt rebuked, and enquired no further.

"Then what do you seek?" asked Gudgeon in his deep tones. A perfect volley of raps seemed to echo from every corner of the darkened room.

"We must ask according to the method," said Dr. Johnson, "as thus: is something to be done by us, or by one of us?" The single rap was almost crisp in reply.

"Which of us?" whispered Mrs. Gudgeon, so far drawn in that she no longer scoffed at Mally's spectre. A sharp rap sounded.

"It said *Yes*," murmured the rigid spinster. "*Yes* to what?"

"Perhaps," suggested the surgeon, "Mrs. Gudgeon is to do something." There was an encouraging knock.

"Alone? —Oh, I couldn't," gasped the frightened matron. Two negative knocks cut her off.

"Not alone," interpreted Mr. Harkebus. "With Gudgeon?" *Rap.* "And Miss Gudgeon?" *Rap.* "And Miss Mally?" *Rap*. "And Dr. Johnson?" *Rap. Rap.* "And Mr. Boswell?" *Raprap.*

"And," added Dr. Johnson, "Mr. Harkebus?" *Rap . . . rap.*

"So," said the surgeon, "it is something all who dwell in this house must do to alay the spectre of White Will. What must they do—leave it?" There was a tremendous heavy rap, and then a long silence.

"Why," says Gudgeon heavily at last, "how can I do

that? Where can I go?" There were no more rappings, but suddenly the charged silence was broken by a series of low moans, that rose in a crescendo to a blood-curdling wail, and then broke off in the horrible gasps of a man strangling in a noose.

"Indeed, Gudgeon, I'll not live in this house another night," cried his wife in terror. "You may e'en pack my boxes in the morning, for with you or without you, out I go before another night falls."

"Look to the child," cried Dr. Johnson, "she can stand no more."

He struck a light. The ladies hastened to burn a feather under the unconscious child's nose, and in the flurry to fetch hartshorn and a hot brick for the feet the first horror of the night's experience passed. Dr. Johnson was firm that the house must be emptied before the next day's twilight. Just as firmly he stipulated that the child was not to be left alone until she could be moved from the house altogether. He drank early tea by her bedside, and had the satisfaction of seeing her fall into a natural sleep before he left her.

We came out of the house into the sunrise, and took leave of Dr. Harkebus on the step. He looked redder than ever in the dawn light; but for the events of the night he had the most respectably philosophical open mind.

"I am perswaded, sir," said he, "that this is no trickery, but a genuine communication; and I hold that in obeying the behest of the rapping spirit Gudgeon shows the truest regard for the welfare of all."

The Manifestations in Mincing Lane

"It is strange," mused Dr. Johnson, "that you were never disturbed by the rappings."

"Nay, sir, they could have no meaning for me, because White Will was never a tenant on this side. I have lived here for many years."

"You may be right, sir," said Dr. Johnson. "Well, I wish you good morning and good repose."

The portly old man bowed with what grace he could muster, and entered his house.

"'Tis a gentle body-snatcher," said I as we strolled along, "and a well-instructed one. But who is this disarrayed youth who seems bent on accosting us?"

The lad in question was a well-made tall-standing youth in the blue apron of an apprentice, and he barred our way at the mouth of Mincing Lane.

"What has gone wrong with Mally Gudgeon," he cried, "that the whole medical fraternity must watch with her till morning?"

"So, George Tucker," cries Dr. Johnson, "you spy on Mally Gudgeon."

"Call it what you will, she needs watching over," replied the lad with spirit. "What has the old witch done to her?"

"Miss Gudgeon?" enquired I.

"Miss Gudgeon is our friend. Not Miss Gudgeon; the step-mother, the cold fish who hates her, the enemy that parted us when we were as good as wed, for lack of ten pounds to buy my indenture with. What has happened to Mally?"

"Walk along with us," said Dr. Johnson. "Mally is

well, and she is in no danger. But if you have a hammer and nails you may do Mally a service tonight."

"I'll do it with all my heart."

"Then bring them under cover of darkness, and a stout crow to boot, to Mally's chamber. Come around by Fenchurch Street and take care that nobody marks you. I will engage that the door shall be unlocked. You must steal in quietly as soon as you shall see Gudgeon and his women-folk depart."

"I will be there," promised the carpenter's apprentice.

As dusk was falling Dr. Johnson and I put Mally Gudgeon and her relatives into a coach and saw them off for their new lodgings. Then we strolled without hurry around the corner into Fenchurch Street, where George Tucker joined us with his tools wrapped in a blue cloth; and so we slipped into the churchyard of All Hallows Staining. Tucker looked uneasily about him, and seemed as if he mightily wished to cross himself, if truth were known, and so did I too; but Dr. Johnson led the way without faltering. I gave him a leg up, and he got his decent brown small-cloathes easily over the wall, and so we slipped into the deserted house by the back passage, and bolted the door behind us.

It took all my friend's intrepidity to hearten me as we stole noiselessly into the haunted room and huddled against the wall in the dark. We sat so without moving for hours, it seemed, while the chimes of All Hallows told the quarters, and my knees prickled because they were asleep and my spine prickled because I was afraid. But nothing rapped, and nothing cried out in the night like a man being hanged. I was beginning to think that we had exorcised the spirit after all, and my eyelids were drooping shut, when there was a screeching sound like a rat in the wainscot, and when I opened my eyes the wall had melted, and It was standing in the air above the level of my eyes. It was swathed in something whitish. It held a corpse-candle in its hand, and I could see its eyes glitter, and the marks of three red fingers stretching along the cheek from the ear. Then it came down and walked on the floor, and bent over the bed, and I heard a rending sound like body-snatchers riving open a coffin. My tongue clove to my palate, and my head swam.

"*Ego te exorciso!*" cried Dr. Johnson suddenly in a sonorous voice. The ghostly apparition stiffened by the bed.

"*Integer vitae, scelerisque purus,*" intoned my intrepid friend appropriately, "*non eget Mauris iaculis neque arcu . . .*"

The white-robed figure was gone. I saw this time how it went through the wall and up the stair, and the panel shut behind it with a squeak like a rat in a wainscot.

"Quick, George," cried Dr. Johnson, making a light, "the hammer and nails."

To my utter astonishment the sturdy carpenter lad proceeded to nail the panel shut and brace it with timbers laid crosswise.

"Sir, sir," I cried, "will you not pursue the marauder?"

"I will not," replied Dr. Johnson. "The unfortunate creature has been hanged once; let that suffice."

George knocked the last nail in place, and none too soon, for there was a mighty wrenching at the other side of the panel, and muffled voices raised in anger.

"Now, my lad," said Dr. Johnson, "let us *detimbrify* this accursed bed, and lay the spectre for good and all."

"Alas," cried the carpenter's boy in professional dismay, " 'tis a shame of so stout a bed! —all of solid oak, and bound with brass besides!"

" 'Twill not be so difficult," returned Dr. Johnson. "See, the spectre has made a start."

He pointed to a breach in the edge, where the side had been forced away. George inserted his crow and pulled mightily. The panel came away with a rending sound.

"Let us see," cried Dr. Johnson, directing the light, "what's within this brass-bound chest."

" 'Tis only a spare feather-bed," said the carpenter's apprentice.

"An odd place to store an old feather-bed," mused I, "while the sleeper lies cold above."

"Pull it out," said Dr. Johnson.

George and I seized each an end, and tugged. The thing was heavy. With a heave it came out onto the floor, clinking as it came.

"Rip it up, my lad," cried Dr. Johnson, " 'tis Mally's dowry, or I much mistake."

George wielded his case-knife, and cried out as he saw the golden guineas among the drift of feathers. He counted them swiftly.

The Manifestations in Mincing Lane

"Sixty-nine—ninety—one hundred and seventeen—'tis a fortune! Pray, Dr. Johnson, how came this money here? Whose is it? Is it Mally's?"

" 'Tis ours, George, we found it," replied my upright friend. "But were you to ask me, whose *was* it, I could only reply, it came out of well-lined pockets on the Great North Road. Come, I will divide it with you."

And sitting on the edge of White Will's bed, holding up the single candle dangerously near to the foretop of his little brown scratch-wig, Dr. Johnson picked up guinea for guinea with the awkward young apprentice. I was too stupefied to protest against this high-handed appropriation of treasure trove, or even to ask for my share.

"And the odd one for you," concluded Dr. Johnson.

"Come," cried the overjoyed apprentice, "let us run and tell Mally."

"Run into Mincing Lane at midnight with a pocket full of guineas!" exclaimed Dr. Johnson loudly. "No, no, my lad! We'll e'en stay here behind locks and bars till the day comes and the good sexton returns with the bailiffs. Pocket your guineas and lock the door behind you. We'll lie in the lower room by the fire till day."

But when the haunted room was locked behind us, Dr. Johnson laid finger to lip and moved his powerful bulk quietly out at the back passageway. The stars were quietly shining in the moonless sky as he went easily over the courtyard wall. George and I scrambled after, and so we came out by the churchyard into Fenchurch Street.

Strolling up Fleet Street the next morning, I met the sturdy Doctor walking out betimes in the sunny day.

"Well met, Bozzy," cried he. "Pray walk along with me."

"To what destination?" I enquired curiously.

JOHNSON: "To Mincing Lane."

BOSWELL: "To what end? The family Gudgeon lie in lodgings in Stepney."

JOHNSON: "Not so; I have already advertized them that their ghost is laid for good."

Though I was eager to review the events of the night as we walked along, not a word would he say, but dwelt upon the advantages of emigration for those ambitious to reform their way and begin a new life. On this matter he was very fluent, until still discoursing eloquently he turned out of Eastcheap into Mincing Lane and knocked peremptorily at the door.

"Sir, sir," I cried, "see how events repeat themselves! This is again the wrong house!"

Already the surly surgeon had wrenched open the heavy black door and was scowling truculently at my venerable companion.

"Sir," said Dr. Johnson, "it has come to my ears that you and your friend have in mind to emigrate and mend your fortunes, which no longer can prosper in London."

"Emigrate!" cried the bonesetter with an oath. "No such thing!"

"You amaze me," replied Dr. Johnson, "for as I hear it, an information is about to be laid against you, and 'twill go hard with you if you and your friend are found in London."

The Manifestations in Mincing Lane

The black scowl grew blacker, but with belated courtesy the burly surgeon stepped back and invited us to enter. I bowed and advanced, but a touch from my intrepid friend deterred me.

"I thank you," replied Dr. Johnson courteously, "but my errand is almost done. There remains only to have a word with your friend."

"I have no friend," said the body-snatcher sullenly.

"I mean your friend," said Dr. Johnson patiently, "who last year was brought to you from Tyburn in a basket, and astounded you by being still in life. You have been a good friend to him. You have kept him in the country this twelve months past, have you not, for the easing of his throat."

"What if I have?" cried Harkebus hoarsely.

"Come, man, lay aside this stubbornness," said Dr. Johnson with asperity. "If I meant harm to your friend I would come with a pack of bailiffs at my back. I mean him only good; but what I have for him I will lay in no hands but his own."

The surgeon favoured my friend with a long searching scrutiny, then bellowed "Will!" There was a light step in the passage, and the sunlight from the open door fell on the veritable apparition of Mincing Lane. I saw the gaunt white face, with the marks of St. Andrew's fire reaching along the cheek from the ear like a map of the Peloponnesus; the head on one side and the twisted neck swathed in white cloth. The gaunt creature was wrapped in a dirty fawn-coloured night-gown and wore a kerchief on his cropped head.

"What's to do, cully?" he croaked hoarsely.

Dr. Johnson extended to him a knitted purse weighted down with something heavy.

"For your journey," said he.

"Journey?" croaked the gallows-bird.

"You are leaving London," said Dr. Johnson, "and I counsel you to amend your ways in your new life."

"The old fogram's honest!" gasped White Will, hefting the purse of gold.

"Middling," replied Dr. Johnson with a smile. "Pray, Mr. Harkebus, satisfy my curiosity."

"If I can, sir."

"How had your friend the good fortune to be brought to you from Tyburn?"

"Why, sir, as an accommodation to a business associate of long standing—I bought the anatomy in advance."

"Did you so? Who was the gentleman's heir?"

"Mumping Mag," said the surgeon, "my friend's—ah—doxy."

White Will let slip an incomprehensible oath.

"Ay," he croaked bitterly, "but she was lagged on Tyburn Hill that very day."

"The better, I tell you, Will," said Harkebus, "or you'd have seen your brass-bound bed no more."

Footsteps came around the corner into Mincing Lane. Promptly the burly surgeon slammed the door, and we stood gaping on the door-step as George Tucker stepped proudly towards us.

He wore his Sunday suit, with a fire-new fire-coloured neckerchief and on his head a cocked hat with lacing. In his hand was something wrapped in a white silk handkerchief, which he handled tenderly.

"For Mally," he said with a grin. "I reckon to be a welcome suitor now."

I thought the fat step-mother scowled at the metamorphosed apprentice, but Gudgeon's melancholy smile gave him candid welcome, and Mally was wearing her Sunday gown. All greeted Dr. Johnson respectfully, and besought him to narrate the laying of the ghost.

"There'll be a ballad made on it," declared Miss Gudgeon fervently.

At the instance of the philosopher we mounted to the back bedroom.

"Alack," cried Miss Gudgeon, " 'twas the Devil after all!"

The brass-bound bedstead was torn apart. In the wall where the sliding panel had been a great hole gaped; on the floor lay George Tucker's timbers in splinters. The circle of chairs was flung about in disorder.

"Why," says Dr. Johnson with a smile, "this was a determined ghost; but I think you'll see him no more."

He poked his head through the aperture; I was not far behind him. We gazed at a pair of shallow steps leading up to a narrow, dusky, airless chamber running the length of the wall.

" 'Tis the priest's hole," said Dr. Johnson. "See yonder niche at the end. This was the Clothworker's oratory."

"How knew you it was there?"

"Why, I was looking for it." His sonorous voice resounded in the enclosed space. "The Master of the Clothworkers had a priest in the house when they took him; in the days of Elizabeth that argues a priest's hole."

Over our shoulders the elder Gudgeons were craning their necks. When we had stared our fill, we turned to the room again. The young folks were sitting demurely, six feet apart, but something was in the air. George's face was all one grin. Though Miss Mally's long lashes were dropped, her cheeks were pink; she wore a posy ring and cradled in her hands a kerchief of white silk.

She seemed to know that the apparition had been White Will in the flesh, and that the young apprentice had been enriched from the highwayman's ill-gotten hoard. I was curious to learn by what processes of ratiocination my astute friend had penetrated the deception practised on her, and Dr. Johnson was ready to enlighten us.

"Sir," said he, "though I am ready to believe in the supernatural origin of the manifestations of such spectres as Scratching Fanny and White Will, yet I am ever as ready to seek out a more natural explanation. 'Twas clear to me, when I had talked with Mally and her kin, that the rapping, the moaning, and even the apparition, might have been engineered from the priest's hole by someone desiring to frighten the child."

"By whom?" I enquired with interest.

"Nay, it was too soon to know. I noted Miss Gudgeon's eagerness to engender belief in the spirit; I noted Mrs. Gudgeon's eagerness to engender belief that the child was somehow responsible; and I resolved—pray excuse me, ladies—to watch the proceedings of both."

"Pray how did I escape notice?" asked Gudgeon in his melancholy voice.

Dr. Johnson smiled.

"You did not escape," he replied, "for though you courted investigation, I bore in mind that perhaps 'twas all done to gain notice to yourself."

"Surely," said I, "those without access to the priest's hole were not under suspicion."

"This is true," replied Dr. Johnson, "but though it was easy to locate the priest's hole, I could not know that it did not have means of entrance from every room in the house, ay, and even out of the house, for when it was made, the surgeon's lodging next door was part of the Clothworker's domain."

"Therefore you summoned Harkebus to watch with us!" I exclaimed.

"Therefore," agreed Dr. Johnson. "Watching with Miss Mally, I had every suspected person under my eye. I was able to make sure that no one of them was actually doing the rapping. There was, then, an accomplice in the imposture—or we had to do with a genuine shade. But before the sitting was over, I was sure I knew who was at the bottom of it, and why."

"I made sure that it was a ghost indeed," said Miss Gudgeon, rather regretfully, I thought. "What told you otherwise?"

"The conduct of Harkebus. Under his guidance we wasted no time in learning the purpose of the imposture. He led us to ask exactly the right questions for his purposes. It must have jolted him when Miss Gudgeon asked who it was, and White Will, not expecting the question, rapped out the truth in answer."

"What was their purpose?" asked Mrs. Gudgeon.

"Why, to frighten Miss from the room, better still from the house. Consider: the first night there come frightening noises only. Miss screams out in terror that she will not sleep here again. Taking her word, the second night a man with a candle enters the supposedly empty room, only to be frightened away by screams. The third night, piloted by Dr. Harkebus, the spirit bids you abandon the house, and by blood-curdling howls frightens you into declaring you will do so. What is bound to happen the fourth night?"

"The man with the candle will again enter the room through the priest's hole. But what for?"

"It seemed as if the departed highwayman had left something behind him of interest to his former neighbour Mr. Harkebus. I determined to watch and know what it was. You know the rest. Recognizing White Will for a living man, I knew the answer to the last question which had puzzled me."

"What was that?" enquired Gudgeon.

"Why Harkebus had not entered the room at his pleasure at any time while the lodgings stood empty."

"Why did he not so?"

"Because he knew naught of what the room contained till White Will returned—in the body-snatcher's basket lest he be seen and recognized—from the Surrey side, where he had been rusticated for the recruiting of his health, since Harkebus received his anatomy more dead than alive from Tyburn Hill."

"Sir," said Gudgeon, "I am your debtor in this matter."

"And I," cried George Tucker, "for I took up my indentures this morning, and I mean to commence undertaker for myself—at All Hallows Staining, if Mally will name the day and father-in-law will have me."

"Done," cried Gudgeon. Mally said nothing, but looked sidewise and for a moment showed a dimple.

"Pray, Dr. Johnson," enquired Tucker, "to what use will you put your share of this treasure trove?"

"I have applied it," replied my philanthropick friend, "to eleemosynary purposes."

"Ah," said the pious sexton, "worthy purposes, I make no doubt."

"Mammy, mammy," cried the little Fragonard, running into the room in excitement, "the men are riding away on big horses, and the skinny one, mammy, his face is all white like flour."

"Worthy purposes?" repeated Dr. Johnson. "Well, no."

Prince Charlie's
RUBY

PRAY, Mr. Boswell," said Flora Macdonald, "what did you do for the Bonnie Prince in the '45?"

"In the '45, ma'am," I replied, "I was a fine boy of five; I wore a white cockade and prayed for Prince Charlie."

"Well done, Bozzy!" exclaimed Dr. Sam: Johnson approvingly.

"But," continued I, "one of my uncles, General Cochran, gave me a shilling on condition that I should pray for King George; which I accordingly did."

"Now I perceive," cried my Tory companion, "that Whigs of all ages are made the same way!"

The company enjoyed a hearty laugh at my expense, for all those present were of the *old interest,* and rejoiced to find the learned Dr. Sam: Johnson kindly affectioned toward the lost Stuart cause; while I looked airy, and whistled a bar or two of "Charlie Is My Darling."

We had but just arrived at Kingsburgh in the Isle of Skye, and now we sat in our host's comfortable parlour by a good fire, comforting ourselves with punch and conversation before taking our rest. In the elbow-chair by the chimney-piece sat our host, Allan Macdonald of Kingsburgh, quite the figure of a gallant Highlander. He wore a brown short coat of a kind of duffle, a tartan vest with gold buttons and gold buttonholes, a bluish filibeg, and tartan hose. He had jet-black hair tied behind and with screwed ringlets on each side, and was a large stately man, with a steady sensible countenance. By his side in a straight chair sat his sister Margaret, a stout-built clever-looking woman with merry dark eyes.

On the opposite side of the fireplace, at Dr. Johnson's right hand, the cynosure of all eyes, sat the wife of our host, the celebrated Flora Macdonald. She was a little woman, of a mild and genteel appearance, mighty soft and well-bred; elegantly attired in tabby, with a gold locket on a chain about her neck.

To see Dr. Sam: Johnson salute Miss Flora Macdonald with a flourish of his glass was a wonderful romantick scene to me. The great lexicographer regarded the Jacobite heroine with reverence, and bent to her level from his ponderous height with a deference touching to see.

The apartment in which we sat might have been in St. James's, rather than in this remote corner of the Hebrides. Two pretty French figurines adorned the delicate scroll-work of the mantel. The room was soft-

ened by hangings of damask, and elegantly lighted by
wax candles in sconces. Dr. Johnson could not forbear
to comment.

"Why, sir, we are not such savages here," said Flora
Macdonald with a smile. "I had the damask from Paris;
and we never lack for wax candles, for my father-in-law
was factor to Sir Alexander Macdonald, and made all
the candles for the big house, and we have the use of
the forms to this day."

I looked at the well-formed tapers. Two of them
burned in sconces beside a bracket whereon stood a
busto in plaster, representing a young man of singular
beauty. Something about it was strangely familiar to
me. I covertly studied the oval face, the beautifully cut
mouth not quite smiling, the broad lofty sweep of the
brows, the keen expression and proud lift of the well-
shaped head. A sly word from my observing friend
brought me out of my reverie.

"For a dog of a Whig, Mr. Boswell," observed he,
"you seem strangely lost in admiration of his Majesty
King Charles III."

With a start I realized why the plaster busto was so
familiar to me. Such effigies of the beloved Prince were
widely dispersed in Scotland; and indeed they were
openly displayed for sale in London, in Red Lion
Square, as long ago as my first visit thither.

"You are a Jacobite indeed," I retorted upon my
quizzing friend, "to recognize your King when you have
never seen him."

"Why, Bozzy," retorted Dr. Johnson, " 'twas no feat
of divination, but the mere use of my eyes. They are not

what they were, 'tis true; but he who will look may see."

He raised the candle before the image, and I saw an inscription on the plaster, traced in faded paint. With difficulty I read it off:

> THEN ALL CLASP HANDS ABOUT THE RING,
> BRING FORTH THE PIPES, LET ALL MEN SING:
> LONG LIFE UNTO OUR PRINCE AND KING!
> THUS SHALL WE MAKE THE WELKIN RING
> WHEN THE KING SHALL COME INTO HIS OWN.

" 'Tis an old song of the '45," said Margaret Macdonald, "of my father's own making. I remember, he taught it me before the battle of Culloden. In later years he limned it above the plaster busto, as you may see, and always kept it bright; but we have not renewed it since he died. 'Tis but doggerel, but he set great store by it."

Dr. Johnson was studying the plaster busto, peering at it with an inscrutable countenance.

" 'Tis a noble countenance," he remarked, "and indeed 'tis a commonplace, that the face of any man is nobler in plaster than in the vicissitudes of flesh."

"Not so," exclaimed Flora Macdonald warmly, with indignation thrilling in her musical voice, "the face of Prince Charles as I saw it last, worn and bronzed and suffused with tears, was nobler and more beautiful than any plaster busto."

To this there was no answer, and Dr. Johnson swiftly turned the conversation to deal with less immediately interesting matters connected with the sculptor's art.

" 'Tis observable, ma'am," he remarked, "that in the

numerous equestrian memorials that adorn our metropolises, the horse is commonly the finer animal. This is because, depicting the same creature over and over, each time with a new rider, the artist perfects and refines his concept of equine nobility."

"You say true," exclaimed Flora Macdonald, whose Edinburgh education and refined travels had equipped her to pass upon the truth of my ingenious friend's observation.

"The like is observable," continued he, pointing to the side of the plaster head, "of ears. Observe the uncommon delicacy and perfection of this ear. This is not Charlie's ear, ma'am; this is *the Platonick ideal of ear.*"

"Nay, Dr. Johnson," replied our hostess, smiling, "there you are out again. This is the bonnie laddie's very ear, for I have observed it myself. Indeed the whole busto is very like. Dr. King relates, that when the Prince was in London in 1750, his serving-man recognized him from just such a head."

"In London in 1750!" I exclaimed incredulously.

Flora Macdonald laughed.

"The Prince," she said, "comes and goes at will. He is totally without fear. He was at the Hanoverian's coronation in '61; and they tell me he was at Inverness not five years past."

"Do you say so!" exclaimed Dr. Johnson. "Now that we have met Miss Flora Macdonald"—he bowed with his rare old-fashioned courtesy—"nothing remained to hope for unless we could meet the Prince himself face to face; you encourage me to believe that even this is not impossible in the Western Islands."

Kingsburgh shook his head.

"Nay, Dr. Johnson," he said, "you must e'en satisfy yourself with gazing on the busto; for we learn that upon his father's death the original is wedded at last, to a beautiful miss of twenty, and a princess to boot, and now he renews his youth as Benedick the married man. Depend upon it, his Majesty the King will come no more to Skye."

"Then, sir," said Dr. Johnson, "we must make do with what we have. I have kissed the hand of the celebrated Flora Macdonald; and now, as the hour grows late and the *poonch*-bowl empty, let me prefer a last request."

"Anything," smiled the lady graciously.

"That I may rest tonight in the very bed that sheltered the Prince so many years ago."

"You ask much," said Kingsburgh doubtfully.

"But not," said Flora quickly, "more than we will grant. Come with me, gentlemen."

We followed her up the stair. At the head she unlocked a door with a key, and we stood in Prince Charlie's room. By the light of the lifted candle we saw that it was a spacious chamber, well dusted and in order. On each side of the fireplace stood a sturdy bedstead, decked orderly with coverlets and hung with tartan curtains. On the hearth a fire was laid; Flora Macdonald lighted it with a spill.

"Ma'am," said Dr. Johnson earnestly, "it seems that the room has been readied for us."

"Not for you, Dr. Johnson," she replied; "for the King. My father-in-law kept it ever aired and redded against the day when Prince Charlie should return to Kingsburgh. The old man died last year; it was his dying wish that we should keep it so."

"So all is unchanged," mused Dr. Johnson, "since the unfortunate fugitive slept here."

" 'Tis the same bed," said Flora, pointing to that on the right of the fireplace. "The hangings are the same, and the coverings. Here is what is left of the linen."

By the light of the candle she carried she showed us an old press in the corner. In a deep drawer, among various strangely-assorted oddments, lay yellowing a sheet of fine linen.

"Pray, ma'am," enquired Dr. Johnson, "did Kingsburgh afford the royal fugitive but one sheet?"

"Not so," replied Flora with a smile, "there was a pair, which we at Kingsburgh have treasured among our dearest possessions. The one which is gone served Lady Kingsburgh for a winding sheet; and this shall do the same for me."

Dr. Johnson peered shortsightedly into the press. It contained a variety of reliques, which Flora Macdonald turned over with a faraway smile.

"Here is old Kingsburgh's punch-bowl," she said, "it suffered an accident on that very night." It had indeed; it was broken clean in half.

"Here is his shoe," said she. "It was worn clear through; old Kingsburgh gave him a new pair."

"Where is the other?" I enquired.

"When the old man died we cut it into strips and gave them away."

Prince Charlie's Ruby

"What is this?" I asked, indicating a roll of pale blue silk.

" 'Tis the Prince's candle," replied our hostess. "Here is his candle-snuffer; and this is his tinder-box."

"Where," enquired Dr. Johnson, drolling, "is the Prince's warming-pan?"

"Here," replied our hostess seriously. Sure enough, it hung bright and gleaming by the fire.

"So, Bozzy," observed Dr. Johnson, smothering a yawn, "tonight we lie royally indeed. I will sleep in the Prince's bed, I will be warmed by the Prince's warming-pan, and I will snuff the candle with the Prince's candle-snuffer."

Flora Macdonald shovelled coals into the polished warming-pan and set it in the Prince's bed between the homespun sheets.

"Good night," said our gracious hostess, "may you sleep soundly, and dream, if you will, of Bonnie Prince Charlie."

We lay in good comfort in the Prince's chamber, but for all that I slept but ill. The wind was in the chimney, and I lay long musing on the melancholy fate of the gallant Stuart prince. At last I slept, but fitfully, and in the phantasmagoria of sleep I dreamt that Prince Charlie returned to Skye. Over the moan of the wind I seemed to hear the subdued murmur of welcoming voices, and footsteps in the long hall. Fitfully through my dream I saw the proud white face of the plaster busto.

We lay late, for no one called us.

"Sir," said Dr. Johnson, "the happiest moments of a man's life are those he spends lying in bed in the morning."

The sun streamed through the leaded panes.

" 'Tis when lying in bed in the morning," said Dr. Johnson, stretching his massive frame, "that a man enjoys the blessings of consciousness, without suffering its inconveniences."

He grunted prodigiously, settled on his head the kerchief that served him in lieu of a night-cap, and with a great creaking of the bed-cords turned over for another bout with Morpheus.

'Twas late when we descended, and found our host and hostess gone, no one could say whither, and the buxom sister left to do the honours, which she did with an abstracted air. We enjoyed an excellent breakfast: as good chocolate as ever I tasted, tea, bread and butter, marmalade and jelly. There was no loaf-bread, but very good *scones*, or cakes of flour baked with butter. Miss Macdonald busied herself pouring out tea for my *tea-ophile* friend.

We were waited upon by a young girl bare-headed but very decently dressed. She kept directing at Miss Macdonald looks full of trouble and appeal, and finally, fetching the barley-bannocks, she burst forth in an odd sort of Gaelick and English:

" 'Tis the Burlow Beanie, ma'am, and not my fault at all, he's pried loose the chimney bricks and turned out the lint we laid up in the old man's time, and now here's one of your Dutch tiles you set such store by gone out of the sitting-room fireplace, and the plaster head is off the bracket and stole quite away, for I can't find it anywhere."

Miss Macdonald dropped the sugar-tongs and stooped to retrieve them, but I was before her.

"You are an ignorant girl," she said severely; "be quiet and fetch some fresh tea."

"We'll all be in our graves," wailed the girl, "for there's a new grave dug by the byre where the old man had the kale-yard . . . Yes, ma'am, fresh tea." The girl retreated before Miss Macdonald's stern visage, only to return in new distress:

"The Burlow Beanie has stole the cheese!"

"That," said Miss Macdonald to us, "sounds more like the Burlow Beanie."

"What is the Burlow Beanie?" I enquired.

"A foul fiend," replied Miss Macdonald, laughing, "which lives under the bed and requires to be placated with victuals; which failing, he takes to stealing and smashing."

"An institution of great utility," commented Dr. Johnson gravely.

"Thus it comes about," replied Miss Macdonald, "that in Scotland no housemaid ever breaks a dish or steals an end of cheese; 'tis all done by the Burlow Beanie."

After breakfast I retreated to our chamber to write up those notes which I am accustomed to keep on the proceedings and discourse of my illustrious friend. No better entertainment offering itself, in the absence of our host and hostess, Dr. Johnson joined me there at the conclusion of the mid-day meal and devoted himself to correspondence.

We supped late with Miss Macdonald, whose discourse proving a little wearisome, we mounted betimes to bed. We were courteously lighted thither by the lady herself, who with deputed zeal must needs inspect the appointments of the chamber.

"Alas, Dr. Johnson," she cried suddenly, turning from his bed in dismay, "you can never lie here tonight!"

"Why not, ma'am?" demanded the philosopher, peering between the curtains.

" 'Pon my soul, sir," exclaimed I, glancing over his shoulder, "you should have spoke better of the Burlow Beanie!"

The bed was sodden with water. Miss Macdonald stared distractedly into the top of the tester.

"A leak—" she cried. "Come, Dr. Johnson, you shall lie in comfort just down the passage."

She marshalled us to the back of the house and installed us in a room which stood providentially ready, two good beds fresh cloathed and a fire laid; and there she left us.

"Hah!" snorted Dr. Johnson. "A leak! The Burlow Beanie! This is mere malice and petty persecution. Someone on this island makes sport of our discomfort."

" 'Tis clear," I returned, "that Miss Macdonald believes in her Burlow Beanie. I met her in the lower passage after dinner, and trust me, she was carrying the lubber fiend the best part of the joint."

Prince Charlie's Ruby

"So do not I," retorted Dr. Johnson, "and I'll lie in the Prince's chamber tonight though I lie with the Burlow Beanie. I'll e'en beg the loan of the edge of your bed, Bozzy, and we'll see what the lubber fiend is after."

Returning stealthily to the Prince's chamber, we lay in tolerable comfort for perhaps an hour, concealed by the tartan curtains close-drawn. Then suddenly there was a light step in the passage, the door opened, and in stepped our gentle little hostess with a candle in her hand. She was followed by her husband and a tall stranger, a slim strong-built man in middle life. Kingsburgh carried a crow, which with no word spoken he applied to the bricks of the chimney-piece.

"Now fie upon my curiosity," muttered Dr. Johnson in my ear, "I had expected the serving-maid." He swept aside the tartan curtain and rose to his feet.

Kingsburgh dropped the crow with a clatter; Flora Macdonald drew in her breath with a little cry. Only the stranger was unmoved. He regarded my friend with a level gaze; I saw his eyeballs gleam in the light of the candle he held beside his head.

"Pray," he said with composure, "make Dr. Johnson known to Mr. Douglas."

I was piqued at the inversion of courtesy by which Kingsburgh *presented* my venerable friend to Mr. John Douglas. However, Dr. Johnson scanned the stranger's face keenly for a moment, by candle light, and then inclined from the waist with his rare stately courtesy.

"If Charles Stuart," he said respectfully, "wishes to be known as John Douglas, 'tis not for me to dispute

149

the appellation. I am your humble servant, Mr. Douglas."

I looked again at the oval face, the eyebrows raised now and the mouth just on the point of smiling. It was a face that had been used hard; the eyes were tired, and the oval was fuller than it had been. But the broad brow, the finely modelled nose, even the keen proud look, were still there.

He was dressed as of old, in Highland costume. He wore kilt and short hose of the red-and-black Stuart tartan. His well-shaped knees were bare; I noted how the full filibeg set off the good shape of his muscular legs. For the rest, he had a black waistcoat and a short cloth green coat with gold cord. On his feet he wore Highland brogues.

He carried himself with composed stateliness. I bowed low as I was presented to him in my turn, meditating on the vicissitudes of fortune that bade Charles Stuart return to the country of his fathers secretly and by night, hiding his presence even from those who in happier times would have been his subjects.

The King was smiling openly now.

"You see I was right," remarked Charles Stuart, "removing the busto from the bracket could not remove it from the memory of Dr. Johnson."

"Yet you were likewise wrong, sir," cried Flora Macdonald, "for you see you stand in no danger from Dr. Johnson, Sassenach though he may be. You might freely have appeared before him in your own person."

"As I do now," said Charles. "The better, for we have need of your counsel, Dr. Johnson."

Prince Charlie's Ruby

"I am wholly at your service," replied my monarchical friend. "What is your difficulty?"

"It is thus, my friend," replied the royal Stuart, "concealed somewhere in this house is a ruby worth £50,000."

"If indeed it be in this house," said Kingsburgh gloomily.

"It is here," replied Charles with confidence. "I trusted it to your father's keeping. I will stake my life that he kept it well. But where?"

"We have had up the fireplace tiles," said Kingsburgh, "we have turned out every chest and press that was here in my father's day, we have dug where the old kale-yard used to be, all to no purpose. Only this room remains to be searched; and I crave your indulgence, sir," he turned to Dr. Johnson, "for the crude means by which we sought to have you out of the way."

"Sir," said Dr. Johnson, " 'tis folly to put your trust in spades and crow-bars. Your father meant that the ruby should never be found by men with mattocks. No, sir; man is the master, not by reason of crows and shovels, but by virtue of the vision in his head."

"Then pray, Dr. Johnson," said the King half humorously, "search in your head and find me my ruby."

"Sir," replied Dr. Johnson seriously, "I will do so. Pray let us conduct this search by the sitting-room fire, with a bowl of *poonch* for the facilitation of the operation."

Accordingly we removed thither. Dr. Johnson brought the candle. Flora Macdonald lit the fire; Miss Macdonald came with the keys and brewed an excellent punch, which Charles Stuart commended heartily; and we sat as snug around the fire at midnight as though we were all old cronies together, and Bonnie Prince Charlie had never lost his kingdom and a ruby worth £50,000.

"But come," said Dr. Johnson when the glass had gone round, "I am not to search in *my* head, for I am a stranger to Kingsburgh; if the ruby is to be found, it must be found in *your* heads. Pray, let me hear the story of the lost gem."

"You must know," replied Charles, "it was one of a pair, the gift of the French King to my granddam Mary Stuart. One of these she gave away; the other descended to my father, and he left it to my brother Henry, the Cardinal. 'Twas the first one which after many years was brought to me at Holyrood and given into my hands for the good cause. I kept it by me for the day of need; 'twas on my person at Culloden."

"This gem was unset?" enquired Dr. Johnson.

"It was set in a ring," replied Charles Stuart.

"After Culloden the Prince fled into the Western Islands," said Flora Macdonald, "and the chiefs of the Isles protected him."

"I remember the day he came to Kingsburgh," said Margaret Macdonald, "though I was then no more than seven. Sir Alexander Macdonald was away at Fort Augustus; and when the military came on Skye, Lady Margaret sent for my father in haste, and he left the forms standing and the wax cooling in the vat and went away to her at Monkstadt. The next day he came back at dusk with a muckle, ill-shaken-up wife in an Irish camlet cape with a hood."

Prince Charlie's Ruby

"Me," said Charles, and laughed to the echo. "What a gawk of a female I made. Old Kingsburgh lost all patience with me. 'They call you a Pretender,' says he as I fell over my skirts, 'all I can say is that you are the worst at your trade I ever saw.'"

"My father was a staunch man," said Margaret softly. "When the Prince had got clean away, we begged him to save himself. 'I'll bide,' says he. 'I'm an old man, and may as well hang as die in my bed; and besides, who will light the great house if I take to the heather?'; and he stayed by the forms till they came from Fort Augustus and took him away."

"I wish," said Allan Macdonald, "that my father could have lived to see this day."

"So do I too," said Charles Stuart, "he was kind and staunch."

"And," added Kingsburgh, "he could have laid your ruby in your hand without ado."

"Have no concern," said I, "Dr. Johnson will lay the ruby in your hand before the night is through."

"I must find it first," said my venerable friend. "Pray, sir, let us hear more of how the gem came to Kingsburgh."

"It came through my agency," said Flora Macdonald. "I will tell you the story. 'Twas in June of '46 that word came to me at my brother's on South Uist, that he for whom we all prayed was hiding in the mountains, and desired my aid to pass over into Skye. We met at Milton by night, and a plan was concerted between us."

"I remember that night," said the royal Stuart, "we met in the byre at Milton. 'Twas black dark; but I remember a soft hand, and a low voice, and a steadfast courage."

"Lady Clanranald got us a boat; but before we could go off," said Flora Macdonald, "the militia had taken me up and brought me on suspicion before the commanding officer."

"Alack," I exclaimed, "how was this remedied?"

"The officer," replied Flora, "was my mother's second husband, and well-affected in secret. He gave me a pass—" she went to the writing-desk—"to carry us all safe into Skye."

She handed my companion a yellowing slip of paper. It was superscribed: "To Mistress Macdonald in the Island of Skye." Dr. Johnson read out the crabbed lines:

"I have sent your daughter from this country lest she should be frightened with the troops lying here. She has got one Betty Burke, an Irish girl, who, as she tells me, is a good spinster. If her spinning pleases you, you may keep her till she spins all your lint; or if you have any wool to spin, you may employ her. I have sent Neil Mackechan along with your daughter and Betty Burke to take care of them."

"A good spinster!" cried Charles. "O Lud, if I had stayed on Skye till I had spun all the lady's lint, I'd be there yet!"

"Prince Charlie," said Flora Macdonald, "in those days and after, was the handsomest man I have ever seen." The King smiled and pledged her in dumb show.

"But alack, sir," went on Flora, and laughed aloud, "in female gear, you were the awkwardest, most impudent jade imaginable, and had us all in terror that you would unfrock yourself before you had made good your escape."

"I submit, sir," said Charles Stuart argumentatively, turning to my venerable friend, "I appeal to your candour, whether any man alive is to be expected to walk from Monkstadt to Kingsburgh, ay and embark in boats and ford burns, clad in a quilted petticoat and an Irish cape with a hood, and still keep his maidenly modesty? 'Tis not in nature, and that's flat."

"Well, sir," continued Flora Macdonald, "modest or no, we took wherry and rowed for Skye, on a night wild with storm. We were all in fear for our lives, all save the Prince; and he sat high in the stern and sang ballads till the day broke."

"I sang," said Charles meditatively, replenishing his cup, "I sang 'Gilderoy.'" He sang softly to himself, in a true clear voice:

"Gilderoy was a bonny boy
Had roses tull his shoon . . ."

"'Twas the worse when day broke," continued Flora, "for the militia spied us from Waternish, and fired on us; and only that the oars were locked in the guardhouse, the adventure had ended there."

"I wished that it had," said Charles, "when we landed at Kilbride, and I had to spend the day lurking among the rocks. All the gnats on the Hebrides devoted the day to me."

"I hastened to Lady Macdonald at Monkstadt," said Flora, "where I found a great company assembled, among them several officers of the militia. I was happy to see old Kingsburgh. My first thought was to ask after Allan, for I could not hear of him since Culloden. Allan's father made me glad with the news that he was safe, and absconding in the heather."

"Ay," said Kingsburgh, "lurking in the heather and thinking of you—and you dining with royalty!"

"Lady Macdonald feared to receive the fugitive," continued Flora Macdonald, "and my father-in-law volunteered to shelter him at Kingsburgh."

"I fared sumptuously in this house," said Charles Stuart. "There was linen on the table. Lady Kingsburgh sat at my right hand, and Flora Macdonald on my left. I dined well on collops, eggs, butter, and cheese."

"And beer," added Flora. "I remember your toast: 'The health and prosperity of my landlord and landlady, and better times to us all.'"

"'Tis still a good toast," observed the royal guest. "Pray, Miss Macdonald, let us have more of your excellent punch."

He raised the replenished glass.

"To the health and prosperity of my landlord and landlady, and better times to us all."

Kingsburgh bowed his acknowledgements. Flora continued with a smile:

"Then our guest produced his pipe, an old thing as black as ink and worn to the very stump, sulphurous as the Pit—and you may be sure the ladies withdrew on the instant."

"'Twas a well-seasoned and deliciously fragrant *dudeen*," said Charles Stuart firmly, "and well it served me in my days of absconding. With it, and old Kingsburgh's famous punch, I comforted myself in talk with my host till nigh on to three. It was then I took the ruby from my bosom and begged him to hide it for me till happier times. He promised; and thus do I know beyond any cavil that the gem is here."

"And this transaction passed here, in this room?" enquired Dr. Johnson.

"Here, in this room," replied Charles.

"There's no hope in that," said Kingsburgh, "for we have turned out the presses and sounded the walls and pried at the fireplace tiles. We must seek further."

"Pray continue your story," said Dr. Johnson thoughtfully.

"I slept that night between sheets," said Charles Stuart, "and never awoke till past noon. Then in came my tirewomen, and inducted me again into the garments of Betty Burke."

"How we laughed, to be sure," said Flora. "The Prince affected to have the *vapours*. I assure you, 'twas more like epilepsy."

"So," said Charles, "by your fair hands I was garbed and shorn."

"Shorn?" I enquired.

Flora Macdonald opened the locket at her bosom.

"There was a great whispering in Gaelick," said Charles with a smile, "and when I enquired what was to do, I learned that Lady Kingsburgh was urging Flora to beg a lock from my devoted head. On the instant I laid it in the lady's lap, and she made a Samson of me."

I looked at the fine curl of light hair with its gleam of red.

"I have worn it in my bosom ever since." The blue eyes and the brown met in a moment of silence. Then Charles drew from his *sporan* a little jewelled snuff-box, turned it thoughtfully in his hand a moment, and then delicately took snuff.

"Kingsburgh fitted me out," he went on, "with new shoes and a stout plaid—"

"My father treasured the old shoes," said Kingsburgh, "you may see one still in the Prince's chamber."

"And where are the clothes of Betty Burke?"

"My father burned them that day," said Margaret Macdonald.

"The rest is soon told," said the King. "Raasay met me with a boat at Portree, and there I took leave of Flora Macdonald. She gave me a snuff-box for a keepsake—"

"You have it in your hand," said Flora softly.

"I carry it always," said Charles. "We took leave without words, and the boat was launched."

"I watched it out of sight," said Flora Macdonald.

"In the end I got clear away," concluded Charles, "and boarded a French vessel at Lochnanuagh, and so ended the adventure."

"And you, ma'am?" enquired Dr. Johnson.

"They carried me off to London," said the lady with a smile, "and lodged me in the Tower with the lions; but after a bit they let me out, and I became a lion in my own right for a while, in the drawing-rooms of St. James's; till at last they tired of me, and so I came away back to the Hebrides and married Allan Macdonald."

Prince Charlie's Ruby

"And lived happily ever after," said the tall Highlander with a tender smile.

"So have not I," said Charles bitterly, "exile and treachery have been my portion since I left Scotland. But now I look for a better day, when my son will be King of England."

"A son," cried Flora Macdonald joyfully, "you have an heir!"

"A fine boy," returned Charles proudly. "The child was born in Italy, but he will be brought up in Scotland. I have committed him secretly to the care of Clanranald. I myself go always in fear of assassination; it shall be otherwise with my child. Let his existence be a secret among us."

"It shall be so," said Dr. Johnson solemnly.

"It is for this," said Charles Stuart, "that I must have the ruby. My brother the Cardinal is a wealthy man; he has taken a fancy to reunite the pair. He will give me its value, which shall serve to educate my son. Well, Dr. Johnson—"

My learned friend was staring into the flame of the candle with an abstracted air, rolling his ponderous frame from side to side. With a start he returned his attention to the royal personage who addressed him.

"You have looked in our heads, sir," said Charles Stuart, "can you look in your own and find my ruby?"

"Sir," replied Dr. Johnson, "to bring our cerebral search to a happy conclusion, I ask only another bowl of *poonch* and a song."

"Sure this is a merry oracle," cried Charles in approval.

Margaret Macdonald brewed the punch, and the royal guest gave us "Gilderoy" with much applause. Still my friend sat with fixed gaze, and Charles Stuart launched into the minor strain of "Lochaber No More."

Midway in the song the candle began to flare and sputter. Flora Macdonald reached for the candlestick, but Dr. Johnson stayed her hand. In another moment there was a light click as something fell from old Kingsburgh's candle into the silver candlestick.

"Man is the master," cried Dr. Johnson triumphantly, "by reason of the vision in his head."

He handed the candlestick to Charles Stuart. In its base, covered with congealing candle-wax, lay a heavy ring set with a huge stone.

"Sir," said Dr. Johnson, "by looking into old Kingsburgh's head, I have found Mary Stuart's ruby as I promised."

"I am your debtor," cried Charles. "By what happy conjecture did you produce it so patly, like a stage play or a conjuring trick?"

"Sir," replied Dr. Johnson, "this house when I entered it was permeated with your presence. Old Kingsburgh and his family had preserved as sacred reliques the bed in which you slept, the sheets that wrapped you, and the ragged shoes you wore. Flora Macdonald wore in her bosom a lock of your hair. But there was one treasure different from these, and therefore mysterious to me—a candle in the room where you had slept. Why was it an object of special concern? Not because you had used it—it was a new candle, never lit. Not because it had been yours—you could not be thought to have burdened yourself with a wax taper in your dangerous journeys through the Highlands. The King's candle already had my curious attention before you entered this house, before you laid your problem before me.

"When we repaired hither, I brought it with me to burn in the King's presence. By its light I listened to the story of the old days in an indescribable state of apprehension. My climax threatened to become an anticlimax; the old man had set the gem further down in the candle than I had looked for. But at last I saw its shape appearing; and as the wax was consumed it fell and so was revealed."

"Pray, Dr. Johnson," I enquired, "how came you to light upon the candle, and not rather upon old Kingsburgh's ditty painted upon the wall? I made sure it was his message to us, and if we could but read it aright we should find the ruby by his direction."

"So did I too," confessed Kingsburgh, "for it repeats the word 'ring' as if by design. I came nigh to wrecking the wall where the word is painted, but 'tis solid, and has never been breached in my memory."

"You might have saved your pains," said Dr. Johnson. "Old Kingsburgh's verses were writ *before Culloden;* how then could they be a guide to the transaction of the ruby, which took place *after Culloden?* But the old man was pouring candles *after* the Prince's visit. No, sir; I have looked in old Kingsburgh's head as he poured the candles for the great house, and set aside for the King a candle worth £50,000."

"Sir," said Kingsburgh, "we are all in your debt."

The dainty mistress of Kingsburgh flung her arms about my astonished friend, and saluted him with a fervent kiss; while Charles Stuart gratefully pressed his hand.

"Bozzy, Bozzy," cried he, "this will be something to tell at the Mitre, that I have kissed the lips of Flora Macdonald and pressed the hand of his Majesty King Charles III!"

"Not so," replied Charles with his affable smile; "for the sake of my son, this episode must remain a part of secret history."

And as such I have respected it; until now the deaths of all the principals, including, alas, that of the last male scion of the House of Stuart, at Ormaclade in the fourth year of his age, sets me free to narrate this romantick episode of our tour to the Hebrides.

The STOLEN Christmas Box

THE DISAPPEARANCE of little Fanny Plumbe's Christmas box was but a prelude to a greater and more daring theft; and was itself heralded by certain uneasy signs and tokens. Of these was the strange cypher message which Mrs. Thrale intercepted; while I myself was never easy in my mind after seeing the old sailorman with the very particular wooden leg.

Dr. Sam: Johnson and I passed him on Streatham common as we approached the estate of the Thrales, there to spend our Christmas. He sat on a stone hard by the gates in the unseasonable sunshine, and whittled. He wore the neckerchief and loose pantaloons of a sea-faring man. He had a wind-beaten, heavy, lowering face, and a burly, stooped frame. His stump stuck out straight before him, the pantaloon drooping from it. That on which he whittled was his own wooden leg.

'Twas a very particular wooden leg. The cradle that

accommodated his stump was high-pooped and arabesqued about like a man-of-war's bow with carvings, upon the embellishment of which he was at the moment engaged. Into the butt was screwed a cylindrical post of about half the bigness of my wrist, turned in a lathe and wickedly shod with iron.

As the carriage passed him at an easy pace, I stared down upon him. He extended his greasy flapped hat, and my venerable companion dropped into it a gratuity.

We found the Thrale household pernitious dumpish, for all it was nigh onto Christmas. The tall, silent brewmaster Thrale greeted us with his usual cold courtesy, his diminutive rattle of a wife with her usual peacock screeches of delight. Of the party also were Thrale's grenadier of a sister, a strapping virago born to support the robes of a Lady Mayoress, and well on her way to that honour on the coat-tails of her husband, Alderman Plumbe. Plumbe topped his brother-in-law in height and doubled him in girth. His features were knobby and his temper cholerick. He scowled upon his children, Master Ralph, a lubber of fourteen, and Miss Fanny, a year older.

Master Ralph was rapidly shooting to his parents' height, but unable to keep pace in solidity. He continually closed his short upper lip over his long upper teeth, which as continually protruded again. He bowed and grinned and twisted his wrists in our honour.

Miss Fanny executed her duty curtsey with downcast eyes. Her person was tall and agreeably rounded, and sensibility played in red and white upon her cheek, playing the while, I own it, on the sensitive strings of my heart. Indeed, I could have been a knight-errant for Miss Fanny, had not I found below-stairs the veriest little witch of a serving-wench, pretty Sally, she who . . . but I digress.

Among the company circulated learned Dr. Thomas, the schoolmaster, assiduously pouring oil, as became a clergyman, on waters that were soon revealed to be troubled. Miss Fanny was in a fit of the sullens ('twas of a lover dismissed, I gathered so much), and Mrs. Plumbe was clean out of humour, and the Alderman alternately coaxing and shouting.

In an ill moment the latter conceived the idea of bribing Miss out of her pouts, and accordingly he fetches out the young lady's Christmas box, four days too soon, and bestows it upon her then and there; a step which he was bitterly to regret before the week was out.

"O Lud!" screamed Mrs. Thrale. "O Lud, 'tis a very Canopus!"

"'Tis indeed," said Dr. Sam: Johnson, "a star of the first magnitude."

'Twas a handsome jewel, though to my eyes scarce suitable for so young a lady—an intaglio artfully cut, and set with a diamond needlessly great, whether for the brooch or for the childish bosom 'twas designed to adorn.

"Sure," screeched Mrs. Thrale in her usual reckless taste, "such a size it is, it cannot be the right gem. Say, is't not paste?"

"Paste!" cried the Alderman, purpling to his wattles.

"I assure you, ma'am, 'tis a gem of the first water, such that any goldsmith in the city will give you £200 for."

Ralph Plumbe sucked a front tooth; his prominent eyes goggled. Pretty Sally, the serving-maid, passing with the tea tray, stared with open mouth. Little Dr. Thomas joined his fingertips, and seemed to ejaculate a pious word to himself. The Alderman pinned the gem in his daughter's bosom, a task in which I longed to assist him. She bestowed upon him a radiant smile, like sun through clouds.

Her fickle heart was bought. She yielded up to him with a pretty grace, those love-letters for which she had previously contested, and the footman carried them over the way that very afternoon to poor jilted Jack Rice, while Miss Fanny preened it with her jewel like a peacock.

'Twas a day or two later that I made one in a stroll about the Streatham grounds. Dr. Johnson and Mrs. Thrale beguiled our perambulation in discourse with learned Dr. Thomas about Welsh antiquities. Master Ralph Plumbe, ennuied by the disquisition, threw stones alternately at rooks and at Belle, the black-and-tawny spaniel bitch.

Coming by the kitchen garden, we marked curvesome Sally, in her blue gown and trim apron, skimming along under the wall. She passed us under full sail, with the slightest of running curtseys. Mrs. Thrale caught her sleeve.

"Pray, whither away so fast?"

"Only to the kitchen, ma'am."

The Stolen Christmas Box

Our sharp little hostess pounced.

"What have you in your hand?"

"Nothing, ma'am."

Mrs. Thrale, for all she is small, has a strong man's hand. She forced open the girl's plump fingers and extracted a folded billet.

"So, miss. You carry *billets doux.*"

"No, ma'am. I found it, if you please, ma'am," cried the girl earnestly.

"Ho ho," cried hobbledehoy Master Ralph, " 'tis one of Fan's, I'll wager."

"We shall see," said Mrs. Thrale curtly, and unfolded the billet.

I craned my neck. 'Twas the oddest missive (save one) that I have ever seen. 'Twas all writ in an alphabet of but two letters:

```
aababababbbbaaaabaaba  ababbabbabbaaaabaaba
abbaa'abbabbaabaaabaabaaab  baabaaabaa
aabbbaaaaaabababaabaabaaabaa  ababa'aabaaaaaaabaabb
abbabbaabbabaaa  ababa'aaaaabaabbabbaaaabaa
abaaabaaaaaabaa  baabaaabaa
aabbaaaaaabaaaaaaabbaabaa  aabbbaaaaaabaaaabbaaaabaa
aaaaaabaaaabababaababaaabaa  aababababaaabaaaaaabaaabbaabaaba
baaabaaaaaababaabababaaabaa  ababaabaaabaaba
```

Learned Dr. Thomas scanned the strange lines.

" 'Tis some unknown, primordial tongue, I make no doubt."

" 'Tis the talk of sheep!" I cried. "Baabaaabaa!"

"No, sir; 'tis cypher," said Dr. Sam: Johnson.

"Good lack," screeched Mrs. Thrale, " 'tis a French plot, I'll be bound, against our peace."

"No, ma'am," I hazarded, half in earnest, " 'tis some imprisoned damsel, takes this means to beg release."

"Pfoh," said Mrs. Thrale, "ever the ruling passion, eh, Mr. Boswell?"

"To what end," demanded Dr. Johnson, "do we stand disputing here, when we might be reading the straight of the message?"

"My husband has the new book of cyphers," cried Mrs .Thrale, "I will fetch it at once."

She sailed off, pretty Sally forgotten; who put her finger to her eye and stood stock-still in the path, until, perceiving how eagerly I followed where Dr. Johnson and the cypher led, she flounced off with dry eyes.

Dr. Johnson made for the drawing-room, and we streamed after him. Seating himself by the window, he peered at the strange paper. Dr. Thomas, Ralph Plumbe, and I peered with him, and Fanny came from the mirror, where we had surprized her preening, to peer too.

As Dr. Johnson smoothed the billet, I threw up my hands.

"What can be done with this!" I exclaimed. "We are to find out the 24 letters of the alphabet, and in this whole message we find but two symbols."

"What man can encypher, man can decypher," replied Dr. Johnson sententiously, "more especially when the encypherer is one of the inmates of Streatham, and the decypherer is Sam: Johnson. But see where our hostess comes."

She came empty-handed. The new book of cyphers was not to be found.

The Stolen Christmas Box

"Then," said Dr. Johnson, "we must make do with what we have in our heads. Let us examine this billet and see what it has to say to us."

We hung over his shoulder, Mrs. Thrale, Dr. Thomas, the Plumbe children, and I. Ralph sucked air through his teeth in excitement, little Fanny's pretty bosom lifted fast.

"Now, ma'am," began Dr. Johnson, addressing Mrs. Thrale, not ill-pleased to display his learning, "you must know, that cyphers have engaged the attention of the learned since the remotest antiquity. I need but name Polybius, Julius Africanus, Philo Mechanicus, Theodorus Bibliander, Johannes Walchius, and our own English Aristotle, Francis Bacon—"

"Oh, good lack, sir," cried little Fanny with a wriggle, "what does the paper say?"

"In good time, miss," replied the philosopher with a frown. "We have here 330 characters, all either *a* or *b;* writ in 16 groups on a page from a pocket book, with a fair-mended quill. 'Tis notable, that the writer wrote his letters in clusters of five, never more, never less; you may see between every group the little nodule of ink where the pen rested. Let us mark the divisions."

With his pen he did so. I watched the lines march:

```
aabab/abbab/baaaa/baaba    ababb/abbab/baaaa/baaba
abbaa'/abbab/baaba/aabaa/baaab   baaba/aabaa
aabbb/aaaaa/ababa/ababa/aabaa . . .
```

"We now perceive," said Dr. Johnson as his pen flicked, "that we have to do, not with a correspondence of letter for letter, but for groups of letters. We have

169

before us, in short, Mr. Boswell, the famous bi-literal cypher of the learned Francis Bacon; as set forth, I make no doubt, in Thrale's missing book of cyphers."

Mrs. Thrale clapped her hands.

"Now we shall understand it. Mark me, 'tis a plot of the French against us."

"Alas," said Dr. Johnson, "I do not carry the key in my head; but I shall make shift to reconstruct it. 'Tis many years since I was a corrector of the press; but the printer's case still remains in my mind to set me right on the frequencies of the letters in English."

"Depend upon it," muttered Mrs. Thrale stubbornly, " 'tis in French."

"You will find," he went on calmly, "*e* occurs the oftenest; next *o*, then *a* and *i*. To find out one consonant from another, remember also their frequency, first *d, h, n, r, s, t;* then the others, in what order I forget; but with these we may make shift."

By this calculation the learned philosopher determined the combination *aabaa* to represent *e;* when a strange fact transpired. Of the sixteen groups, representing perhaps the sixteen words of the message, nine ended with that combination! Dr. Johnson considered this in conjunction with the little marks like apostrophes, and glowered at Mrs. Thrale.

"Can it be French after all?"

In fine, it was; for proceeding partly by trial and errour, and partly by his memory of the cypher's system, the learned philosopher made shift to reconstruct the key, and soon the message began to emerge:

"Fort mort n'otes te—"

The Stolen Christmas Box

" 'Tis poetick!" screeched Mrs. Thrale. "*Strong death snatch thee not away!* Alack, this is a *billet doux* after all, a *lettre d'amour* to some enamoured fair!"

"Oh, ay?" commented the philosopher drily, penning the message:

"Fort mort n'otes te halle l'eau oui l'aune ire te garde haine aille firent salle lit."

" 'Tis little enough poetick," I muttered, translating the strange hodge-podge:

"Strong death snatch thee not away—market—the water, yes—the alder—anger—keep thee hatred—let him go—they made room—bed."

"O lud, here's a waspish message," cried Fanny.

"Yet what's this of a market, water, and an alder tree?"

"There's an alder tree," cried Ralph with a toothy inspiration, "by the kitchen pump!"

Infected by his excitement, we all ran thither. There was the water, sure enough, in the old pump by the kitchen garden, and drooping its branches over it, not an alder, but a hoary old willow, whose hollow trunk knew the domesticities of generations of owls. There was nothing of any note in the vicinity.

This strange adventure made us none the easier; the less, as we encountered, at his ease on the bench by the kitchen door, the one-legged sailorman. He pulled his forelock surlily, but did not stir. His very particular wooden leg was strapped in its place, and the iron-shod stump was sunk deep in the mud of the door-yard. Belle snapped at it, and had a kick in the ribs for her pains.

The adventure of the cypher much disquieted the

Alderman, who incontinently decreed that Miss Fanny's brilliant must be made secure in Thrale's strong-box. Now was repeated the contest of pouts against Papa; Miss Fanny moped, and would not be pleased. At last by treaty the difficulty was accommodated. Let the Alderman make the gem secure today, and Miss Fanny might wear it in honour of the twelve days of Christmas, to begin at dusk on Christmas Eve precisely.

Christmas Eve came all too slowly, but it came at last. We were all in holiday guise, I in my bloom-coloured breeches, Dr. Thomas in a large new grizzle wig, Ralph in peach-colour brocade with silk stockings on his skinny shanks. Even Dr. Sam: Johnson honoured the occasion in his attire, with his snuff-colour coat and brass buttons, and a freshly powdered wig provided by the care of Mr. Thrale.

The ladies coruscated. Mrs. Alderman Plumbe billowed in flame-colour sattin. Mrs. Thrale had a handsome gown in the classick stile, with great sleeves, and gems in her hair. Miss Fanny wore a silken gown, of the tender shade appropriately called maiden's blush; 'twas cut low, and her brooch gleamed at her bosom. Even Belle the spaniel was adorned with a great riband tied on with care by the white hand of Miss Fanny.

'Twas Thrale's care to uphold the old customs, and play the 'squire; while at the same time he had a maccaroni's contempt for the lower orders. 'Twas decreed, therefore, that we should have our Christmas games in the library on the lower floor, while the servants might have their merry-making in the servants' hall, and the strolling rusticks had perforce to receive their Christmas gratuities withoutside.

We supped upon Christmas furmety, a dish of wheat cakes seethed in milk with rich spices. I relished it well, and did equal justice to the noble minced pyes served up with it.

Supper done, we trooped to the library. Impeded by an armful of green stuff, Dr. Johnson came last, edging his way to the door. On the threshold, as he sought to manœuvre the unmanageable branches through, the crookedest one fairly lifted his fresh-powdered Christmas wig from his head, and as he clutched at it with a start, precipitated it in a cloud of white onto the floor. I relieved him of his awkward burden, and good-humouredly he recovered his head-covering and clapped it back in its place, all awry.

In the library all was bustle. It was my part to wreathe the mantel with green. Pretty Miss Fanny lighted the Christmas candles, looking the prettier in their glow, her sparkling eyes rivalling the brilliant at her breast. Thrale ignited the mighty "Yule clog."

Dr. Johnson was in great expansion of soul, saluting his hostess gallantly under the mistletoe bough, and expatiating on the old Christmas games of his boyhood.

"Do but be patient, Dr. Johnson, we'll shew you them all," cried Thrale with unwonted vivacity. He was busied over a huge bowl. In it heated wine mingled its fumes with orange peel and spices, while whole roasted apples by the fire were ready to be set abob in it.

'Twas the old-time *wassail bowl*; though Dr. Johnson persisted in referring to its contents, in his Lichfield accent, as *poonch*.

> "Here we come a-wassailing among the leaves so green,
>   Here we come a-wandering, so fair to be seen . . ."

The notes of the song crept up on us gradually, coming from the direction of the common, till by the time the second verse began, the singers stood in the gravel path before the library windows; which we within threw up, the better to hear their song:

> "We are not daily beggars, that beg from door to door,
>   But we are your neighbours' children, whom you have
>   seen before . . ."

Past all doubt, so they were. The servants had crowded to the door-step in the mild night, and merry greetings were interchanged as they found friends among the waits. A light snow was drifting down. The rusticks were fancifully adorned with ribands, and wore greens stuck in their hats; they carried lanthorns on poles, and sang to the somewhat dubious accompaniment of an ancient serpent and a small kit fiddle. In the ring of listening faces I spied the surly visage of the one-legged sailor. Belle the spaniel spied her enemy too. She escaped from the arms of Miss Fanny, eluded the groom at the house-door, and dashed out into the mud to snap at his heel. She came back with a satisfied swagger, the more as she had succeeded in untying her riband and befouling it in the mud. Miss Fanny admonished her, and restored the adornment.

The Stolen Christmas Box

"Now here's to the maid in the lily-white smock
  Who slipped to the door and pulled back the lock,
  Who slipped to the door and pulled back the pin
  For to let these merry wassailers walk in."

There was no suiting the action to the word. Thrale
passed the cup out at window, keeping the lower orders
still withoutside. The waits wiped their mouths on
their sleeves, and sang themselves off:

"Wassail, wassail all over the town,
  Our bread it is white and our ale it is brown,
  Our bowl it is made of the green maple tree —
  In our wassailing bowl we'll drink unto thee!"

Next the mummers came marching. Like the waits,
they had been recruited from the lads about Streatham.
Though every man was disguised in fantastick habili-
ments, among them the canine instinct of Belle uner-
ringly found out her friends. His own mother would
not have known the *Doctor*, he presenting to the world
but a high-bridged nose and a forest of whiskers; but
Belle licked his hand, the while he acknowledged the
attention by scratching her ear and making her riband
straight. She fawned upon *St. George* (by which, " 'Tis
the butcher's boy!" discovered Mrs. Thrale) and put
muddy foot-marks on the breeches of the *Old Man*,
before her attentions were repelled. She came back with
her tongue out and her riband, once again, a-trail. Miss
Fanny, defeated, neglected to restore it. She crowded
with the rest of the company in the window as the link-
boys lifted their torches, and upon the snowy sward the
rusticks of Streatham played the famous mumming
play of *St. George and the Dragon*.

"Pray, sir, take notice," said the pleased Dr. Johnson, "is not this a relique of great antiquity, the hieratic proceedings of yonder sorcerous *Doctor* with his magick pill? Pray, my man—" out at window to the *Doctor*, "how do you understand these doings?"

"Nor I don't, sir," replied the player huskily, and carried on his part to a chorus of laughter from within.

"And God bless this good company," concluded *St. George* piously. He caught the heavy purse that Thrale threw him, weighed it, and added in his own voice, "God bless ye, sir."

The guests added their largesse. Plumbe hurled a piece of gold; Dr. Johnson and I scattered silver; even withered little Dr. Thomas must needs add his half-crown. 'Twas scarce worth the trouble he went to, first to fumble in his capacious pocket for the destined coin, then to wrap it in a leaf from his pocket book, finally to aim it precisely into the hands of *St. George*. His heart was better than his marksmanship; his shot went wide, and a scramble ensued.

"God bless all here," chorused the rusticks, and made off with their torches as we within closed the windows and clustered about the fire. Then the bowl was set ablaze, and we adventured our fingers at snapdragon, catching at the burning raisins with merry cries.

"Fan, my love," said the Alderman suddenly, "where is thy Christmas box?"

Everybody looked at the flushed girl, standing with a burned finger-tip between her pink lips like a baby.

"The man," she half-whispered, "the man, Papa, he

looked at it so, while the mummers played, I was affrighted and slipped it into a place of safety."

She indicated an exquisite little French enamel vase.

" 'Tis here, Papa."

The Alderman snatched the vase and turned it up. 'Twas empty. Miss Fanny's Christmas box was gone.

The Alderman turned purple.

"The servants—" he roared.

"Pray, Mr. Plumbe, calm yourself," said Dr. Johnson, "we must look for Miss Fanny's diamond within this room."

He pointed, first to the snow now lightly veiling the ground beneath the window, then to the splotch of powder on the threshold. In neither was there any mark of boot or shoe.

But, though the cholerick Alderman turned out the chamber, and though every one present submitted to the most thorough of searches, though Plumbe even sifted out the ashes of the Yule clog, little Fanny's Christmas box was not to be found.

"This is worse than Jack Rice a thousand times," sniggered her brother in my ear.

It was so. Poor pretty Fanny was in disgrace.

" 'Tis a mean thief," cried Dr. Johnson in noble indignation, "that robs a child, and be sure I'll find him out."

Poor Fanny could only sob.

'Twas enough to mar the merriment of Christmas Day. Little Fanny kept her chamber, being there admonished by good Dr. Thomas. The lout Ralph wandered about idly, teizing Belle until the indignant spaniel nipped him soundly; upon which he retired into the sulks. The Alderman and his lady were not to be seen. The master and mistress of the house were busied doing honour to the day. I was by when they dispensed their Christmas beef upon the door-step; pretty Sally handed the trenchers about, and there in the crowd of rusticks, stolidly champing brawn, I saw the one-legged sailor. He seemed quite at home.

Dr. Johnson roamed restlessly from room to room.

BOSWELL: "Pray, sir, what do you seek so earnestly?"

JOHNSON: "Sir, a French dictionary."

BOSWELL: "To what end?"

JOHNSON: "To read yonder cypher aright; for sure 'tis the key to tell us, whither Fanny's brilliant has flown."

BOSWELL: "Why, sir, the words are plain; 'tis but the interpretation that eludes us."

JOHNSON: "No, sir, the words are *not* plain; the words are somehow to be transposed. Now, sir, could I but find a French dictionary printed in *two* columns, 'twould go hard but we should find, in the *second* column, the words we seek, jig-by-jole with the meaningless words we now have."

Upon this I joined the search; but in twenty-four hours we advanced no further in reading the cypher.

After dinner the next day I came upon Dr. Johnson conning it over by the fire, muttering the words to himself:

"Te halle l'eau oui l'aune ire te garde haine . . ."

I was scarce attending. An idea had occurred to me.

"Yonder hollow willow near the garden—" I began.

"How?" cried Dr. Johnson, starting up.

"The hollow willow near the garden—"

"You have it, Bozzy!" cried my companion in excitement. "Te hollow willown ear te gard en."

So strange was the accent and inflection with which my revered friend repeated my words, that I could only stare.

"Read it!" he cried. "Read it aloud!"

He thrust the decyphered message under my nose. I read it off with my best French accent, acquired in my elegant grand tour.

"Can't you see," cried Dr. Johnson, "when you speak it, the words are English—the hollow willow near the garden! 'Twill be the miscreants' post-office, 'tis clear to me now. See, they had cause to distrust the maid who was go-between."

He pointed to the last words: *aille firent salle lit*, I fear Sally.

"How did you do it, Bozzy?"

"I, sir? Trust me, 'twas the furthest thing from my mind. It had come into my head, perhaps by the alder was meant yonder hollow willow—"

"No, sir," returned Dr. Johnson, "there came into your mind, a *picture* of the hollow willow, because you heard, without knowing that you heard, the words I uttered; and when *you* spoke the words, *I* recognized that you were repeating mine. But come, sir; let us investigate this thieves' post-office."

He fairly ran out at the door.

Coming suddenly about the corner of the house, we

surprized the sailorman standing under the wall of the kitchen garden; and I could have sworn that I caught the swirl of a skirt where the wall turned. As we came up, the one-legged man finished knotting something into his neckerchief, and made off with astonishing speed. He stumped his way across the common in the direction of the ale-house on the other side.

"Shall we not catch him up?" I cried.

"In good time," replied my friend. "First we must call for the post."

Accordingly we lingered to sound the hollow tree. Save for some grubs and beetles, and a quantity of feathers, it was empty.

Our fortune was better when we passed under the wall where the one-legged man had stood. There we picked up the second of the strange messages that came under our eyes at Streatham.

'Twas a strip of paper, scarce an inch wide and some twelve inches long. Along both its edges someone had made chicken-tracks with a pen. One end was roughly torn away. Search as we might, the missing fragment was not to be found. At last we repaired to the house.

In the library we encountered Mrs. Thrale, in philosophical discourse with Dr. Thomas. She looked at the strange piece of paper, and gave a screech.

" 'Tis Ogam!"

The Stolen Christmas Box

"Ogam?"

"I know it well, 'tis the antique writing of the Irish," said Dr. Thomas, scanning the page with interest. "You must understand, sir, that the untutored savages of Ireland, knowing nothing of pen and paper, had perforce to contrive some way of incising letters upon wood, stone, horn, and the like. They hit upon a system of scratching lines on the edges of these objects, as perpendicular or oblique, and grouped to represent the various letters. Thus it was said of many a deceased Irish hero, 'They dug the grave and they raised the stone and they carved his name in Ogam.'"

"Why, this is a learned jewel-thief. Pray, Dr. Thomas, translate these triangles and dashes."

"Alack, sir, I cannot do it extempore. I must first have my books."

"*You*, ma'am," says Dr. Johnson to the volatile matron, "*you* are mighty familiar with Ogam, pray read it off for us."

"O Lud, sir, not I, I am none of your antiquarians."

"Why, so. Then I must extract the meaning for myself. 'Twill be no harder than the bi-literal cypher."

But try as he would, the strange marks on the edges of the paper would not yield to the theory of the printer's case. At last he leaned back.

"Let us begin afresh."

"No, sir," I begged, "let us have our tea. I am no Spartan boy, to labour while a fox is gnawing my vitals."

"Spartan!" cried my companion. "You have earned

your tea, Mr. Boswell. Do but answer me one question first, we may begin afresh and I think proceed in the right direction. Pray, what shape is this paper?"

"Sir, long and flat."

Dr. Johnson dangled it by one end.

"No, sir, 'tis helical."

Indeed as it dangled it coiled itself into a helix.

"Let us restore it to its proper shape," said Dr. Johnson. "Pray, Mr. Boswell, fetch me the besom."

I looked a question, but my sagacious friend said nothing further, and I went in search of the pretty housemaid and her besoms. After an interlude of knight-errantry, which taught me somewhat about women, but naught at all about our puzzle, I returned with such brooms as the house afforded.

I found my learned friend surrounded by stocks and staves, thick and thin, long and short. Around them, one after one, he was coiling the strange paper as a friseur curls hair about his finger. The results left him but ill satisfied.

"Could I but recall it to mind," he muttered, "there is a thing missing, that is germane to this puzzle; but now 'tis gone from my memory."

"Why, sir," said I, "we are to question the one-legged sailorman."

"Well remembered, Mr. Boswell." He stuffed the coiled paper into his capacious pocket. "Come, let us be off."

I bade farewell to my tea as I followed him. We found the publick room of the Three Crowns nigh empty, its only occupants being the idling tapster, and two men drinking in the ingle; but one of them was the man we sought. His companion was a likely-looking youth with a high-bridged nose, who pledged him in nappy ale.

"Good day, friend," Dr. Johnson accosted the maimed sailor.

The fresh-faced youth rose quietly, pulled a respectful forelock, and made off. Dr. Johnson looked at the sailorman's tankard, now empty, and signed to the tapster.

Not that the sailorman's tongue wanted loosening. Previous potations had already done the business. He was all too ready to spin his yarn.

"Nine sea fights I come through," he cried, "and lost my peg in the end, *mort dieu*, in Quiberon Bay."

He dealt his wooden member a mighty thump with the again emptied tankard. My worthy friend, ever ready to relieve the lot of the unfortunate, once more signed to the tapster. As the can was filling, he animadverted upon the wretchedness of a sea-life.

"I marvel, that any man will be a sailor, who has contrivance enough to get himself into a gaol; for being in a ship is being in gaol with the chance of being drowned."

"Ah," said the peg-legged sailor mournfully, and buried his nose in his pot.

My friend pressed upon him a gratuity in recognition of his perils passed. The sailorman accepted of it with protestations of gratitude.

" 'Tis nothing, sir," replied my kindly friend. "Do you but gratify my whim, I'll call myself overpaid."

"How, whim?" says the sailorman.

"I've a whim," says Johnson, "to borrow your wooden leg for a matter of half an hour."

I stared with open mouth, but the sailorman shewed no flicker of surprize. He unstrapped the contrivance immediately and put it in my friend's hand.

"Pray, Bozzy," said Dr. Johnson, "see that our worthy friend here lacks for nothing until I come again."

Before I could put a question he had withdrawn, the unstrapped peg in his hand. I was left to the company of the tapster and the loquacious sailorman. He insisted upon telling me how he had made his peg himself, and how it had often been admired for its artistry.

"Here's this young fellow now," he rattled on, gesturing vaguely across the common, "he thinks it a rarity, and but this morning he had it of me for an hour at a time."

This statement but doubled my puzzlement. What in the world could a two-legged man want with a peg-leg? Surely my learned friend was not intending to personate the one-legged sailorman? Had the high-nosed youth done so? I tried to recall the glimpse I had had of the one-legged beggar by the kitchen garden.

When Dr. Johnson returned, he returned in his own guise. We left the sailorman, by this time snorting with vinous stertorousness in the corner of the ingle, and walked across the common back to the house.

"Pray, sir, what success? Did you find the diamond?"

"Find the diamond? No, sir, I did not find the diamond; but I know where it is, and I know how to lay the thief by the heels."

He dug from his pocket the strange strip of paper. Between the lines of Ogam he had penned the message:

"£140 tonight 12 a clock y° oak nighest y° 3 crowns"

"What shall this signify?"

"Nay, Bozzy, 'tis plain. But here comes our friend Dr. Thomas. Pray, not a word more."

I was seething with curiosity as we supped at the Thrales' sumptuous table. The talk turned, willy-nilly, to the strange way in which the Christmas gem had been spirited from the library. Dr. Johnson admitted himself baffled. He was in a depression from which he could not be wooed even by the blandishments of the spaniel Belle, who, spurred by hunger, begged eagerly for scraps; until a new larceny, committed against himself, restored him to good humour.

It must be said that Dr. Sam: Johnson is scarce a dainty feeder. He is a valiant trencherman, and stows away vast quantities of his favourite comestibles.

"Ma'am," says he on this occasion, unbuttoning the middle button of his capacious vest and picking a capon wing in his fingers, "ma'am, where the dinner is ill gotten, the family is somehow grossly wrong; there is poverty, ma'am, or there is stupidity; for a man seldom thinks more earnestly of anything than of his dinner, and if he cannot get that well done, he should be suspected of inaccuracy in other things."

"Oh," says Mrs. Thrale, not knowing how to take this, but willing to turn it against him, "did you never, then, sir, huff your wife about your meat?"

"Why, yes," replied he, taking a second wing in his fingers, "but then she huffed me worse, for she said one day as I was going to say grace: 'Nay, hold,' says she, 'and do not make a farce of thanking GOD for a dinner which you will presently protest to be uneatable.'"

At this there was a general laugh; under cover of which Belle the spaniel, tempted beyond endurance, reared boldly up, snatched the capon wing from the philosopher's fingers, and ran out of door with it.

"Fie, Belle," cried out Mrs. Thrale, "you used to be upon honour!"

"Ay," replied the Doctor with his great Olympian laugh, "but here has been a *bad influence* lately!"

Not another word would he say, but devoted himself to a mighty veal pye with plums and sugar.

Yet when we rose from the table, he sought out the guilty Belle and plied her with dainties.

"'Tis a worthy canine, Bozzy," cried he to me, "for she has told me, not only *how* Miss Fanny's diamond was spirited from the library, but by *whose* contrivance. Between the good Belle, and yonder strange paper of Ogam, I now know *where* the conspirators shall meet, and *when*, and *who* they are, and *what* their object is; to prevent which, I shall make one at the rendezvous. Do you but join me, you shall see all made plain."

I was eager to do so. Muffled in greatcoats, we crossed the common and took up our station under the great oak a stone's cast from the Three Crowns. As the wind rattled the dry branches over our heads, I was minded of other vigils we had shared and other miscreants we had laid by the heels.

The Stolen Christmas Box

The darkness was profound. Across the common we saw window after window darken in the Thrale house as the occupants blew out their candles. Then I became aware of motion in the darkness, and towards us, stealing along the path, came a muffled shape, utterly without noise, flitting along like a creature of the night. For a moment we stood rigid, not breathing; then Dr. Johnson stepped forward and collared the advancing figure. It gave a startled squeak, and was silent. Dr. Johnson pulled the hat from the brow. In the starlight I stared at the face thus revealed.

'Twas Dr. Thomas! I beheld with horror his awful confusion at being detected.

"Alas, Dr. Johnson, 'tis I alone am guilty! But pray, how have you smoaked me?"

"Ogam," says Dr. Johnson, looking sourly upon the clergyman. "Trust me, you knew that was no Ogam. Ogam is incised on *both* edges of a right angle, not scribbled on paper."

"That is so, sir. You have been too sharp for me. I will confess all. 'Tis my fatal passion for Welsh antiquities. I have pawned the very vestments of my office to procure them. I took Miss Fanny's gem, I confess it, and flung it from the window wrapped in a leaf from my pocket book."

"I see it!" I exclaimed. " 'Twas thrown at hazard, and the one-legged sailor carried it thence hid in the hollow of his wooden leg."

"Nothing of the kind," said Dr. Johnson. "The role of the sailor and his wooden leg was quite other. But say, how much had you for the gem?"

"Two hundred pounds," replied the fallen clergyman. "Two hundred pounds! The price of my honour! Alas," he cried in a transport of remorse, falling on his knees and holding up his hands to Heaven, "had I, when I stood at those crossroads, gone another way, had I but heeded the voice within me which cried, *Turn aside, turn aside, lest thou fall into the hands of thine enemy,* had I but gone swiftly upon the strait way, then in truth we might at the grave's end have met together in the hereafter . . ."

Dr. Johnson heard this piteous avowal unmoved, but not so I. 'Twas a solemn sight to see the unfortunate man wring his hands and cry out with anguish, turning up his eyes to Heaven. Suddenly, however, his gaze fixed eagerly upon the darkened inn. In the same instant Dr. Johnson whirled, and ran, swiftly for all his bulk, to where a light coach was just getting in motion. I heard the harness jingle, and then the startled snort of a horse as my fearless friend seized the near animal by the bit and forced it to a halt.

"So," he cried angrily, "you'll meet them hereafter, at *Gravesend!* Never a whit. Come down, sir! Come down, miss!"

For a moment there was only the jingle of harness as the nervous horses pranced. Then a figure stepped to earth, a tall young man muffled to his high-bridged nose in a heavy cape, and lifted down after him the cloaked figure of—

Miss Fanny Plumbe!

"Pray, Dr. Johnson," she said statelily, "why do you hinder us? What wrong have we done?"

The Stolen Christmas Box

"You have diddled your father, and all of us," replied my companion sternly, "sending Bacon's cypher to Jack Rice here with those letters you gave up so meekly —once you had the diamond that you might turn into journey-money."

The chit's composure was wonderful.

"Why, sir," she owned with a smile, "you gave me a turn when you decyphered my last message by the hand of Sally; whom indeed, Mr. Boswell—" turning to me—"I no longer dared trust when she became so great with you. But confess, Dr. Johnson, my French held you off, after all, until I was able to convey a new cypher to Jack by the hand of the sailorman."

"And Dr. Thomas was your accomplice in making away with the gem?" I cried in uncontrollable curiosity.

"Be not so gullible, Bozzy," cried my companion impatiently, "trust me, Dr. Thomas knew never a word of the matter until Miss here opened her mind to him in their close conference on Christmas Day. 'Twas the hussy herself that conveyed her diamond to her lover, that he might turn it into money for their elopement."

"Nay, how? For she never left the room."

"But *Belle* did—and carried with her the diamond, affixed to her riband by the hand of Miss Fanny. Out flies the dog to greet her friend the neighbour lad in his mummer's disguise; who apprised of the scheam, caresses his canine friend and removes the brilliant in the same operation."

"That is so, sir," said Jack Rice.

"Surely," said Miss Fanny, "surely I did no wrong, to convey my jewel to the man I mean to wed."

"That's as may be," said my friend, unrelenting, "but now, miss, do you accompany us back to the house, for there'll be no elopement this night."

"Pray, sir," said Dr. Thomas earnestly, "be mollified. The lad is a good lad, and will have a competence when once he turns twenty-one; and I have engaged to make one in their flight and bless their union, which the surly Alderman opposes out of mere ill nature."

"To this I cannot be a party," began my authoritarian friend. The little clergyman was fumbling in his pocket. He brought forth, not a weapon, but a prayer-book.

"Do you, John, take this woman . . ." he began suddenly.

"Hold, hold!" cried Johnson.

"I do," cried the lad in a ringing voice.

"And do you, Fanny . . ."

Jack Rice pulled a seal-ring from his finger.

"I do."

"Then I pronounce you man and wife."

The ring hung loose on the girl's slim finger, but it stayed on.

"You are witnesses, Dr. Johnson, Mr. Boswell," cried the little clergyman. "Will not you salute the bride?"

Dr. Johnson lifted his great shoulders in concession.

"I wish you joy, my dear."

As the coach with its strangely-assorted trio of honeymooners receded in the distance:

"Pray, Dr. Johnson," said I, "resolve me one thing. If the strange message was not Ogam, what was it?"

JOHNSON: "Simple English."

BOSWELL: "How can this be?"

The Stolen Christmas Box

JOHNSON: "The triangles and scratches along the edges of yonder paper were halved lines of writing, and had only to be laid together to be read off."

BOSWELL: "Yet how are the top and bottom of a single strip of paper to be laid together?"

JOHNSON: "The Spartans, of whom you yourself reminded me, did it by means of a staff or *scytale*, around which the strip is wound, edge to edge, both for writing and for reading."

BOSWELL: "Hence your search for a staff or broomstick."

JOHNSON: "Yes, sir. Now it went in my mind, yonder one-legged man had a strange wooden leg, which did not taper as they usually do, but was straight up and down like a post. Was he perhaps both the emissary and the key? At the cost of a half-crown I had it of him—carried it out of his sight that he might not babble of my proceedings—and read the communication with ease."

BOSWELL: "This is most notable, sir. I will make sure to record it this very night."

JOHNSON: "Pray, Mr. Boswell, spare me that; for though the play-acting clergyman with his two hundred pounds and his Welsh antiquities failed to deceive me, yet 'tis cold truth that under my nose a green boy has conspired with a school-girl to steal first a diamond and then the lass herself; so let's hear no more on't."

The Conveyance of
EMELINA GRANGE

"Sir," said Dr. Johnson, "'tis the best function of the law, not to punish, but to forestall, deeds of violence and fraud."

"What, sir," I exclaimed, rallying my learned guest, "do you tell me I must go forth like the beadle into the byways of Edinburgh, rather than to the Court of Session like the responsible advocate I am?"

"Ay must you," retorted Dr. Johnson in the same spirit, "and well you'll look with a staff in your hand!"

'Twas the eve of our departure for our long-expected visit to the Hebrides. How I rejoiced to see my respected friend so cordially at home in my house in Edinburgh, sitting by the fire as easy and jovial as ever I saw him at the Mitre.

"But, sir," I continued in more serious vein, "how is this to be done? 'There's no art,' says the poet, 'to find the mind's construction in the face.'"

The Conveyance of Emelina Grange

"Nor would I find it in the face," replied Dr. Johnson, "but in the betraying actions, the necessary arrangements, which must come as the forerunners of a contemplated crime."

"Mr. Boswell," said my servant, appearing at the door, "here's a fellow below-stairs with a message, which he'll trust to no ear but yours."

"Admit him," said I. "Pray excuse me, Dr. Johnson."

"Willingly," said Dr. Johnson, "I will devote my attention to Miss here."

My daughter Veronica, then kicking her heels in her nurse's arms by the fire, was at four months of age a great favourite with my majestic friend. As he peered into her small face and nodded his head repeatedly, she crowed with joy; when he stopped, she fluttered and made a little infantine noise, and a kind of signal for him to begin again; which he delighted to do.

" 'Tis strange indeed, Bozzy," commented Dr. Johnson in a mellow voice, "to see the complaisance with which Miss is pleased to accept of my poor attentions."

Miss gurgled with joy, and reached for my learned friend's impressive nose. The door opened to admit a hulking, weather-beaten, red-headed countryman who made a leg to the company at large.

"My good friend Saunders!" I cried in surprise. "What brings you from Kincardon?"

"I'm no from Kincardon, sir, only from the Canongate," replied the man in a rich Scotch accent which I despair of reproducing. He handed me a folded paper. "My master sends you this billet, sir, and begs that your famous friend Dr. Johnson will accept of his hospitality as well as you, Mr. Boswell, and he begs that you will honour him with your presence, and—and so do I too, sir."

This strange harangue was delivered with a tone and look of desperate urgency.

"Is your master in trouble?" I enquired.

SAUNDERS: "He'll no say so, Mr. Boswell, but all's very ill in that house."

BOSWELL: "But why does he send to me? Surely there's those he could sooner turn to than me."

SAUNDERS: "*He* invites you to sup with him, sir. But *I*, sir—I make so bold as to beg you, for the sake of the old days at Kincardon, to come down to that dreadful house and try to set things straight if you can, sir."

BOSWELL: "What do you complain of, Saunders?"

SAUNDERS: "Nothing for myself, sir. I will tell you what I ken. I was close to Master Jamie, sir, for we were of an age, and hunted together at Kincardon in the old man's time. Then Master Alick was laird, and brought the estate very low with his gaming and his tricks. My heart bled for Master Jamie, for he loves Kincardon, and it turned him glowering mean to see it racked for his brother's pleasure. He's had no education, Master Jamie, and none to care for him, and all he loves is Kincardon."

"Yet he left Kincardon," said I, who held a less romantick notion of Jamie Grange of Kincardon, "he left so soon as he inherited the estate."

"He did so, sir," admitted Saunders. "He went to London and married the Sassenach woman with all the

The Conveyance of Emelina Grange

siller, and brought her back to Scotland. But the lady herself, nor nane o' her siller, never came to Kincardon till the day I'm to tell you about. Of a sudden one night, now two months gone, he rode up to the old house at Kincardon that's falling to ruin, and the Sassenach lady with him, and her Sassenach maid that's own cousin to her, and there they lay till morning."

"So he did return to Kincardon," I remarked.

"No more than I've told you. For it stormed that night, and I heard the lady weeping and crying, and swearing she'd no be buried in the country to be drowned under a leaky roof, and Master Jamie give in to her, and in the morning he carried her back again to Edinburgh, and me along with them."

"Come, Saunders, my man," cried I, laughing, "here's no cause for disquiet. Nay, this is pure comedy, this tale of the lady who abhors the country."

" 'Tis not comick at the Canongate," said honest Saunders pitifully. "He's turned off all the servants, sir, and sits there all day glommering with only me to do for him. And the lady's gey ill, and lies in the dark with only Master Jamie to carry her her bit parritch. I'm fair frighted, sir, what he'll do."

"Has the lady no woman to wait on her?" I asked thoughtfully.

"None, sir, for they turned off the fat Sassenach woman at Kincardon, and my brother Geordie rode her on her way before the day dawned."

"So the companion's sent back to England, eh?" I mused.

"No, sir; Geordie told my mother he was for the Western Islands. 'Tis like a tomb in the Canongate. Do come down, sir, and see my master."

He looked at me with the appeal of a hungry spaniel, then hastily made a leg as my dear wife entered from an inner door and seated herself by the fire. Veronica made a little crow of pleasure and waved hard at my learned friend as I turned to consult him.

"How say you, Dr. Johnson, shall we sup in the Canongate?"

"Let us do so, sir," replied my sagacious friend. "I have a fancy to see this lady out of Congreve, who fears to be buried in the country."

"Say to your master," said I to the honest messenger, "that we will come."

Faithful Saunders withdrew covered with gratitude.

"Where," said my wife, "will you come, Mr. Boswell?"

"To dine with Jamie Grange of Kincardon."

"Surely, Mr. Boswell, you'll not go to Jamie Grange!" cried my anxious spouse. " 'Tis notorious he's mad, and a miser to boot."

"How can he be a miser," I enquired reasonably, "if he's married an heiress?"

"And if that be madness, ma'am," added Dr. Johnson, "then half London is mad or aspires to lunacy."

"Nay, sir," replied my wife, "I never thought him mad at Kincardon, though he was a surly churl enough; nor when he scraped together a few pounds to take him to London, nor when he brought back his English heiress in April and took the house in the Canongate and summoned all Edinburgh to wish him joy."

"Who will ever say that the prosperous man is mad?" enquired my sententious friend.

"'Twas in May," pursued Mrs. Boswell, "that she gave her last rout. You was in London, Mr. Boswell; but I was there when Jamie denounced her to her face for a spendthrift, and turned all the company out of doors. 'You're ruining me,' cries he, 'with your frivolity and extravagance!' And she a great heiress! Is not this madness?"

"'Tis a kind of madness," observed Dr. Johnson, "all too scarce in London."

"And since then," concluded my wife, "she's never shewed her face out of doors, nor has any of their former acquaintance ever supped there. I had thought them gone to Kincardon."

"Well, my dear," said I, "we shall see how they go on."

"'Tis great folly, Mr. Boswell," objected she. "Saunders is a gloomy fool. There'll be no more amiss than the misconceived œconomy of a miser's household. Depend upon it, Jamie Grange will give you a bad dinner and then want something of you—he's going to law, as like as not, and wants a lawyer's advice without a lawyer's fee."

"Then I'll eat his bad dinner and give him bad advice."

"And I," struck in Dr. Johnson, "shall pay my respects to the lady."

"Fie, sir," cried my wife, "ever the gallant to the fair, be she four months or forty years."

The infant Veronica gurgled imperiously, and waved a tiny hand toward my venerable friend's massive nose.

Jamie Grange received us civilly enough, and set us down to a bad dinner of kale and boiled mutton. 'Twas coarse fare, coarsely served by the niggardly light of two candle-ends. Waiting against the gloomy wainscoting, the man Saunders was uneasy. His little eyes darted about in the gloom, and he continually wiped his clammy palms on the crumpled serviette he carried.

Jamie Grange, the Laird of Kincardon, was at his ease. His thick bull neck, his weather-beaten complection, his heavy hands, marked the country-bred laird. He was the same as I remembered him from the old days at Auchinleck, only for the marks of age gathering upon him, and a certain composed, waiting stillness about him. He ate little and spoke little, beyond uttering without grace the necessary civilities to his distinguished guest. He had never read *The Rambler* nor heard of *Rasselas*, so his compliments were without substance.

"Sir," said the learned lexicographer perfunctorily, "you are most obliging."

After this exchange conversation languished till the uncouth servitor placed on the table the cheese-ends and the thin wine, and withdrew. It then transpired that my domestick Cassandra had been doubly right. Jamie Grange followed his bad dinner by laying a legal problem before me. He spoke of his lady's illness with concern.

"She is to bring Kincardon an heir," said the laird

quietly, "at her age the shock and strain have prostrated her. She is filled with concern for the child to come, and is feverishly anxious to provide for the little one's material welfare. I fear for her reason unless she is enabled to effectuate her desire without delay."

"Surely," said I, "this is a matter for the Court of Session."

"So I take it," agreed Kincardon, "but she is impatient of delay. Surely it is possible to draw up an instrument which, signed by reputable witnesses, would hold good until she is delivered. The Court of Session has just risen. She will be delivered in four months time, and then we may do all things orderly. But for the interim she is bent on executing a document which she has prepared; and begs that Mr. Boswell and Dr. Johnson will wait on her to witness such a conveyance."

"I shall be happy to wait on the lady, the more since I understand that she is my countrywoman," assented Dr. Johnson with an eagerness that forestalled the more cautious reply which I had framed.

"That is true," replied Kincardon, rising. "She is the only daughter of Sir Hampton Boon."

"Do you say so!" exclaimed Dr. Johnson. "Sir Hampton is well known to me, for his seat lies in the neighbourhood of my native Lichfield, and I have more than once been obliged by the use of his very extensive library. I remember Miss Boon as a child."

"Do you so?" exclaimed Kincardon, seating himself abruptly.

"A bonnie blue-eyed lass," said Dr. Johnson, "I hope

the years have used her well. I fear her present indisposition may be aggravated by her apprehensions concerning her father's state of health."

"Is he then no better?" enquired Kincardon with some emotion.

"He grows daily more dropsical," returned Dr. Johnson. "When I last saw Lichfield 'twas said to be only a matter of months, perhaps weeks. Yet if the old man would but heed his physicians and amend his way of life, all might be changed."

"We have been in continual apprehension for him," said Kincardon, "fearing that every packet will bring news of his dissolution."

"'Tis most sad," agreed Dr. Johnson. "But come, I am longing to present my respects to my old friend."

"I am sorry, Dr. Johnson," said Kincardon calmly, without moving, "but I fear this meeting cannot be. The shock of meeting an old friend, and one who must give such a gloomy account of her father's state of being, would only too surely prove fatal to my hope of posterity. I am sure Dr. Johnson will understand my position."

"Nay, sir," said Dr. Johnson, "I pledge myself to console, rather than distress the lady."

"It is out of the question," said Kincardon, unmoved. "Saunders shall supply Dr. Johnson's room."

"So be it," assented Dr. Johnson without further importunity. Saunders was summoned, and inadequately lighted by one of the guttering candle-ends, we mounted the creaking stairs of the narrow old house, leaving the learned philosopher sitting at the untidy table, deep in meditation.

We found Emelina Boon, the English heiress, lying in the dark in the upper chamber of her husband's gloomy old house. Her outlines, dimly seen under the wavering shadow of the tester, were thin and sharp in the great bed. The light of the candle as we brought it in caught gleams from her eyeballs as she rolled her prominent blue eyes on us.

"My dear," began Kincardon, "set your mind at rest. Mr. Boswell will attest the authenticity of the instrument you wish to execute."

She turned her eyes on me.

"Thank you," she whispered. "Give it me and let me sign it."

Kincardon presented a paper already indited.

"Pray read it, ma'am, before you sign," said I. I held the document before her eyes, and she scanned it painfully line by line to the end. Kincardon pressed a quill into her hand. Thrice she brought the point to the paper, and thrice her hand fell powerless.

"I cannot write," she whispered. "I will make my mark here—so—" with Kincardon guiding her wrist she did so and fell back exhausted.

"And Mr. Boswell," she resumed weakly, "shall be my witness that I did so with my own hand."

"Gladly, ma'am," I assented in pity, taking the document to the table to sign in my turn.

"What's this, Kincardon?" I said in an undertone. "This form is quite irregular," and I began to read: *I,*

Emelina Grange, Lady Kincardon, being of sound mind and mindful of the uncertainty of life, do confess and declare, that my child . . .

Kincardon twitched the paper out of my hand.

"Don't distress my wife," he muttered. "This is the form she dictated. When she is better, all can be done anew. Let us leave her alone."

He turned to the door, and a change passed over his blunt face.

"Dr. Johnson!" he cried. "This is too bad of you!"

"I beg your indulgence," said Dr. Johnson softly, "I could not control my eagerness to see my old friend's daughter."

He advanced to the bed. Kincardon gave way with ill grace.

"Here is an old friend, my dear," he cried with unnecessary loudness. "You remember Dr. Samuel Johnson, of Lichfield."

The sick woman turned her great blue eyes on him. Her mouth formed his name inaudibly. Dr. Johnson scanned the gaunt face long and sadly by the light of the one candle.

"I am glad to see you again, my dear," he said at last. "It is long since we met."

The wan face in the shadow assented mutely.

"How well I remember, 'twas at Boon Park, in the Gothick grotto by the lake," pursued Dr. Johnson sentimentally. A puzzled shadow passed over the invalid's face, and she moved restlessly.

"No," she whispered, "no. There is no Gothick grotto at Boon Park."

The Conveyance of Emelina Grange

"Of course there is not," returned Dr. Johnson, abashed by this slip of memory. "Forgive an old man's faulty recollection, and tell me what I can do for you."

"My father—?" articulated the invalid.

"He was very well when I saw him last."

The head never moved, but the blue eyes slewed sideways and fixed themselves on Dr. Johnson's face.

"Don't deceive me," came the sharp whisper. "He is dying."

"You need not perjure yourself, sir," broke in Kincardon, "Emelina knows there is no hope. Come, shall we leave her to her rest? This has been a great strain for her."

He folded the signed document into an inner pocket, and made as if to lead the way to the door.

"A moment," said my benevolent friend.

He bent his massive head close to the motionless figure on the bed.

"You may trust me, my dear," he murmured. "Can I do nothing for you?"

"Nothing," said the pale lips.

"You are without a servant. May I not send a woman to watch over you?"

The head moved in sharp negation.

"No—no, no," came the answer. "I sent my woman away because she spied on me. I'll have no spies about me." The voice rose hoarse and intense.

"Farewell," said Dr. Johnson sadly. "Remember that I am your friend. Send to me at Mr. Boswell's should need arise."

The head was averted, the frame tense, but her whisper followed us as we withdrew.

"I shall not need."

James Grange of Kincardon was through with us. He uttered the briefest of adieux and turned on his heel, leaving Saunders to light us to the portal.

Standing in the frowning doorway in the light of the niggardly candle, my benevolent friend bestowed a generous gratuity upon the honest countryman, saying,

"My honest friend, watch over your mistress, and let no man harm her."

"Nay, sir," returned the faithful Saunders, "no man can harm her, for my master tenders her dearly. Whiles I hear them laughing together, for all she's so low. Will she live, think you, sir?"

"That she will, if you but care for her well."

"I will, sir, I will. Goodnight, gentlemen."

The heavy door closed. I glanced back at the gloomy, ill-lighted old pile.

"What's to do there?" I mused aloud.

"Nay, I know not," said my companion shortly.

He touched the palings with his hand as we walked along the narrow street, rolling his head and articulating "Too, too, too," as is his manner when disturbed in mind.

He touched the last post, and shook his head discontentedly.

"I know not," he repeated. " 'Tis a bad match, that's clear."

The Conveyance of Emelina Grange

" 'Twas a niggard entertainment," I commented, "in a house of poverty. Is the lady in truth an heiress?"

"A very great heiress," returned my friend. "Sir Hampton Boon is one of the richest men in England."

"And 'twill all be hers when he dies? Or has he left it away from her?"

" 'Tis well known that all is settled on herself and her child after her."

"Then Jamie Grange may soon mend the roof at Kincardon."

"Ay may he, for what's hers is his by the law of the land."

A thought struck me: "Then why is the roof not mended already?"

"If she brought Kincardon any portion," replied Dr. Johnson thoughtfully, "I'll wager my head it was but small. Emelina Boon has long lived out of her father's favour."

"How so?" I enquired.

"She flouted his wishes to marry a rakish young lieutenant, it's now twenty years ago. Worse still, when he would have forgiven her she'd not be forgiven, but followed her soldier and lived on his pay. He fell under Braddock in '55, and still she'd not go home to Boon Court, but lived in London with her son, and only her female cousin to companion her."

"What became of the boy?"

"He means to follow his father's profession. Sir Hampton has bought him a commission. I hear he's with the 37th, and gazetted for India."

"Think you the lady is in any danger?" I enquired.

"I cannot conceive it," replied Dr. Johnson, "for Kincardon will enjoy her fortune only as long as her life lasts. He may attempt to browbeat her, but he'll tender her life as dear as his own. To harm her would be but to enrich her son."

"Yet she looks very ill."

" 'Tis pitiful to see her so. I should never have recognized the blue-eyed child of Boon Court; but her relationship to Sir Hampton is writ clear on every feature. Age and emaciation have brought out the resemblance only latent in the plump young miss."

We walked in silence over the cobbled street. The night sky gleamed between the roofs of the crowding old houses.

"I don't trust Kincardon," said I presently.

"Nor do I," agreed Dr. Johnson, "but he can't touch her money, and he won't touch her. He'll behave himself, for the sake of Kincardon."

"Is she mad, think you? Trust me, I saw no sign in that skinny frame of a coming confinement."

"I cannot take upon me," pronounced my philosophical friend, "the function of a panel of matrons. 'Tis evident they both believe it."

" 'Twill be a sad blow to Kincardon if the lady fails him," I reflected. "He is mad for an heir, for the sake of Kincardon. Does he know, think you, that her fortune is entailed away from Kincardon?"

"If he has just learned," suggested Dr. Johnson, " 'twould explain his sudden rage and the new parsimony of his household. Well, he's a disappointed man, but we may be sure she'll not be the one to suffer for it."

The Conveyance of Emelina Grange

"She's under no duress," I observed, "for she made it clear that she signed her preposterous paper of her own free will, and she read it through before she signed."

"And she positively declined my aid, which I proffered with some such possibility in mind."

"Then," I concluded as we ascended the steps of my house, "we may safely put Emelina Boon out of our minds, and think of our coming journey to the Western Islands."

Our journey, so long planned, took us northward by chaise to Aberdeen, thence to Banff and Inverness, where we took horse. It was a pretty thing to see the ponderous author of the Dictionary jogging along on one of our little Scottish ponies. Dr. Johnson was in great spirits, and we had many a curious conversation by the way.

We drove over the very heath where Macbeth met the witches, according to tradition. Dr. Johnson repeated solemnly "How far is't called to Forres" etc. I had purchased some land called Dalblair; and, as in Scotland it is customary to distinguish landed men by the name of their estates, I had thus two titles, 'Dalblair' and—from my father's estate—'Young Auchinleck.' Dr. Johnson parodied the poet to me: "All hail Dalblair!"

At Inverness we visited Macbeth's castle. I had a most romantick satisfaction in seeing Dr. Johnson actually in it. It answers to Shakespeare's description, "This castle hath a pleasant" etc., which I repeated. When we came out of it, a raven perched on one of the chimney-tops and croaked. Then I repeated, "The raven himself is hoarse," etc. As we rode away, we fell into solemn converse concerning the awful crime of murder. Dr. Johnson quoted solemnly:

"Between the acting of a dreadful thing

And the first motion, there's an interim," etc.

" 'Tis in that interim, I dare say, sir," I remarked, harking back to our conversation at Edinburgh, "that you would have the law catch and restrain the intending malefactor."

The learned philosopher assented.

I pulled up my pony and patted his neck. Dr. Johnson reined in beside me, and we silently surveyed the prospect as we breathed our mounts. The sky was lowering, the country treeless and bare; but that diversion which Nature failed to afford, Dr. Johnson was able to supply from the storehouse of his boundless knowledge.

"I wonder, sir," I remarked when we were again in motion, "at your command of the laws, not only of your own country, but of other systems past and present."

"I hold it true," returned Dr. Johnson, "that he who would live respected, must acquaint himself with the law under which he lives."

"How few," I lamented, "are so acquainted. At least it is so in Edinburgh, where everyone is half-informed, or misinformed, but no man really knows the laws of Scotland, still less those of England, which touch him so nearly."

"Yet every Scotchman fancies himself a lawyer," said Dr. Johnson.

The Conveyance of Emelina Grange

"To the detriment of the legal profession," I agreed. "You saw this foolish neighbour of mine, Kincardon. He would neither go to court nor take advice, but I must witness the extraordinary legal hodge-podge that he scratched together himself."

" 'Twas a hodge-podge, eh?" commented Dr. Johnson.

" 'Kincardon,' I said to him, 'this won't do,' but he cut me short. I would have bettered it for him, if I'd been let. *Being of sound mind, and mindful of the uncertainty of life*—though 'tis a conveyance, he starts it off like a will, because he has read a will or two—"

"Hey, hey?" cried Dr. Johnson. "Was it her will the lady signed?"

"No, sir, it goes on with a bit from some confession he's read on a broadside in a tavern somewhere—*do confess and declare*—'tis legal, d'ye see, if it has two verbs—"

"Confess?" repeated Dr. Johnson.

"Ay, confess," said I contemptuously. "In a conveyance it should be *give and devise to* my child—and mark you 'tis a non-existent child, but she is not to indicate that—instead of *confess that my child* etcetera etcetera."

"Bozzy, Bozzy, don't teize me!" cried Dr. Johnson in powerful excitement, "confess that my child what?"

"Nay, sir, I don't know. Kincardon did not care for my strictures, and snatched his misbegotten document from my hand."

"Misbegotten indeed!" cried my companion. "Why did not you read it through?"

"Though I did not, yet the lady did. I suppose Emeline Boon can read?"

"Oh yes, and writes a dainty hand," replied Dr. Johnson. "Alas, alas, sir, why do I hear this only now, so far away?"

"Why, sir, you were there and saw the lady."

"Ay, but I knew not what she signed."

"Why, she signed a worthless paper, no more."

"Does Kincardon know that?"

"No matter; she'll provide for her child when the time comes, before a Scottish court."

"How will she so, when all's entailed for her oldest boy?"

"Nay, let the courts decide of that."

"If it come to the courts. But were I in Edinburgh, I would smell out the shape of things to come. Let it rest, naught will happen until the lady's brought to bed. When she brings Kincardon an heir—I'll be there, Bozzy, I'll be there!"

We came that night to Fort George, where lay Sir Eyre Coote's regiment, the 37th. Sir Eyre, a most civil man, shewed us the fort. At three the drum beat for dinner. I could for a little fancy myself a military man, and it pleased me; only for my father's determination to make a lawyer of me, I had followed the colours in my youth.

There was a pretty large company. We had a dinner of two complete courses, and the regimental band of musick playing in the square before the windows after it. Dr. Johnson was much sought after by all the officers

The Conveyance of Emelina Grange

present. I noted a very young lieutenant, fresh and handsome of face, watching my learned friend eagerly. At last Sir Eyre brought him before us.

"Sir, I present Lieutenant Hampton Ballinger."

"Your servant, sir," said the fresh-faced boy ceremoniously. "I made so bold as to seek your acquaintance—I make bold to enquire, sir—" the ceremonious manner was lost in eagerness—"Are you not lately from Lichfield, sir?"

"Within the month," replied my learned friend.

"Pray tell me then, how goes on Sir Hampton Boon? Does he yet live, sir?" asked the young soldier earnestly.

"Sir, I left my old friend yet in life," returned Dr. Johnson gravely. "But you must know the dropsy gains so upon him, that it cannot long be so." He scanned the boy's face narrowly. "Are you not kin to him, sir?"

"He is my grandfather," said the boy, "and since my father's death, my protector."

"Do you say so, lad!" exclaimed my benevolent friend, shaking his hand cordially. "This is indeed a thing of note, that I must come to Scotland to see first the daughter, now the grandson, of my old benefactor at Boon Court!"

"How, sir!" exclaimed the young lieutenant. "You have seen my mother? Were you then in Ayrshire?"

"Nay, lad, your mother is in Edinburgh."

"I might have guessed so much," rejoined young Ballinger with a smile. "My mother would never dally long in Ayr. Her spirit was made for the great world. Pray, sir, how does she go on? Routs, eh? Kettledrums and assemblies? And does she make up a good company at cards?"

Dr. Johnson and I exchanged glances.

"Not these days," returned Dr. Johnson guardedly. "She is to bring Kincardon an heir."

"Ho ho!" cried the young soldier in high spirits; "then I wager there's the Devil to pay! The vapours, I'll be bound, and the waiting-women running with the smelling-bottle, and all the lap-dogs turned out of my lady's bed-chamber! Ay, and new bed-gowns for my lady's levee, and the bluff Laird to fetch and carry. This will be something to see!"

"You draw too rosy a picture, sir," returned Dr. Johnson reluctantly. "Your mother is ill and gaunt and out of spirits, and sees no company at all. Were I you, sir, I would hasten to her side."

"Why, I'll do so, sir," returned the young soldier readily, "if they don't whisk us off to India. But sure you mistake, sir, my mother's a lady of spirit, and a fine rosy buxom woman. Gaunt and out of spirits, you say? Believe me, sir, you are deceived."

"I saw her not a week gone," replied Dr. Johnson, "and trust me, her face might have been Sir Hampton's, so emaciated was it."

"A gaunt face like Sir Hampton's?" returned the young man. "See, now, I was in the right of it. That's Kathy."

"Kathy?"

"My mother's cousin, Katharine Boon. *She's* gaunt and vinegary, and I swear my mother keeps her about just to laugh at her jealousy and envy; for Kathy's ugly and ignorant and unhandy, and can't even write. Depend upon it, sir, you've taken the maid for the mistress, and that's ever a poor bargain. This is my mother."

The boy pulled out a miniature. Emelina Boon had indeed matured rosy and buxom.

"Well, sir, I see I was deceived indeed," remarked Dr. Johnson. "You may set your mind at rest."

"Concerning my mother, my mind is always at rest," said the young man carelessly. "She can fend for herself."

"I hope so indeed," returned Dr. Johnson soberly; and as the bugle sounded in the square, the young Lieutenant withdrew.

We lay that night at the fort. For want of space, I lay in a little truckle bed in Dr. Johnson's room.

"So," remarked Dr. Johnson, extinguishing the candle, "we were befooled after all."

"Ay," I rejoined, "'twas the companion who can't write that set her mark to Kincardon's bastard document; and you and I were to be his dupes, to swear to it when the child should be born."

"I smoaked so much," muttered my friend, "I smoaked it, when he would have prevented me seeing her. I saw her in spite of his teeth, and she diddled me to my face. Only that she had Sir Hampton's features, and knew Boon Park so well, I had had her then and there."

"Hence your vapouring about the Gothick grotto that does not exist!" I exclaimed.

"'Twas but to test her," replied Dr. Johnson. "I should have remembered, that such knowledge was not a *note*, but an *accident*, of Emelina Boon's personality. I should have sought a more exclusive test."

"No matter," said I, "what's to do now?"

"Sir," returned Dr. Johnson, "this is just such a plot of violence and fraud as I would have the law catch a-making. There's time and to spare before its consummation. We must go about to prevent it."

"Time," said I, "what time?"

"Why, time till Kincardon's heir be born. Which of the women, think you, is to bear the child?"

"Not the vinegary companion, I'll be bound."

"I am with you there," conceded Dr. Johnson. "Then Emelina Boon yet lives, and we must find her."

"How may we do so?" I enquired hopelessly. "We cannot run about Scotland in search of a missing heiress. Best entrust the search to her son."

"Nay, sir," replied Johnson, smiling, "I do not mean to run about like a beadle with a staff in my hand. I sit here at Fort George and look into my mind, and it tells me where to find Emelina Boon."

"Does it so, sir!" I exclaimed. "Sure your mind is a seer's crystal indeed, a very *black stone of Dr. Dee!*"

"He who is capable of memory and reason, sir," replied Dr. Johnson, "needs no seer's crystal."

"Where, then, sir," I enquired, "do memory and reason bid us seek the missing heiress?"

"Cast your memory back," replied my acute companion. "When was Emelina Boon last seen?"

"When Jamie Grange carried her to Kincardon, and my simple friend Saunders heard her proclaiming she'd not be buried in the country."

The Conveyance of Emelina Grange

"I think you are right, that was surely Emelina speaking in her own voice. But the 'fat Sassenach woman' was gone before morning, and the thin Sassenach woman returned to Edinburgh as Jamie's wife, with simple Saunders for their only attendant; and there they lived so retired that none of their old acquaintance ever laid eyes on the lady."

"And for that he pitched upon you and me, because he thought us strangers to her."

"'Tis so. Well, Saunders' brother Geordie, with fewer scruples and it may be more brains than Saunders, carried off the fat Sassenach woman. But before he went he blabbed to his mother, and she to Saunders, and he to us. Whither went he, by his story?"

"I remember now!" I cried: "To the Western Islands!"

"To the Western Islands," assented my companion. "Well, 'twill go hard but we shall find out where dwells a Sassenach woman among the wild Highlanders. Then young Hampton may take his mother under his protection; and once she's safe we may spoil their games in Edinburgh."

So saying, my wise companion blew out the candle and with a creaking of the bed-cords composed himself to slumber.

Accordingly we went over into the Western Islands. We were cordially received everywhere, but could get no tidings of a Sassenach woman newly come among the Hebrides, until we came to Coirechatachan in the Isle of Skye, a comfortable farm-house ruled over by one

Lachlan MacKinnon, a jolly big man who had hospitality in his whole behaviour. 'Twas at his house my famous friend received a deputation.

" 'Tis the catechist from St. Kilda," said Coirechatachan, "and with him his little daughter."

"Which, sir," says the catechist, a gnarled stump of a man with a grin, "the child has a gift to lay in Dr. Johnson's hand."

He pushed forward a half-grown, frightened-looking lass. She dropped an awkward curtsey, thrust something into my friend's hand, and backed off in confusion. Dr. Johnson looked in puzzlement at the gift, a clew of coarse St. Kilda yarn.

"How come you to bring me so particular a gift, child?" enquired he.

" 'Tis from the Sassenach lady," whispered the girl.

Dr. Johnson turned it about in his hand. There was a crackle of paper. In a trice he had out a crumpled billet, and was smoothing it upon the table.

"Who told them on St. Kilda, Dr. Johnson was in the Hebrides?" I puzzled.

"Me, sir," said the catechist proudly.

Dr. Johnson read out the words on the paper:

"They've carried me off to St. Kilda. I pray you send a boat to take me off, for I'm nigh seven months gone and tho I'm well serv'd the life is hard. Say nothing to Jamie Grange. I'll have a word with him when I see Edinboro again.

EMELINA GRANGE"

Before Johnson could speak, Coirechatachan had ordered up his boat, well manned, for the voyage to St. Kilda, and the unfortunate lady was brought off.

The Conveyance of Emelina Grange

Though exhausted by hardship, she told her strange story. She could say no more, than that she had been seized by night at Kincardon, and driven hard night and day till they took ship for St. Kilda.

"'Tis pity," exclaimed the roly-poly matron, "that you left Geordie upon St. Kilda, for he was an amusing rustick, and I had taught him a vast deal about piquet."

"Ma'am," says Dr. Johnson, "you amaze me."

In that mood we left her and set sail for Coll, leaving her to the care of her son, come in hot haste from Fort George.

We heard no more of the Boon Park heiress until we were once more in Edinburgh. There, alas, we received a melancholy communication from the young lieutenant. Kincardon's heir had been prematurely born, and both mother and child had perished. He saved less melancholy intelligence for a postscriptum:

"Grandfather has had in Mr. Bathgate the surgeon, and writes himself out of all measure recovered. The 37th sails for India this day week. Adieu!"

Silently my friend handed me the ill-omened missive.

"Pray tell me, ma'am," says he off hand to my dear wife, "how go on the mad Kincardon and his heiress wife?"

"They continue their sullen life in the Canongate," she replied. "The lady keeps close; and 'tis rumoured she will soon go down to Kincardon to be brought to bed in the country."

"Is it so?" rejoined Dr. Johnson. "Well, Bozzy, you and I must once more wait on this friend of yours."

"To what end?" I enquired.

" 'Twas an ill document the lady signed. She shall sign a better, before she brings Kincardon an heir."

I stared.

"Bring him an heir?" I stammered.

"Even so," said my friend, "for when all is known, by hook or by crook she will bring him an heir. To what end was all this plot, save to make it seem that the heiress disowned young Ballinger, thus bringing the entail to light on Kincardon's child? So, by fair means or foul, Kincardon must have a child; and how long, think you, will his pretended wife live, after an heir is found?"

"You are right," I confessed, "we must go down to the Canongate."

Dr. Johnson knocked loudly with his heavy oaken cudgel. Red-headed Saunders admitted us. After a space Kincardon came to us in the dingy sitting-room.

"How does your lady?" enquired Dr. Johnson courteously.

"Indifferently," said Kincardon suspiciously. "We think to go down to Kincardon for the country air."

"Do so," replied Dr. Johnson cordially. "But first, my friend Boswell desires to clear up the little irregularities of your lady's conveyance. He has prepared a new paper—"

"What ails the old one?" demanded Kincardon truculently.

"A mere matter of falsehood, sir," replied my friend cheerfully.

Kincardon half rose, then thought better of it.

The Conveyance of Emelina Grange

"Saunders," said Dr. Johnson, "pray summon the lady."

Katharine Boon came accordingly, muffled in a loose bedgown that neither concealed secrets nor revealed the lack of them.

"We witnessed a document for you some months gone, Miss Boon," the thin woman looked up at the name—"Pray be so good as to affix your signature—I crave pardon, your mark—to this one. Mr. Boswell will read it out for you."

Katharine Boon opened her mouth, but no sound came. I unfolded the paper with a snap, and read out:

"I, Katharine Boon, do confess and declare, that coming into this kingdom with my cousin and mistress, Emelina Boon, wife of James Grange of Kincardon, I did plot and covenant with the said James Grange: to kidnap the said Emelina and hold her in seclusion until the birth of her child, the heir of Kincardon; by supplying her room to make it appear as if she affixed her signature—"

"Only you could not write, but must make your mark," said Dr. Johnson. "I should have had warning from that."

"—make it appear as if she affixed her signature to a document—" ("And a beggarly fustian document," I interjected) "designed to prove her eldest son no true heir, and so secure the reversion to Kincardon; upon her delivery to procure the murder of the said Emelina Boon—"

"No! No!" cried the woman wildly.

"—and to supply her room in perpetuity."

" 'Tis false," cried Katharine Boon, "I was only to sign the document, and take her place until her return with the child."

"You are a dupe after all," said my penetrating friend in disgust. "She would have died when the child was born, and you before your false 'lying-in' was over. How else could Kincardon gain control of the money?"

Jamie Grange sat like a man of stone under Katharine Boon's startled gaze.

"Cancel the last article," said Dr. Johnson. "What did Kincardon promise you, Miss Boon?"

"A sum of money," she said, "and a competence when he should have got the handling of the old man's fortune."

"He'd have given you six feet of earth at Kincardon," said Dr. Johnson grimly. "Proceed, Mr. Boswell."

"And I further state, that if I die while in the house and under the protection of the said James Grange of Kincardon, I denounce him as my murderer, and pray that justice may be done upon him."

"She'll not stay in my house," uttered Kincardon between his teeth, "nor will I protect her."

"I think you will, sir," said Dr. Johnson. "If she seeks other protection, how will you stop her mouth?"

I wrote "Katharine Boon" under our extraordinary document:

"Pray affix your mark here, Miss Boon."

She did so with shaking fingers.

With a sudden clumsy surge Kincardon fell upon me, snatching at the paper. There was a sharp crack of wood against bone as my powerful friend felled him with one mighty blow. I put the table between us as I bestowed the paper in safety.

Slowly Kincardon rose to his feet, his face black with baffled rage.

"I bid you good day, sir," said Dr. Johnson as I backed towards the door.

He looked into the two faces.

"I wish you much joy of one another."

As he gently closed the door behind him, I heard his quiet laugh.

The Great Seal of ENGLAND

ON THE NIGHT of March 23, 1784, the Great Seal of England was stolen out of Lord Chancellor Thurlow's house in Great Ormonde Street, and was never seen again. In August of that year, Lord Chancellor Thurlow very graciously intimated to the friends of Dr. Johnson that that learned philosopher might draw against him at need for as much as £600.

The connexion between these two events forms a part of secret history. In that history I, James Boswell of Auchinleck, advocate, played a not inconsiderable part; and my learned friend, Sam: Johnson, displayed at large his inimitable powers of ratiocination and penetration, the more that he was then confined to his dwelling with a dropsical condition, complicated by asthma, that was soon to prove mortal.

In early March I was at York, and in two minds

whether to press on to London or to retreat to Edinburgh. News that Parliament was about to be prorogued, with a general election to follow, inclined one of my broad principles to return to my home port to weather the storm; but then I should miss seeing Mannering hang. Mannering was the last of the Tyburn hangings, a gallant and a duellist, and he was to hang for spitting his man and missing the French packet.

I sat long in the ordinary at York, weighing my principles against the last of the Tyburn shows; and in the end I rode post for London to be in at the death. I rode up to Tyburn as dawn was breaking, and saw all from the spectator's gallery.

Had I not done so, I had missed the greatest of Dr. Johnson's feats of ratiocination. For coming away from the gallows while the mob was still shouting, I encountered George Selwyn in the press, and he carried me in his coach as far as St. James's Street; and there I met Lord Chancellor Thurlow coming out of Brooks's arm in arm with Charles James Fox; and that in itself was a portent of stranger things to come.

The Tory Chancellor was composed and sardonick. His swarthy skin was cool and his black eyes were watchful under their bushy brows. The Whig leader was deucedly foxed, his usual condition at that hour of any morning. He was rumpled and bleary, and his bushy hair stood on end. He was also in a complaining frame of mind.

"Look at him," he complained, gesturing at Thurlow in a way that threatened him with immersion in the kennel. "Look at 'm. Been standing by the gaming tables all night long. Wha's he got? Got his pockets full, tha's what. Looka me. Been standing by him all night long. Gaming? No. Mustn't game, Mrs. Armistead says. Gaming's ruin. Me, I been drinking. Stanning right by him, he's gaming, I'm drinking. Wha's he got? Got his pockets full. Wha've I got? Got my snout full. Armistead's all wrong. Never make that mistake again. Whoosh."

A final windmill gesture set him on his broad rump on the pavement. His grievances continued to run through his head.

"Pocket full o' money, and going to pro—prorogue Parliament tomorrow an' send all the Whigs home to stay."

"You say true, Mr. Fox," replied Thurlow icily, "for there's not a borough in England will return a Whig to the new Parliament."

Fox slewed him a quick look. It occurred to me that he was not so incapacitated as he seemed.

"A wager," he cried. "A rump and dozen that I'm returned for Westminster. Guineas to shillings Parliament an't prorogued. My head to a turnip you lose the seals, you trimming half-faced Tory."

He swayed to his feet. His contorted face was diabolick in the red light of dawn. Then it dissolved into a silly grin. He wagged his head to himself.

"These proposals," says Thurlow, still calmly, "would hardly meet the approval of Mrs. Armistead."

"Keep your tongue off Armistead," said Fox surlily. "Who are you to talk?"

The Great Seal of England

Thurlow's eyebrows went up; then he shrugged and turned his back.

"A night at Brooks's," he remarked, "is a night wasted among Whigs and scoundrels; and a pocketful of guineas off the gaming tables is poor enough pay. Pray, Mr. Boswell, will you ride along with me to Great Ormonde Street and break your fast?"

I accepted with alacrity; and so it fell out that I played a part in the strange events of secret history which I am about to narrate. The Chancellor entered his coach, and we were carried at a smart pace towards Great Ormonde Street.

As I drove along at Thurlow's side, I reflected with some awe on the inscrutable ways of Providence, that I, a poor Scotch advocate, should be breaking my fast on terms of intimacy with the Lord Chancellor of England and the Keeper of the Great Seal. I thought with indescribable emotion of the sacred nature of the Great Seal, and I resolved to beg a sight of it, that I might record for posterity the feelings of a man of sensibility on beholding that awful symbol of kingly authority.

Accordingly I led the discourse subtly in that direction.

"Pray, my Lord," I began, "inform me whether the Great Seal is not necessary to the dissolution of Parliament?"

"It is always affixed to the King's writ of whatever kind," replied Thurlow. "Ha! 'Twill *seal* the fate of the d——d dastardly Whigs, I promise you."

Lord Thurlow is noted for his profane swearing. I ignored it, and followed him as he stepped from his carriage and mounted his elegant stair in Great Ormonde Street.

"Pray, my Lord," I continued as best I could for climbing, "could you not gratify me with a sight of the Great Seal, for I have never seen it?"

"Nothing is easier," replied Thurlow, "for when all is said and done 'tis no more than a handful of soft metal, and I always keep it by me. Pray step this way."

I followed the saturnine Chancellor into a study on the first floor. The walls were lined with elegant authors in calf bindings. Opposite the door stood a graceful writing-bureau, its drawer half open. Beside it stood something covered with a green baize cloth. Thurlow twitched away the cloth, and with an easy movement handed me a heavy club surmounted by a crown. My wrist snapped with its weight.

" 'Tis the Mace!" I cried between awe and delight.

" 'Tis the Mace," assented Thurlow carelessly, "and well it is that 'tis borne before the Chancellor by a bravo with a porter's knot, for I've known many a d— —d puny little monkey of a Lord Keeper who could not have wielded it to save his life. Now the Seal is lighter."

He drew out the half-open drawer, and his face changed. A sickly green came up in his swarthy cheeks, and his voice dried in his throat. I made bold to peer over his shoulder. The drawer was empty.

Or rather, not quite empty. In it lay two bags, turned back and tossed down like carelessly drawn-off gloves. One bag was of leather; the other was a precious and costly purse of silk, richly embroidered and bejewelled.

Both bags were empty. The Great Seal was gone.

The Great Seal of England

The Lord Chancellor stood like one struck to stone while one might have counted to three. Then he damned the Whigs. He damned them for a thieving, scoundrelly pack of highway robbers, with no fear of their God or their King. He damned them for breaking and entering, for debauching the electorate, and for picking pockets. He promised to have them pilloried, lampooned, and disfranchised. All the time he was turning out the drawers of the bureau and searching the room. 'Twas useless. The Great Seal of England was gone.

"Boswell," cried Thurlow, "do you mount guard here, lest the d——d thieving Whigs come back for the Mace. I charge you, don't stir for your life. If the dogs are in the house, I'll rout them out." With a solemn sense of responsibility, I kept close watch over the sacred symbol of majesty.

I thought long till Thurlow returned. The house was quiet as the grave. Once I thought someone stood in the doorway behind me; but when I whirled, there was nothing. Once I thought Thurlow had apprehended the Whigs indeed, for there was a great clatter belowstairs and the sound of Thurlow swearing. But again the solemn silence supervened; and in a few moments more the troubled Chancellor returned.

"All is clear, Boswell," said he, his old truculent composure restored. "The miscreants have escaped. Come with me."

He dusted the rusty streaks from his palms, locked the drawers of the cabinet, and led me below to the domestick offices. There he showed me how the bars of the back kitchen window had been wrenched loose. I looked at the loosened bars lying in the court below under the open window, and shook my head over the pools of plaster lying on the kitchen floor.

"With bars at every window, surely a man ought to be safe from the d——d Whigs," he muttered.

"This is clearly a matter for the philosophical mind of Dr. Johnson," I cried. "I will wait upon him at once."

" 'Tis a matter for the bailiffs," responded Thurlow surlily, "they shall wait upon the b——y b———y Whigs at once."

I wondered if he meant Mr. Fox, and so my mind turned to Parliamentary affairs.

"What will come of this?" I queried. "How is Parliament to be prorogued?"

"I'll prorogue 'em," cried Thurlow grimly. "I'll find a way to send the scoundrels home. But I must search out precedents. I'll go straight off to Downing Street and consult Pitt."

"And I," said I, "will go straight off to Bolt Court and consult Dr. Johnson."

"Do so," responded Thurlow, "and I'll come after you as swiftly as I may."

I found Dr. Johnson lying late in his bed-gown, with a kerchief on his grizzled head. He stared as I burst into his chamber.

"Bozzy!" he exclaimed. "What brings you to London? 'Pon my life, 'tis some weighty affair of state. By the bulging of your eyes, you are big with news of the great world. Well, well, I will hear it."

The tone of raillery piqued me. Composing my countenance, therefore, I seated myself and enquired politely for my venerable friend's state of health.

"The indisposition is abated," replied Johnson impatiently. "Come, Bozzy, your news! What brings you to London?"

"To see Mannering hang."

JOHNSON: "And did he hang with a good grace?"

BOSWELL: "He did not hang."

JOHNSON: "So you were cheated of your entertainment after all."

BOSWELL: "No, sir, my entertainment was very well. All the world and his wife was there, with my Lady Lanchester that Mannering fought for supported by three gallants in the forefront, and the dead man's brothers glowering at the gallows foot. 'Twas a noble sight to see Mannering smile on them and never turn a hair, with his arms bound at his sides and the man of God mumbling beside him and the cart ready to move off and leave him dangling."

JOHNSON: "Why, is not this better than turning a man off hugger-mugger at Newgate, as the new law requires? Why must we do without the procession to Tyburn? The publick is gratified with the procession; the criminal is supported by it. Why must it be swept away?"

BOSWELL: "I know not; but so it must be."

JOHNSON: "But come, Bozzy, be not so close-mouthed. How came Mannering so near the other world, and yet remains in this?"

I own I was tired of my tale, and longed to astound

my friend with the grave news which was agitating me. I had no more time for Mannering.

"Why, sir," said I, "thus it was. At the very point, when Mannering had perforce to give over his strutting and his ogling and let the handkerchief fall, comes a cry from the crowd *A reprieve, a reprieve;* though 'twas in truth no reprieve, but the King's pardon engrossed at large with the yellow wax on the tapes; and Mannering kissed the boy that had brought it, and rode away in his coach as he had come, with never a glance at my Lady Lanchester. As for her, she let out a screech and fell into a swoon; and 'tis all the talk that it has come to mortal hatred between them, and that the dead man's brothers will kill Mannering sure if he remains in England."

"Why, so," says Dr. Johnson, "this is a docket indeed, and George Selwyn himself could not have told it better; though indeed it falls something short of the great affairs I thought you big with."

This was my opportunity.

"Pray, sir," I said quietly, "what news would content you? How if I tell you that the Great Seal of England has been stolen, and that I was by when the loss was discovered?"

Dr. Johnson was thunderstruck. A staunch Tory, and a great supporter of kingly authority, he appreciated to the full the infamy of the deed. I presented Lord Thurlow's request for the assistance of my friend's known acumen; to which he replied:

"I am an old man, Bozzy, and my infirmities gain upon me; but I solemnly declare that I will neither repose nor recruit till I shall have put the Great Seal of England into Lord Thurlow's hand."

Rising, he summoned Francis Barber to bring his cloathes; and as he dressed and broke his fast with me, I told him all the circumstances of the audacious theft.

He heard me through in silence, shaking his head and rolling his great frame the while. Only when I had finished did he question me.

"The domestick offices are on the lowest floor?"

"Yes, sir."

"And the writing-bureau on the floor above?"

"That is so, sir."

"The bars of the window were dislodged and fell to the ground?"

"Yes, sir. I ought to say that the window faces the open fields, whence the house-breakers are supposed to have come."

"And plaster and rubbish lay on the kitchen floor? Sparse, or thick? Under the window, or more generally dispersed?"

"Thick, sir, under the window, and sparser where it had been tracked into the passage."

"Footprints?"

"No, sir, only a line of faint smudges, as it might be off the boots of a man who had stood in plaster; and indeed Lord Thurlow and I made such another track when we came away from the window."

"The servants?"

"All in their beds. Lord Thurlow rouzed them as we came away."

"Had they heard aught in the night?"

"Nothing, they said."

"Yet a band of Whigs broke in and abstracted the Great Seal. Pray, whom of his household has Lord Thurlow about him?"

"I know not. His irregular connexion with Mrs. Hervey is well-known; but I never saw her, nor any of her children."

Dr. Johnson shook his head in dissatisfaction. There was a summons below, and my friend's black servant announced Lord Thurlow. We descended to him in the panelled drawing-room, where the sage and the politician greeted one another with great mutual respect.

Though separated in age by upwards of twenty years, these two famous men were not unlike: Thurlow tall, strong-built, of a saturnine cast, with sharp black eyes under beetling brows; Johnson as tall, but more massive, his heavy face marred by the King's evil. If Johnson roared, Thurlow thundered. The one had met his match in the other, and they were mighty civil and polite together.

"Well, Dr. Johnson, what think you of this outrage?" demanded the Lord Chancellor. "But the d— —d thieving Whigs shan't make good their purpose, I promise you. I have taken the opinions of Gower and Kenyon; a new Seal is making, and Parliament shall be prorogued tomorrow. So all is happily resolved, and we'll send the d— —d Whigs home to stay in spite of their teeth. Mr. Boswell, Dr. Johnson, I thank you for your good offices in this matter, and beg that you'll discommode yourselves no further over it."

"Surely, Lord Thurlow," protested my Tory friend, "the matter is not to end thus. Have you taken no steps for the apprehension of the thief?"

"You mistake me, Dr. Johnson," replied Lord Thurlow, "one Lee, a notorious receiver of stolen goods, is under our eye. We think to take him in the fact, if we but have patience. But my first care is to send the rascally Whigs packing; and this we may do, for the new Seal will be ready by nightfall."

"Pray, Lord Thurlow," replied Dr. Johnson, "indulge me. I am no thief-taker; but I have had my successes as a detector of cheats, and I have sworn to lay the stolen Seal in your hand. Pray let me have your answer to a question or two."

"I will do so, Dr. Johnson; but pray be brief, for I have yet to wait upon his Majesty."

"Tell me, then: the Great Seal was customarily preserved in a bag?"

"Two bags, Dr. Johnson, of silk and of leather, the one within the other."

"How were they secured?"

"With a thong or draw-string."

"The silk bag was costly?"

"That is so. It is enriched with gems and bullion, and cost upwards of fifty guineas."

"So that the thief," said Dr. Johnson meditatively, "though 'twas worth his life to be found there, lingered so long as would serve to untie, not one bag, but two, that he might leave behind him fifty guineas worth of booty; when he might in a single motion have pocketed bags, Seal, and all, and made good his escape. This is a strange sort of thief, and one who cannot hope to rise in his profession. A practised thief will disdain no loot that comes to his hand."

"Nor did he so," said Lord Thurlow quickly, "for he carried off my silver sword-hilts, and a matter of £35 in fees, that were laid up in the writing-bureau."

I looked my surprise at this news.

" 'Tis a bagatelle, to the loss of the Seal," continued Thurlow, "and I have given it scant attention; but such is my personal loss, out of the drawers that were ransacked."

"One more question, then," said Dr. Johnson. "Who of your family were at home with you in Great Ormonde Street?"

Thurlow looked like a thundercloud.

"How can this be to the purpose, Dr. Johnson?" he enquired stiffly.

"Pray, my lord, do not hinder me," said Dr. Johnson firmly, "for I am resolved to get to the bottom of this matter, whatever I may find there."

Thurlow looked blacker still, but he replied to the question:

"Why sir, Mrs. Hervey is taking the waters at Bath, and my little girl with her. My household at present is only my daughters Catharine and Caroline, and my cousin Gooch's boy, Ned Durban."

"What's he?"

"Why, sir, he's a young springald come to me for old times' sake to be made a man of fashion; though indeed 'tis all in vain, for the d——d stubborn young dog is a

Whig and a gamester, and I can make nothing of him."

"Pray, Lord Thurlow, make these young people known to me."

Lord Thurlow rose from his place.

"Very well, Dr. Johnson, if you wish it. Will you come down to Great Ormonde Street?"

"No, sir, I will not. I am a dropsical old man, and I cannot gallop about London like a Bow Street runner. You must be my courier, and send Great Ormonde Street to me."

"Let it be as you wish," said Lord Thurlow coldly; and left us with scant ceremony.

The morning was half gone when a coach deposited a young lady and a young gentleman at the mouth of Bolt Court. I watched them from the two-pair-of-stairs window as they crossed the court. The young lady was sombrely dressed and cloaked in black to her heels. Her companion, thin and shambling, was gorgeous in mulberry brocade from his wig to his buckled shoes. He made play with a muff and a clouded cane. He handed his companion carefully up the steps and supported her into the withdrawing room, where Dr. Johnson received them.

"Your servant, Dr. Johnson," lisped he of the clouded cane, and made a leg, "Ned Durban at your service. Here's Caroline."

"Miss Thurlow," said Dr. Johnson gently, "I bid you welcome."

The girl in the black cape looked at him mutely. She was very young, not more than fifteen, with pale ivory skin shewing dark shadows under the eyes. She wore her own soft dark hair, not a made head, but swept back any how. She was dressed in grey tabby, without ornament.

Gravely Dr. Johnson led her to his deep wing chair. She sat gingerly on the edge, and looked at Ned Durban. The exquisite youth came to her, and took her hand.

"Never fear, my dear," he said gently, "you are to answer what Dr. Johnson asks; he won't hurt you. He only wants to find the Great Seal."

The dark eyes turned to Dr. Johnson.

"Truly, truly, sir, I know nothing of the Seal."

"Nor I, sir," added Durban; "but ask me what you please."

I was liking the shambling exquisite a little better, when he fell to sucking the head of his cane.

"Then tell me, pray," began Dr. Johnson, "how you have spent your time since yesterday."

Durban left off sucking his cane, and replied:

"Strap me, sir, 'twas a rare night for me, for I never once saw the inside of Brooks's, though I have a card there, and seldom miss. But last night I carried my cousins to sup at Ranelagh, and so on to the masquerade; and so it fell out we three were together till the east shewed grey."

"All the time?"

"From supper till morning."

"Pray tell me, sir, is it your custom to squire your ladies so closely?"

Durban cackled, and replied:

"There you have me, Dr. Johnson. 'Twas the first masquerade from which I have failed to follow one or other devastating little mask and let the rest go hang. But, d'ye see, sir, little Caroline here was half beside herself, and Cathy and I in dejection, and we just sat one by another and watched the masquers, until near dawn we could bear it no longer and came away home together."

"How late?"

"Perhaps an hour before sunrise."

"And you then retired?" enquired Dr. Johnson.

"Yes, sir. I had half a mind to the hanging, but the thought of it was so deuced dumpish and depressing, in the end I carried a bottle to bed with me, and the next thing I remember my Uncle Thurlow was shaking me and bidding me rise and come down to Bolt Court."

"And you, my dear?" Dr. Johnson turned to Caroline Thurlow.

She looked at Ned, and he squeezed her hand and nodded at her.

" 'Twas as Ned said," she faltered.

"And after? When you came home?"

"I went to my bed."

"Do you lie alone? Or with your sister?"

"With my sister," whispered the white-faced girl.

"Well, my dear, and so you fell asleep and slept till mid-morning."

"No, sir. I lay awake and watched the day break. I couldn't sleep."

"And you heard nothing?"

"Yes, sir, I heard a great clatter and a rending sound. It made me afraid. My window fronts the fields, and sometimes men fight there."

"Did you look out?"

"Oh, good lack, no sir. I hid my head under the counterpane."

"What an unlucky chance," I exclaimed. "You might else have detected the thieves."

"When was this rending sound, my dear?" enquired Dr. Johnson.

"I cannot say, sir. I had lain awake for hours, and the sun was risen."

"And your sister slept by you?"

"All the night, sir. But it was morning before I slept, and when I awoke she was gone."

"Whither?"

Caroline looked at my benevolent friend without speaking. Durban answered for her.

"O lud, sir, who knows where a lady goes o' mornings? To the milliners, to pay calls, I know not what. She is to follow us when she returns."

"She comes pat upon her cue, sir," I reported from the window, "for here is Lord Thurlow crossing the court, and with him a most exquisite lady of fashion."

" 'Tis Cathy," said little Miss Thurlow wistfully, "for Cathy's eighteen, and a reigning toast."

Cathy came into the sombre panelled room like a queen. She wore lavender lutestring, and a made head full twelve inches high, powdered and picked out with plumes. She was a sparkling girl with her father's eyes.

I bent over her hand as Dr. Johnson saluted the Lord Chancellor.

"Why, Cathy," said Caroline. "Where ever have you been? All the time I lay awake you were snoring, and as soon as I slept you rose up and left me."

"Nowhere," said Cathy. "Everywhere. What do you think, Carly, the mantua-maker has the impudence to be indisposed! What am I to wear to the ball tonight?"

Thurlow greeted his little daughter tenderly.

"What, poppet, look up, my dear. Never fret about the Seal. The new one is as good as made, and there's no harm done."

"Nevertheless the Seal is to be found," said Dr. Johnson. "I have taken so much upon myself."

"I take this resolve very kindly of you," said Thurlow cordially, "nevertheless I would not have you fatigue yourself unduly."

"Nay, sir," replied Dr. Johnson, "we progress, and without fatigue. I have learned much about this strange thief, who does his house-breaking by daylight, who takes the Seal and leaves the Mace and the jewelled bag. Pray, answer me one question more: when did you last see the Great Seal?"

"Why," says Thurlow, "last sealing-day."

"Recollect yourself, sir. I think it was when you sealed Mannering's pardon."

"That is so, sir," replied Thurlow instantly.

"And I think that was done last night, else how comes it that it nearly came too late?"

"Prodigious, Dr. Johnson! Again you are right. The

document came late from the engrosser's. 'Twas close on midnight, and I sealed it then and there and sent it by hand to the unfortunate man's friends."

"And did you then deposit the Seal in the bureau?"

"I did, sir," replied Thurlow.

"And was anybody by to observe these transactions?"

"Sir!" began Thurlow angrily.

"Pray, Papa, no heroics," said Cathy languidly. "I was by, Dr. Johnson. I helped. I served as chaffwax, as I have often done before—haven't I, Carly?—*Carly!*"

Every head turned to the winged chair. Caroline's face was the colour of lead. Her eyes were closed, and her breath came shallow.

"The child's fainted!" cried Thurlow angrily. "Come, Dr. Johnson, a truce to this inquisition."

Catharine moved stiffly to her sister—stiffly from the effort of carrying her stately powdered head—and cut her stays with despatch and decision. Ned Durban laid her tenderly on the sofa, and gradually her breath and her colour returned. She opened her eyes, looked into his face above her, and burst into a storm of weeping. As he smiled tenderly into Caroline's eyes, muff or no muff, I liked the boy.

Miss Thurlow's indisposition put an end to my acute friend's researches for that while. Catharine donned a green baize apron belonging among Francis Barber's kitchen gear, and with her own hands made a posset for her sister; and very strange she looked in her lavender lutestring with the plumes in her powdered head.

Soon Caroline was sitting up. Her weeping fit had done her good. There was pink in her cheeks, and a smile began to play about her lips. Nevertheless, Dr. Johnson swore that she must not be moved, but the whole company must stay and dine. Thurlow excused himself on the ground of much business; but Caroline consented, and Ned and Catharine elected to stay with her. Francis Barber was to be sent to the ordinary to bespeak chickens and sweetbreads.

The Lord Chancellor then took his leave, promising Dr. Johnson a sight of the new Seal before supper-time. I offered to accompany him, if I could be of use; and he gratefully closed with my offer. So I departed with the Lord Chancellor; and of my doings that afternoon suffice it to say, that my usefulness was all in fetching and carrying, fetching and carrying.

I returned to Bolt Court as evening was falling. I found Dr. Johnson on the step taking leave of a visitor; and so I greeted for the second time that day Charles James Fox, the fascinating and beloved Whig leader.

This was a different Fox, however; fresh from the hands of his man, wigged and point-device; with his irresistible smile on his broad lively-looking face.

"You may set your mind at rest, sir," Dr. Johnson was saying. "I promise you no one shall suffer for the sequestration of the Great Seal, save alone him who destroys it."

"Then I will promise you," rejoined Fox in his rich voice, "that no Whig has it, no Whig took it, and no Whig will destroy it. 'Tis my belief, Dr. Johnson, that the surly Chancellor himself could tell us much, if he would."

"Lord Thurlow has already told me much," replied Dr. Johnson, "and the matter approaches its end. But pray gratify my curiosity in one particular. Boswell here tells me that Thurlow spent last night with you at Brooks's. How can this be, that a staunch Tory should be found in the Whig stronghold?"

Fox laughed.

"He came by that way after supper," he replied, "to threaten me, in his amiable way, about Ned Durban, who is personally attached to my party, and of great use to me. When he was announced, Jack Wilkes tipped me a wink, and laid me guineas to crowns I could not make so good a Whig of him as to keep him in the club till dawn. Well, sir, I never refuse a wager; and a hundred guineas is more than curling-paper money. It took all my finesse to get him to the tables; and there I guarded him like gold till the night was spent. 'Twas hardest of all to see him winning, and lay no stakes myself, but I dared not. Had I begun gaming, he might have walked away, and I would never have followed. Jack Wilkes was by, and saw fair play; and when the light began to come in at the windows, he paid down my guineas on the nail, and I got Thurlow out of Brooks's and consigned him to the Devil, for I don't like the man."

"You never left his side?"

"I stood by the black-browed Tory from ten in the evening till daylight, and 'tis a task that's ill-paid at a hundred guineas."

"One question more: how knew you that I was employed in the matter?"

Fox smiled blandly.

"Nothing Thurlow does," he replied, "is unknown to the Whig leaders; and at this very moment, I'll lay a guinea, someone is telling Thurlow that Fox has called at Bolt Court."

"Well, sir," says Dr. Johnson, "I will serve you, if I may serve justice at the same time."

" 'Tis all I ask," replied Fox, "for indeed whether the old curmudgeon has made away with it himself, and blames the Whigs, or whether a thief has it indeed, and Thurlow has put about this Whig story to turn it to his own ends, 'tis all one to me; the Whigs have it not."

"You may set your mind at rest, sir," replied Dr. Johnson; and the Whig leader took his leave.

"What, Bozzy," exclaimed Dr. Johnson, peering into my face as he gave me welcome, "you're again great with news."

"That is so, sir," I exclaimed eagerly as we mounted the stair.

"Stop, I will tell you," said Dr. Johnson, "there was a felonious entry at the Petty Bag in Rolls Yard last night."

"There was indeed," said I, dumbfounded, "but—"

"But nothing was taken," finished Dr. Johnson.

But I still had a couple of crumbs.

" 'Tis thought," I told him, "that they looked to find the Great Seal there, for 'tis there they have the engrossing of pardons and such-like; but they had their labour for their pains, and so went away to the Chancellor's house, and there fared better."

"Do you say so?" said Dr. Johnson politely.

"Furthermore," I concluded triumphantly at the drawing-room door, "Lee, the receiver of stolen goods, is taken, and will be arraigned for purchasing the stolen Seal. 'Tis said he had it of a woman for forty guineas."

"So the Seal is found!" exclaimed Johnson, thunderstruck.

"No, sir. 'Tis feared it is into the melting-pot already."

Johnson opened the panelled door, and we entered the room. I bent low over Catharine Thurlow's hand. She had been crying, but she was more beautiful than ever with a last tear sparkling in her eye, and her glossy dark hair in little ringlets all over her proud little head. She reminded me of an ancient statue—or a portrait—what was it?—something I had seen recently.

Dr. Johnson was most assiduous in his attentions to both the ladies. The Whig maccaroni fondled his muff and smiled at vacancy. I had my mouth open to sound the opinion of the Great *Cham* on the strange events just passed, when Francis Barber announced Lord Thurlow, the latter coming in briskly on his heels with a leathern bag in his hand.

"Now, sir," says Thurlow, "we'll prorogue 'em," he brandished the leathern bag, "we'll prorogue 'em and send the d——d dog-stealing Whigs back to their kennels. Here's the little beauty will do it."

"The new Seal!" I exclaimed.

"Ay," said Thurlow, handing the leathern bag to my learned friend, "the new Great Seal. 'Tis a replica of the old one, and equally as handsome, brass though it may be."

The Great Seal of England

My near-sighted friend carried the bags to the window. The leathern bag yielded a silk purse of exquisite workmanship; the silk purse yielded a heavy disk of yellow metal.

"You say true," remarked Dr. Johnson, hunching his shoulders as he peered at it in the light from the sky, "this is not to be told from goldsmith's work."

He passed the heavy thing to me, and I at last beheld, albeit of brass and hastily constructed, the GREAT SEAL OF ENGLAND.

I gazed with indescribable emotion on the sacred person of George III, represented as seated on a charger; on the obverse the same, seated in state. I handed the heavy metal disk to the young ladies. Caroline regarded it with wondering eyes; but Catharine shrugged her slim shoulders.

"This is no nine-days' wonder," she said indifferently. " 'Tis no different from the other one."

She yielded it back to my friend.

"Francis," called Dr. Johnson from the passage, bagging the Great Seal the while, "pray let us have our tea."

"I cannot drink tea with you," said Thurlow instantly, "for I am on my way to Downing Street with the new Seal; but my daughters may do so, and I will send the carriage back for them."

"Very well, my Lord," responded Dr. Johnson, "I rejoice that the crisis is happily over, and we may drink our tea with light hearts."

"So?" says Thurlow. "Have you, then, given over your determination to lay the Great Seal in my hand?"

"Sir," says Dr. Johnson, "the Great Seal is but metal,

till the King's will gives it life; and so I hold that the disk you carry there in its bag is in very truth the Great Seal and no other; and in that belief I rest from my labours."

"Now," says Thurlow, "you speak like a man of sense. Sir, I am obliged to you. Pray command me. Give me the pleasure of serving you to requite your trouble in this matter."

"I thank you, my Lord," replied Dr. Johnson. "I have but one request: freedom for Lee the receiver."

"Freedom? For the tool of the Whigs? The man who melted up the Great Seal of England? Sure, sir, you jest."

"Not so, my Lord. I counsel you, Lee must not be brought to trial."

"Not? When twenty witnesses stand ready against him?"

"No, sir. There might come a twenty-first witness you would not wish to hear."

Thurlow looked sharply at Johnson. Then he lifted his shoulders.

"I can see," he remarked, "that I am in your debt indeed. Lee shall go free."

"I thank your lordship," said Dr. Johnson; and Thurlow took his departure. I attended him into Fleet Street and so we parted.

As the Lord Chancellor mounted his coach, I took note of a young man who was lounging in front of the Dolphin, smoking a church-warden and watching the mouth of Bolt Court. No sooner had the Lord Chancellor driven off, than he shook out his pipe and put himself in motion. To my surprize he caught me up at Dr. Johnson's door. I stared at him. It was Mannering.

Mannering had elected to hang in peach-coloured velvet, picked out with gold. He was still in peach-coloured velvet, and he was still smiling.

"Exit the heavy father," he murmured; "enter the lover. We should all make our fortunes at Drury Lane. Pray sir, is this the right stair for Dr. Johnson? And who are *you?*"

"James Boswell, at your service, Mr. Mannering. Pray come with me."

"Oons, nothing like hanging to get oneself known," drawled Mannering, mounting the stairs before me. There was no handsomer man in England. He carried himself like a grenadier; his handsome sallow face was like a player's, melancholy and sentimental, with shades of sensibility constantly playing over it.

Like a player he threw open the drawing-room door and stood motionless on the threshold. He got his effect.

The languid Durban leaped to his feet, crying:

"Tom! Stap me, 'tis Tom!"

Catharine Thurlow applauded softly, saying,

"Bravo, well timed, Tom!"

But Caroline Thurlow crossed the room in one motion, and threw herself on his breast. Dr. Johnson peered at the newcomer, who seemed to be mightily relishing the scene.

"Permit me," said Catharine sedately, "to make Mr. Mannering known to Dr. Johnson." Though Caroline's head was pressed tight against the peach-coloured chest, Mannering managed a graceful salutation.

He touched Caroline's dark hair gently.

"Be satisfied, little one," he said, "they can't hurt Tom Mannering." He set her gently in her chair.

"How come you so pat, Tom?" said Durban.

It was Catharine who answered.

"I sent to him," she said, "by Francis, when he bespoke the chickens at the ordinary."

"And I," said Mannering, "came when dusk fell. I have enemies in England."

"Had you but come a little sooner," says Caroline in a dreamy voice, "you might have thanked Papa for your pardon."

"Papa!" cried Mannering. "Trust me, I will give Papa a wide berth."

"Pray, sir," said Dr. Johnson, "be seated and take a dish of tea with us."

"I thank you, no. I ride for Dover in an hour, and so over into France. 'Tis safer so, I think."

He looked directly at Catharine Thurlow.

"I had not looked to speak before an audience," he said (I thought he minded us little enough), "but time presses. I thank you for my life. Will you marry me and come with me into France?"

Catharine Thurlow returned as level a look.

"I have not changed my mind," she said. "I couldn't see you hang; but I will not marry you, Tom, tonight or ever."

Mannering scowled.

"You'll be the death of me," he said. "Whose fault was the Lanchester affair?"

"I've made amends, I think, for driving you into her

arms," replied Catharine. "Go over into France, Tom, and God take care of you, for I won't again."

Caroline stood up. "I'll come with you, Tom."

Mannering looked at her.

"No, no, little one, you're too young and tender. I'll go alone." He touched her hand; looked a long moment at Catharine's vivid face; bowed, and was gone.

Catharine Thurlow went to her sister and set an arm about her shoulders.

"Catharine," said Caroline wonderingly, "what did he mean, about Papa?"

"Why, you little goose," cried Catharine, "where did you think I went, when I left you weeping your heart out in the darkness and went off dressed like a link-boy?"

"You said you were going to fight a duel," said Caroline doubtfully.

"That was to keep you quiet, you little moppet," said her elder sister. "I lay there in the dark listening to your sobs, and wished I could have got father to save Tom; and it came over me that if I were bold enough I could do it myself."

"How?" said Caroline.

"By sealing a pardon and carrying it myself. It wasn't hard. I carried the Seal to Rolls Yard, and engrossed a pardon in form as best I could. 'Twas a botch, but a bold botch. I sealed it with yellow wax, and then I had to run all the way to get there in time. The hangman never looked at it; how could he, with the press shouting *A reprieve, a pardon,* and Tom Mannering getting into his coach as cool as a cucumber."

I stared at the intrepid girl.

"All had gone well," she continued, "had my father not taken a freak to look at the Seal at six o'clock in the morning."

" 'Twas I," I said, "who took that freak."

"You have given me a bad day, Mr. Boswell," she replied; "but all's well that ends well."

"Yet give me leave," I begged, "to know the answer to a question or two. Pray how had you a boy's suit by you?"

"I had gone to the masquerade as a link-boy."

"Did your father know of this?"

"Not when 'twas done; but like Dr. Johnson he saw that 'twas not the work of a thief, but of a member of his household. Therefore he wrenched out the bars of the kitchen window, that it might look the more like a house-breaking."

"And therefore he was so fierce against the Whigs?" I added.

"No, sir; he is fierce against the Whigs from long practice."

"Pray, Dr. Johnson, was this known to you?"

"Sir, by little and by little. At your first account I saw plainly, from the rust on his palms, from the clatter below-stairs, from the plaster *inside* the window though the bars had been cast *outside*, that 'twas Lord Thurlow himself who had breached his own defenses. Therefore I summoned to me all who lived above-stairs, and learned that all had been in company with others till nigh on dawn. I was puzzled to know which of the young people had abstracted the Seal upon their return home, and why. Then I mentioned Mannering's pardon, and father and daughter immediately lied in concert. Lord Thurlow pretended to have sealed Mannering's pardon and Miss Catharine to have served as chaff-wax. Obviously both lied, for Lord Thurlow was at Brooks's all night long, though he knew not that I knew it, and Miss Catharine was at the masquerade. Then Mannering's pardon was forged. And by whom? Not Lord Thurlow—he could have procured a genuine pardon, had he so wished. Therefore Miss Catharine was the forger; Lord Thurlow guessed so much, and lied to cover her. 'Twas all news to Miss Caroline that Mannering had got off; she fainted away with the revulsion of feeling."

"Pray, Miss Thurlow," I enquired, "did you indeed steal £35 and two silver sword-hilts?"

"No, indeed, Mr. Boswell. I now hear this accusation for the first time."

" 'Twas a detail your father invented to lend verisimilitude to his version of the house-breaking," explained Dr. Johnson, pouring his fifth cup of tea.

"Now sir," said I rallying him, "what's this supping of tea? Did you not swear not to rest nor recruit until you had laid the Seal in Lord Thurlow's hand?"

"Why, sir," returned Dr. Johnson, "you saw me do so."

I stared.

"Why, Bozzy," exclaimed Dr. Johnson, "did you think I would let the King's writ pass under base metal? Here is the brass one." He drew it from the capacious old-fashioned pocket of his snuff-coloured suit.

I continued to stare.

"But, sir, how came you by it," I exclaimed, "without stirring out at the door all day?"

"I detected its hiding-place, and asked for it."

"Where—?"

Catharine Thurlow laughed aloud.

"Pray, Mr. Boswell, is it the custom in Scotland for ladies of the *ton* to wear a made head before breakfast? 'Tis not so here; but when a lady has chopped off her hair in a hurry to pass for a boy by daylight, she must needs don a wig; and what better hiding-place for a thing she must conceal on her person till the hue and cry is over than the inner reaches of that same wig?"

"Pray, Mr. Boswell," said Dr. Johnson, "accept of the brass seal as a memento of this day's transactions. As for me I desire no better reward than to have saved a lady from the consequences of her rashness."

In fine, Dr. Johnson was true to his word; for though all became known to the Chancellor through the agency of his younger daughter and though he made the proffer with the utmost delicacy, Dr. Johnson was steadfast not to touch Lord Thurlow's £600.

NOTES

on Historical Background

ACH ONE of the nine stories in this book is embroidered upon the fabric of history. For those readers who, like myself, prize fact equally with fancy, I here append a few brief notes distinguishing the one from the other as they are woven into my tales.

The Wax-work Cadaver pictures Mrs. Salmon's famous Wax-Work as it was during the interregnum (1760–65) of Dr. Clarke the surgeon. Dr. Clarke died in 1765, needless to say in less sensational circumstances. His fate, which I have invented, springs naturally from the locale and the association of surgery and working in wax. I have taken minor liberties with Boswellian chronology in order to place Boswell on the spot at the right time. With the opening handbill, which is abridged from a real one, I have also taken liberties; the idea of immortalizing criminals in wax was not Dr. Clarke's, but Mme. Tussaud's, several decades later.

Of all my stories, *The Second Sight of Dr. Sam: Johnson* contains the most pure, unadulterated Boswell. First published in his *Journal of a Tour to the Hebrides* were the description of Dr. Johnson; the conversation about the second sight; the fox and the cave. Into the actual events of Dr. Johnson's visit to Raasay I have embroidered only the sinister Kelpie Pool and what was found in it.

It was in conversation with Professor Frank Krutzke of Colorado College that I first suggested the "detector" possibilities of Dr. Sam: Johnson. In this story those possibilities were first exploited. It and every subsequent story owe much to Professor Krutzke's criticism and suggestions.

"Robberies," lamented the *Annual Register* for 1761, "were never perhaps more frequent about this city. . . . One highwayman in particular, by the name of *The Flying Highwayman,* engrosses the conversation . . ." The rather drab career of this real rapscallion I have enlivened with details culled with lavish hand from a century of famous highwaymen.

"A highwayman," records the same *Annual Register,* "having committed several robberies on the Highgate road . . . two thief-takers, in hopes of entrapping the highwayman . . . set out . . . in a post-chaise, like travellers, upon the same road, with a view of being attacked by the highwayman at the usual place . . ."

Notes on Historical Background

The thief-takers bungled the job. Needless to say, they were *not* Johnson and Boswell. Neither were they attached to the horse patrol of the famous "blind beak of Bow Street," a heroic figure of eighteenth-century London who deserves to be better remembered.

In *The Monboddo Ape Boy* I have invented a story calculated to display Dr. Johnson's impatience with the eccentric evolutionary and alimentary theories of the inimitable James Burnet, Lord Monboddo. The character of Monboddo is drawn from the life; it transcends invention. He anticipated not only the Darwinian theory, but also modern linguistic science. He did not, however, anticipate the atom, nor was he suspected of alchemy. He was fascinated by Memmie Le Blanc and Peter the Wild Boy, both of them real people; but he never really had the good fortune to acquire a real wild boy of his own.

The Manifestations in Mincing Lane duplicate those which Dr. Johnson investigated in Cock Lane. I have made a new story, because the outcome of the Cock Lane investigation is so well known that I wished to offer a new and entirely different solution. In case any reader finds the denouement incredible, I would refer him to *The Newgate Calendar*, where many such cases are chronicled.

Although there is no record that Dr. Johnson ever found *Prince Charlie's Ruby*, he really did visit Flora Macdonald in the Isle of Skye; he really did sleep in

Prince Charlie's bed with its tartan curtains; he really did see most of the Jacobite relics described in the story; and he really did hear from Flora Macdonald the moving story of the days of the '45. The rest of the story is invention, carefully framed upon hints in history: Prince Charlie's visits in disguise to his lost kingdom, the rumoured birth of his son and heir, his brother's actual possession of a pair of fabulous matched rubies.

The Stolen Christmas Box is a fictitious adventure of real people, Dr. Johnson's Mrs. Thrale and her relations by marriage. Boswell did not like Mrs. Thrale; he considered her his rival for "that great man." The portrait here given as from his pen must be taken with a grain of salt. The "new book of cyphers" is a real book, *The Art of Decyphering and of Writing in Cypher,* by Philip Thicknesse, London, 1772. Though the cipher messages and the missing diamond are fictitious, they are woven into the real romance of Fanny Plumbe and Jack Rice; and the final and most unbelievable detail, the elopement *à trois,* is a matter of history.

The Conveyance of Emelina Grange to St. Kilda actually pre-dated Boswell by quite a bit. It has been laid at the door of that wicked old rake-hell, Simon Fraser, Lord Lovat. The fact that the abducted lady with her clew of yarn ended up in the Hebrides has caused me to flout chronology and Johnsonize the tale.

The disappearance of *The Great Seal of England* from the house of Chancellor Thurlow is one of the great classic mysteries. The circumstances of its disappearance are faithfully reproduced, although Boswell was actually not by to record them. In the light of those circumstances the solution here offered is a good guess, made better by the fact that Lee the receiver not only got off, but later sued his captors for false arrest, and made it stick. The tantalizingly respectable reticence of contemporary chroniclers about Thurlow's irregular household has forced me to invent his daughters, known to me by name alone, out of whole cloth. Ned Durban and Tom Mannering are cut from the same bolt; "the last of the Tyburn hangings" had taken place some months earlier, on November 7, 1783.

In this story Dr. Sam: Johnson, detector, was first presented to the world by Fred Dannay, with a loyal faith and enthusiasm which place me deeply in his debt. Six of the nine tales first saw the light under his cordial sponsorship in *Ellery Queen's Mystery Magazine*.

DE LA TORRE'S
LIFE OF JOHNSON

Samuel Johnson was born at Lichfield, in the English Midlands, on September 18, 1709. His father was a bookseller, and Samuel, although he managed to study at Oxford for a while before poverty put an end to it, got the most of his great store of knowledge by reading his father's stock.

In 1732 his father died, leaving him to make his own way. Sam was a raw-boned, ungainly youth, with congenital bad health and a nervous tic, and he found it hard to establish himself in any learned calling. In 1735, at the age of 26, he found and married the love of his life, Elizabeth Porter. Mrs. Porter was a widow some 21 years his senior; but they suited each other very well. She thought he was the most sensible man she had ever met. He thought she was the most enchanting creature that ever existed, and he thought so to the end.

Once more failing as a schoolmaster, the bridegroom soon set off for London to seek his fortune. He found 25 years of literary drudgery. He tried his hand at every kind of writing, gaining a good deal of admiration but very little cash. He wrote for the *Gentleman's Magazine.* He produced satires in verse, and a sensational biography, and a tragedy called *Irene.* For two years he published a weekly essay called *The Rambler,* which was highly prized for its sage observations and stately prose; but it brought him very little money.

Johnson's great life work was his Dictionary, a landmark in the history of the English language. In 1746, when he was 37, a coalition of booksellers commissioned him to produce this work; but the advance they gave him barely supported the crew of thread-bare scholars he put to work on it in a garret in Gough Square. In the midst of his labors, Elizabeth died, and left him to life-long mourning.

At last, in 1755, the Dictionary appeared, winning Johnson his place as the undisputed "Great Cham of Literature." But he angrily repelled patronage, and remained as poor as ever. When in 1759 his aged mother died, he had no money to settle her affairs. He had to dash off a novel, *Rasselas,* to raise the cash he needed. At his mid-century point, after years of literary achievement, Johnson was as impecunious as ever.

Three years later, all that changed. The government granted Johnson a pension. Thus freed from the wolf at the door, he settled back to enjoy what he loved best in life — good friends and good talk. His writings, wise and humane, had brought him many friends. Soon they brought him one more, James Boswell, a Scottish youth who came to London determined to win the friendship of the "Rambler," won it, and became his biographer.

So Samuel Johnson lived out his remaining years at his ease. He founded the Literary Club. He travelled, visiting the Hebrides with Boswell and France with his wealthy friends the Thrales. He published an edition of Shakespeare and a set of Lives of the Poets. In 1784, valiantly as he had lived, he died.

ADDENDUM:
THE GREAT CHAM

CHAM, pron. kam, variant of khan, as in Genghis Khan, Turkish. Current in Johnson's day, both for the Cham of Tartary and fig. for any big shot.

It was Tobias Smollett the novelist who applied the term to Dr. Johnson. The circumstances form a little human interest story. On March 16, 1759, Smollett wrote to his friend, the politician John Wilkes:

> "I am again your Petitioner in behalf of that great Cham of Literature, Samuel Johnson. His Black Servant, whose name is Francis Barber, has (218) been pressed on board the Stag Frigate, Capt. Angel, and our Lexicographer is in great distress..." (Lewis M. Knapp, *Tobias Smollett, Doctor of Men and Manners,* Princeton, N.J.: Princeton University Press, 1949, pp. 217-218)

Wilkes quickly rescued the lad from a servitude which Dr. Johnson regarded with horror as being in jail with the prospect of being drowned.

ABOUT THE AUTHOR

Lillian de la Torre was born in New York on March 15, 1902, and christened Lillian de la Torre Bueno (subsequently shortening the name to provide her pseudonym). She was brought up in a house full of books, including a rich collection of early detective stories, which marked her for life. In graduate school her field of special interest was the Age of Johnson, soon to provide both the inspiration and the materials for her continuing short story series about Dr. Sam: Johnson, detector.

As the wife of George S. McCue of Colorado College (now retired), Miss de la Torre has spent almost fifty productive years in Colorado Springs, Colorado.

Half of her twelve published books are in her chosen field of historical mystery and crime, including *Elizabeth Is Missing, The Heir of Douglas, The Truth about Belle Gunness,* and a play, *Goodbye, Miss Lizzie Borden.* Two biographies for teens, an anthology, and two cook books (co-authored), and a collection of verse, with numerous articles both ''learned'' and otherwise, complete the list.

Her hobbies are amateur theatre as actress and playwright, choral singing, travel for pleasure as well as research, and cooking, a daily adventure.

Still active, Miss de la Torre is now working on the mystery of the ''Kidnapped Earl,'' and her ''Dr. Sam: Johnson, detector'' short stories continue to appear now and then in *Ellery Queen's Mystery Magazine.*